PLANTATION

Books by Fern Smith-Brown

FICTION

COPPER KELLY
WHAT MADE SARAH CRY
WHISPERING WINDS
THE CABALLERO BANDIDO

NON-FICTION

THE BECKONING HILLS- Chronicles of the Hamlet of
Darlington
TOUCH ME WITH YOUR SMILE
SPEAK TO ME OF LOVE
GOD IS ON THE MOUNTAIN

CHILDREN'S BOOKS

IF I COULD BE ANYTHING - I'D BE A FISH
IN A CHILD'S GARDEN
SILLY RHYMES FROM FATHER MOOSE

GoldenIsle Publishers, Inc.
2395 Hawkinsville Hwy,
Eastman, Georgia 31023

Library of Congress Catalog Card Number: 98-73652

Fern Smith-Brown, 1939-
Plantation/Fern Smith-Brown

ISBN 0-9666721-3-5

1. Plantation life - Virginia, mid-1800's - fiction. 2. Slavery - fiction. 3. Civil War - fiction. 4. Race relations - fiction. I. Title. II. Title: Plantation.

Printed in the United States of America

First Edition

10 9 8 7 6 5 4 3 2 1

PLANTATION

FIC

FERN SMITH-BROWN

**GoldenIsle Publishers
Eastman, Georgia**

Many thanks to my family for their support and encouragement. And to J. P. J. who shared his vision.

PROLOGUE

Yesterday brought to today so lightly!
(A yesterday I find almost impossible to lift.)
                                    E. Bishop

"If you can't handle this story, girl, I want you to tell me now." The gruff voice rasped across Laura Townsley's nerve endings.

"I can handle it, Mr. Worthington." She tried to ignore the scowling features. But, Stanley Worthington was very hard to ignore.

The burley editor seemed to expect a more subservient response. His bushy brows drew together in one black line, and he leaned forward across the massive oak desk.

Laura smiled. She knew her boss was actually quite kind and very caring of his staff. He just liked to pretend otherwise in the belief it helped him get his own way. And, to him, the Right Way for *COUNTRY,* a slick magazine published in Richmond, Virginia, was His Way.

Laura knew she wasn't his first choice to handle the story. Mavis Holmes, a fixture at *COUNTRY* for many years, would normally have had this assignment. But Mavis was unavailable having gone on a long postponed honeymoon, leaving this feature story to fall right into Laura's lap. Laura smiled inwardly at her good fortune, thankful for the opportunity to prove that she could produce a piece every bit as good as the seasoned Mavis.

"We've made arrangements for you to interview the owner of Stafford Hall," Worthington said, making no effort to hide his doubt of her getting the type of story he desired. "It's about a hundred miles from here, sitting on a bluff overlooking the Potomac. It's been through several owners since it passed out of the Hamilton family after the Civil War. But it's been vacant now for years. It was recently put on the market, and a descendant of the original family has purchased it."

"What is the new owner's name?" Laura asked casually.

"Austin James Hamilton. Sounded personable over the phone," Worthington murmured absently. "Started out as a historian, but ended up in computers. Made a fortune, I hear. He has plans to restore the property to its former state of grandeur. Wants it to be a working farm again. Be interesting to see how he manages to accomplish that," Worthington mused.

"How big is this plantation?"

"Only a thousand acres."

"Only," she murmured.

"The original was several times that."

Laura whistled through pursed pink lips. "Can you imagine running an estate that size?"

Her editor shook his head. "He's going to have his hands full just getting the place restored. He's also compiling information on his ancestors and Stafford Hall from old documents and diaries. He wants to get everything catalogued for future reference."

"Sounds interesting. I always thought I'd like to dabble in genealogy."

"He's not dabbling. He's one of the best historians around and he's been cataloging information from those diaries and old papers, since he arrived. It's a project he's putting his heart into. By the way," he said leaning forward, "you've been invited to stay at Stafford Hall. He has a housekeeper, gardener, various other employees, so you won't be alone. Do you have a problem with that?" He knitted his brows at her.

"No, Sir." She answered the old-fashioned gentleman blithely, focusing her sight on the tip of her high-heeled shoe.

"It will make it easier to work if you don't have to run back and forth from a motel to the plantation."

"Certainly," she agreed, "and it was thoughtful of him."

Stanley Worthington nodded absently, his mind on other matters he wanted to discuss. "I want a comparison piece on plantation life around the Civil War era. Give me a piece that shows me what plantation life was all about then. I want you to read every word of those diaries -- read between the lines -- delve into every document. I want you to put yourself in that time frame and live it so you can bring me back a piece that will make our readers feel they've been there." He leaned across the desk. "I don't want just words. I want feelings," he barked. His bushy black brows were literally jumping up and down in emphasis.

Mr. Worthington stood, strode around the desk, and sat back down, giving his words time to sink in. "I want the readers to feel the soil between their bare toes," he said dramatically, scrunching up his fist. "I want them to feel like they can hear the slaves singing in the fields and to understand the tragedy of what it meant to be master and slave. Do you understand, Miss Townsley?" he asked, then gave her no time to respond. "I want you to move them with this piece as you've never done before. Do I make myself clear?" he intoned, glowering at her from beneath the bushy black line.

"Yes, Mr. Worthington," she mumbled.

"I want you to leave first thing in the morning," he said, standing and thus dismissing her.

Early the next morning, she was on her way to Stafford Hall to compile the masterpiece that Mr. Worthington requested.

To Laura, it seemed far from an April day in early spring. The frosty air made her shiver despite the warmth in the small car. Though the grass had begun to turn a vivid green, it had rained all night, soaking the fields and wooded stretches along the roadside, and now they glistened with ice particles that shimmered in the light. The trees were weighted down with icy mantles clinging tenaciously to their branches. She saw a row of pines that had been uprooted from the sheer weight of ice on their wide-spreading limbs. The freak ice storm was a frigid reminder of the whims of Mother Nature, wreaking her power at a time when spring flowers should have been waving in the breeze and fresh air wafting through the treetops.

Laura's eyes roved pensively over the fields that had once glistened with the sweat of the slaves who worked them, and again with the blood of soldiers who fought without glory in the Revolutionary and Civil Wars. A row of daffodils danced along a fence row as though mocking the universe with their vivid yellow hues that contrasted brightly with heavy boughs glistening in crystal gowns.

The road was bleak and fog was gathering in the distance. She frowned, her shoulders shrugging beneath the padded shoulders of her deep-green suit. She had thought it warm enough for traveling and had tossed her raincoat into the backseat. Folly to trust the weather for even a moment, she thought, reaching to turn up the heat, hoping the plantation had some kind of heating system. She smiled. Fireplaces. Didn't every room always have a fireplace? She was sure they did. She gained a measure of comfort from the thought of logs crackling in a wide fireplace.

The wind shrieked in protest to the cold front upsetting the natural course of Mother Nature's seasons. A small, jagged tree limb came sailing over the hood of her car and Laura cringed in momentary fear. Only months ago, she had purchased her sporty, sleek white Corvette. She liked the low-slung lines and hated to think of dents before the smell of new leather was even gone.

She turned her thoughts to the article Mr. W. wanted, mulling over the gut-wrenching slant he desired. Her dark chestnut-colored hair bounced as she moved her head up and down, a light shining in her dark brown eyes. She'd write this article so damn well that Mr. W. would never have doubts about her ability again. He would never have to ask her if she could handle it, because he would know she could. She'd read every word of those diaries, walk every inch of the grounds, absorb it all through her pores and every cell of her body, until she knew it thoroughly. Her words would be so vivid and convincing that before he read the last page, Mr. W. would think that she had lived through every moment of it.

Finally, amid the rain and whistling wind, she arrived. She turned from the main road onto an unpaved drive. Traveling round a bend, she guided the car between a double row of magnolia trees flanking the winding driveway. Laura felt that she had crossed an invisible line into the long-ago past. Minutes later, at the end of that brown ribbon road, she saw the manor house, a Georgian-style mansion that epitomized a grand lifestyle.

Two white oaks of enormous girth stood aside from the double row of magnolias, overshadowing the end of the lane in front of the house. Laura stopped her car there, just as hundreds of carriages must have done a century ago, and felt that the modern vehicle was a rude mockery to the serenity of a gracious age. Her glance roved over the red brick structure with two sets of chimneys at each end. The platform between the two had been restored with, as yet, unpainted boards.

She wondered where Mr. Hamilton would want her to park her car. The wind blew hard, bouncing raindrops against the windshield like popcorn in an electric popper. She decided to make a dash for the front porch, and reached into the backseat for her briefcase, dragging it over the top of the front seat to her lap. With a deep breath, she opened the door, bracing herself for the onslaught. Amid the slamming of the car door came the ripping sound of a limb tearing loose from the trunk of the nearby tree. Despite the din of the wind, the noise was horrendous, and she paused to look up. A broad tree branch sailed toward earth, breaking off smaller limbs in its path as it careened downward. Laura screamed and started to run, but the spreading branches at the end of the limb struck her, knocking her to the ground.

The sound of the limb crashing to earth was audible even beyond the thick walls of the mansion. Austin Hamilton strode down the front hall, peering through the window at the driveway. He saw Laura's car and the limb beside it. He uttered a swear word as he jerked open the wide front door, and ran down the steps. He saw the journalist's feet protruding from beneath the ice-covered leaves of new spring growth.

He ran to the inert figure, and shoved aside the smaller limbs covering her petite frame. His long fingers groped among the leafy branches, moving over her slender neck. Relief swept over him to find the white column intact. Her head lolled to one side and Austin saw the dark red streak trickling down the side of her face from a gash at her temple. It stood out in stark contrast to her fair complexion. Austin looked up at the sound of running footsteps. Edwin, his newly hired gardener, came running toward him.

"Holy hell! Is she dead?" Edwin yelled above the whistling wind and pelting rain.

"No, but she's hurt," Austin replied, indicating the blood oozing from the gash on her temple. Above the wrath of the storm, he shouted, "Help me get this off her."

Edwin rushed to help. They pulled the limb aside. Austin bent down to Laura's small form. "I don't think anything's broken," he murmured, slipping his arms beneath her body and lifting her. Edwin sprinted up the walk, hurrying to open the wide front door. He called to Ada, the housekeeper.

Austin carried Laura into the back bedroom, and laid her gently on the bed. Ada bustled in, carrying a pan of warm water and a soft cloth. Clicking her tongue over the young woman's injuries, she wrung out the cloth, and turned to wash the cut on the girl's head. Austin took the cloth from her hand and proceeded to attend to it himself. When the bleeding was slowed, he could see the wound was not deep. His long fingers, probing and feeling for broken bones, moved swiftly over her arms, and unself-consciously down her legs to her slim ankles. Though she was definitely out cold, and may have suffered a concussion, he murmured to the two in the room, "Nothing's broken."

He sat on the edge of the bed, observing the journalist who had made a less than grand entrance. He had known she was coming, of course, but he had expected a bespectacled, timid librarian type to write the article her editor had been so excited about. He smiled. He hadn't expected one so young or so pretty. He bent forward and smoothed back the waves of chestnut hair from her forehead. Her eyes flickered open for a moment, and he saw they were a dark, velvety brown. When they encountered his, he could have sworn a small smile momentarily curved her lips upward as though in recognition. And then, as if contented, her eyes fell shut again. Austin felt that he had looked into those eyes before. His brow furrowed in puzzlement, for her name meant nothing to him. He shook the feeling off quickly, his face registering concern. Laura's eyes flickered as though she watched a rapidly moving scene on a movie screen.

He saw her lips move and bent down to them. "You're going to be all right," he whispered.

Laura heard his voice, but she couldn't force her eyes open. From somewhere in the fog-shrouded recesses of her mind, she heard herself crying in a childish voice, "Mama! Don't let them take me away from you!"

And Mama saying softly, "Hush, Baby. Hush, Tilda."

Laura tossed on the bed, fighting to draw back from the long-buried memories clutching at her possessively like magnetic tentacles determined to draw her forward. She was powerless to stop the pain pounding in her head. Confusion engulfed her as tenaciously as the cloying web that closed around her. Why did Mama sound so different? Her voice was strangely jumbled. And why had she called her "Tilda"?

Laura looked up, saw Mama and herself quite plainly, saw her childish mouth quiver as she peered up at her mother. Understanding streaked across her senses. Mama was a slave! She, too, was a slave! And she sank into the dark depths of oblivion.

1

THE YEAR 1849

The cry of a child by the roadway,
the creak of a lumbering cart,
Are wronging your image that blossoms a rose
in the deeps of my heart.

Wm. Yeats

*M*atilda and her mother, a tall, striking mulatto, stood on a high platform. Men, women, and children joined them on the platform the slaver called an auction block. Matilda had never seen one before, but she had heard of them. Every child had. That is, every child who was a slave. Oftentimes, the auction block was only an old stump of a log, but the stories the slave children heard were frightening. There were plenty of tales to strike terror in the hearts of those held in bondage, for the auction could tear you away from those you love and change your life forever.

White men and women clustered round, invited by the slave trader to look over his merchandise before the auction began. The people below them wore fine clothes, the men in long, dark coats, fitted at the waist, and broad, silken bow ties at their necks. An array of silks and satins and velvets adorned the women, all of them in a rainbow of deep, vibrant colors.

Matilda's fingers longed to touch the softness she imagined the cloth to have. She could hear them whispering about the slaves on the platform, could see them pointing with gloved hands, and her heart skipped a beat when she saw a finger pointed at her. She tucked her hand in the comforting hand of her mother's and watched with frightened dark eyes as a woman below bent her head to hear the whispered words of her companion. Matilda knew they spoke of her, and she willed herself to turn away from the curious stares.

To be more thorough in his inspection, a portly, middle-aged man climbed up to the platform. He passed by the other Negroes, making his way to the far end where eight-year-old Matilda stood with her mother.

The child stood out from the group, for she didn't look like a Negro at all. Her long, full hair, lacking the stiffness and kinky curl of the African, hung in a cloud of softness down beyond her thin shoulders. Her eyes were velvet brown, like her mother's, but her features were slender like the planters' and their families'. Her skin was no darker than a child who had played in the sunshine while on holiday. She clung to the hand of the Negro woman at her side, proclaiming that here was yet another plantation child that fate had deemed to look like her father. It was an old story, one heard too often, of an unfortunate child born of the union between slave and master. Most of the gentlemen turned away, embarrassed to acknowledge that the situation existed. The women averted their eyes, pretending not to notice.

The middle-aged man did not stop until he reached the end of the platform where he slowly circled Matilda's small figure. He stroked her hair and ran his hand down her arm. "Five hundred dollars for the girl. I'm not interested in the woman."

Tilda was terrified, but she knew better than to speak. The man ran his big hands across her chest. She froze where she stood, willing herself to stare out into the crowd, trying desperately to separate herself from reality. She focused on a young man just swinging down from his horse. She knew he had to be a planter's son by his clothes, his proud, straight carriage, and his aristocratic manner. She wondered what it would be like to be dressed in such fine clothing, to ride such a beautiful, prancing horse. She even dared to wonder what it would be like to be on the other side of this platform.

The young man turned, glancing up at the slave block just as the elder man plucked at Matilda's shift and peeked beneath. He was repulsed to see the man run his tongue over thick lips that were stretched into a lecherous grin. His anger mounted when he heard him call out to the slave trader, "Six hundred dollars and you can keep the woman."

Stark terror registered in the velvet-brown eyes. The young man held the little girl's wild-eyed gaze for a moment. His senses were assaulted by the look of fear and despair. His hand went up, and James Hamilton called out abruptly, "Eight hundred dollars for both of them."

The slave trader, conducting his own auction, cast a satisfied look from the elder man beyond, to the young man standing below him. No accounting for taste, he thought, pleased that there was such interest in the white child. Light skinned children were an embarrassment and often difficult to sell. He flung a look of expectancy to the elderly man on the platform, but uninterested in bidding higher, the man sneered and waved the auctioneer away. Unabashed, the slave trader was quick to note that the man had now turned his attention to a light-skinned, well-proportioned young female on the block. With a complacent smile, he went on with his business of inviting those interested to take a closer look.

While the young man tended to completing the transaction, Tilda and her mother stood on the side waiting for him. Tilda turned her back on the auction block, hardly able to bear the sounds of anguished cries as husbands were separated from wives, and children were separated from parents. She reached for her mother's hand.

"There, there, chile," her mother murmured, "everythin' gonna be all right."

The man who had purchased them strode up. "I'm James Robert Hamilton from Stafford Hall," he announced. "We'll be leaving for the plantation in a few minutes. What is your name?" he asked the woman.

"Beulah, Suh."

"And the child's?" he asked softly.

"Matilda, Suh, but I calls her Tilda."

"Well, Tilda," he said cheerily, bending down to the little girl, "where are you from?"

"Over in Maryland, Suh. On Wyndley Plantation."

"Did you know this is Virginia? You're going to be living here now." He took off his hat, ran a hand through black wavy hair, tousling it pensively, then replaced the hat. "You see my horse tied up over there by that wagon?"

The child nodded.

"You run on over there and climb up into the wagon. There's a basket of apples in the corner. You may have one if you hurry along and be good."

"One without a worm?" she asked seriously.

James laughed. "One without a worm," he said.

The child scurried as fast as a rabbit, and selected a large red apple from the contents in the basket. Laughing, she held it up for her mother to see before sinking even white teeth into the juicy fruit.

James turned his attention to Beulah. "Why did you leave your last home?" he asked.

"Didn't leave. Was sent. Marsa Webb would never have sent me and my baby away. He died. Ol' Missus couldn't wait to be rid o' us," she said bitterly.

"Master Webb. Was he Matilda's father?" James asked quietly.

The woman drew herself erect, holding her head upright. James sensed, not defiance, but a strong sense of pride for who she was, what she had been to her master. She would apologize to no one for the way she felt about her child's father. She looked him directly in the eye and said, "Marsa Webb was Tilda's daddy. He never wanted nothing to happen to his little girl. He was gonna see that she was taken care of. He didn't want her to live like no slave. Soon as she was older, he was gonna send her up no'th where she could have a better life. An' I was gonna have a place near him, but he died and . . ." Her words trailed off in despair.

"I'm sorry," James murmured. "Come along, now," he said gently. "We have to be heading home." He moved toward the wagon.

"Marsa James?"

He turned back, looking at her over his shoulder.

"Thank yo' fo' saving Tilda from dat man."

He nodded, and she moved past him and climbed into the wagon.

James swung astride his horse.

From his wagon seat behind the horses, old Uncle Abrams thumbed a battered hat back from his head, and called down, "We ready to go, Massa James?"

Before James could reply to the aged black man on the buckboard, Tilda's childish voice turned every head back to the auction block.

"There's Tansy, Mama," the child said, pointing to a tall, thin woman on the auction block who had been near the head of the line.

The mulatto woman was too dark to be white, and too white to be black. Those of mixed blood had their own private hell, belonging in neither the slave's world nor the planter's world. They were often scorned by both races.

A tall, graying man, standing midway back from the platform, called out, "One thousand dollars for the mulatto woman."

A loud guffaw rose from somewhere in the front row. From the back came a sharp question, "Whatcha gonna do with the pretty mulatto, Stranger?"

The man's eyes grew steely. He reached into his breast pocket, withdrew the notes, and marched to the forefront. He shoved the money at the slave trader, then asked curtly for a piece of paper. Accepting the small scrap of paper, the man reached up to the makeshift podium for the writing pen and ink, scrawled a short note onto the paper, then handed back the pen. The slave trader's helper had released the woman from her shackles, and she had joined the man on the ground. Without fanfare, he handed Tansy the paper, accompanied by some bills folded discreetly in his palm.

The woman's dark eyes were puzzled.

"Can you read?" the stranger asked quietly.

"Jus' a bit, Suh," she said, glancing down at the scrap of paper. She didn't need to know much to understand what this paper meant. Unbidden, tears began to run down her cheeks.

The man smiled. "You are now free, young woman. Go somewhere up North. Make a life for yourself. You will not be anyone's slave, ever again. But keep this paper with you. It proves that you are now a free woman."

Tansy nodded, a dumbfounded expression mingling with the tears that streaked her face.

The stranger turned away, disappearing into the crowd. He carried himself with his head held high, and perhaps a sigh of relief echoing in his heart for a wrong finally made right. A small smile played about his mouth. It was just one step in assuaging the sins that rested on his shoulders and festered in his soul. There would be other towns, other auction blocks.

The crowd that had been awestruck suddenly regained its voice. Some cursed him, accusing him of setting a bad example. Others walked away quietly, their hearts constricting, knowing they lacked the courage to emulate his deed. James turned back to the wagon and saw Tilda and her mother looking at him.

"I wish I could do the same for you," he said softly, "but you don't belong to me. You belong to Stafford Hall. If it were up to me, all slaves would have had their freedom years ago."

Old Uncle Abrams saw the sag of his young master's shoulders and knew of the heaviness that lay on his heart like a stone. "Time to go home, Massa James," he said softly.

James nudged his horse gently, falling into step beside the rumbling wagon.

It was late afternoon when they turned into the long tree-lined drive of Stafford Hall. James knew he would have some explaining to do to his father and mother, Andrew and EmiLee. He had been away for two days on an entirely different mission, that of selling a load of lumber from Stafford Hall to a smaller planter farther north. While he knew his father would accept the new slaves, especially since Old Aunt Sallie had been retired several months ago, his mother would not be happy about Tilda's white features. There were too many incidences where a light-skinned slave, resented by the Negroes, created friction in the quarters. Tilda was just a child. How much trouble could she cause? His mother was a good woman. He'd simply have to appeal to her motherly instincts.

As the wagon drew up to the landing, James saw Mammy Ticey and his sister, Jane, crossing the yard. When the little girl saw him, she let go her nurse's hand and ran to meet him, calling his name.

James leaned down, scooping the child up in front of him. "Did you miss me?" he asked, kissing her temple.

Shoulder-length blond curls bounced as she shook her head vigorously. Wrapping her small arms around his neck, she kissed his cheek. "Did you bring me something?" she asked winsomely.

"I sure did." He fished into his breast pocket and withdrew a length of wide blue ribbon. "Did I hear you say you needed a blue hair ribbon to go with your new dress?"

"Oh, thank you, James," the child squealed. "You're the best brother in the world."

James chuckled, handing her to the round-faced mammy that had been nursemaid to them both. "You all right, Mammy Ticey?"

"Now that you's safely back home, Jimmie-James, ol' Mammy Ticey's jus' fine."

"Where will I find my mother and father?" he asked, and she noted the seriousness in his voice. "I brought them a surprise." He indicated the two in the buckboard behind Uncle Abrams.

Tilda had gotten to her feet to watch when she heard Jane's young voice, and she stood now holding onto the side of the wagon, watching the homecoming with dark, interested eyes.

"Oh, good Lawd!" Mammy Ticey drawled, seeing the white child in the wagon. "You done done it dis time Jimmie-James." She shook her head from side to side. "Dey ain't gonna like dis surprise, honey-chile. Dey ain't gonna like it a' tall."

"I couldn't leave her there, Mammy Ticey," he said hurriedly. "They were going to separate her from her mother, and some lecherous old fool had his hands all over her," he snapped angrily. "What else was I to do?"

Mammy Ticey shook her head again, wobbling the red bandanna that covered it. "Chile, you gotta stop thinkin' with yo' heart. Ain't no way to run a plantation. Ain't no way a' tall," she mumbled, letting Jane slide to the ground. "Massa and Missus in the front room. Want I should come in dere with you?"

James shook his head. "Thanks, Mammy Ticey, but I can handle this."

He smiled to himself. Old Mammy Ticey had been with the Hamiltons since she was a young woman. From a plantation in South Carolina, where she had been the slave of a harsh master, she had been separated from her husband and sent to Virginia, where James' grandfather had purchased her. Soon after that, she lost her only child during birth. She'd been Andrew's nurse, and then James' and now Jane's, and over the years had become firmly instilled in the family's lives and hearts. She made no bones about the fact that James was her favorite. She doted on the boy, championed him even when she knew he had done wrong. She had never called him Massa, always using her pet name of Jimmie-James. Mammy Ticey had never had another child, and had transferred all her love to the planter's children, but it was James she loved the most. Mammy Ticey commanded respect for herself, and her opinions in the Hamilton household did not go unnoticed. James knew she would have made her presence known, on his behalf, should he have allowed her to accompany him in this confrontation. Something deep inside James, a feeling that gnawed at him like a rat, was pushing him to do this on his own.

He glanced up at Uncle Abrams. "Wait right here for a few minutes."

He strode around to the back of the wagon. "If you want to get out and stretch your legs, you can," he told Beulah. "Let Tilda play if she wants, but keep her close by. I'll be back in a few minutes."

Beulah's liquid eyes searched his face. She hadn't been treated so nice since Massa Webb died. She watched the young master walk toward the big house. Nearby, a small group of slaves stopped to stare curiously at them.

Beulah wondered where the overseer was. The plantation was strangely silent. These folks just ambled along like they had all the time in the world. She raised her face to the heavens, murmuring, "If I's dreamin', Lawd, don't ever let me wake up!"

James' long stride soon fell into step beside Mammy Ticey and his sister, Jane. Inside the wide hall, Mammy Ticey held the door open, peering up at him with an anxious look on her face. "I sho' go with you, chile, if you needs me," she whispered.

James shook his head, laying a hand on her shoulder, giving it a warm squeeze before striding down the hall. Without hesitation, he pushed open the door to the library.

"James," Andrew acknowledged, coming forward to greet his son with a handshake.

"James Robert Hamilton," his mother intoned, using his full name just as she had when as a child he had committed some wrongdoing. "How could you?"

"How could I not, Mother?" he countered, surprised that they already knew of his purchase. "How did you know so quickly?"

"Your approach was obvious to all of us -- as was

your baggage. We're waiting for your explanation."

"I passed a slave auction on my way home. My intent was to stop for just a few minutes, more to rest than anything else. An obnoxious, man was pawing the child. He made an offer for her -- without her mother." James' eyes met his mother's. "I couldn't stand by and allow him to take an innocent child like that." His words implored his mother to understand.

"James, you must stop allowing your heart to rule your actions. She is a slave."

"She is a little girl of mixed blood. She is as white as we are."

"No, James," his mother said. "She is not as white as we are. Her mother is black."

"Her mother is a mulatto," he interjected.

"One drop of black blood makes her a nigra," his mother intoned firmly. "The child is born a slave and will always be a slave." Her words were not spoken unkindly, simply truthfully.

"Does that mean, Mother," James asked quietly, "that we should close our eyes to her plight, that I should have left her to the evil and suffering that awaited her?"

"We cannot be responsible for those things or all the injustices committed around us."

"It's not right! None of it is." James turned abruptly and strode over to the fireplace. Resting his elbow on the mantle, his chin on his thumb and forefinger, he stared into the embers of the flickering firelight without really seeing them. His brow furrowed in anger and frustration.

Andrew, looking from wife to son, understood her reasoning, but silently agreed with his son. Too bad more of us don't stand up for what we believe, he thought.

"Now, Emi," he began. "James is right. This is not the child's fault. The boy did what he thought was best. In fact, I think I would have done the same myself. It's amazing. The child looks as white as any of us."

His wife turned on him. "Andrew Hamilton! How can you take his part?"

Andrew put his arms about his wife. "I think, Emi, we must make the best of the situation. The money is already spent -- "

"It's not the money," Emi interrupted, her face showing how horrifying that was to her senses. "That's not it at all."

"I wasn't intimating that it was," he replied softly, putting a finger beneath his wife's chin. "You know how some of the planters treat quadroons -- and this child looks white. Under the circumstances, she will have a better life with us."

"Andrew, you know as well as I do," she reasoned, "that these children can create problems in the quarters. Our plantation is running so smoothly now, I just hate to see it upset by taking a chance like this."

"You're not afraid of a challenge," he teased. "You took a chance on me," he said, winking at her.

"Andrew, you are incorrigible," she said, a false gruffness to her words.

James had moved to the window overlooking the front drive. He could see Tilda playing by the wagon, the sunlight dancing off her dark hair. "Look at her, Mother," he invited. "How can you turn her away?"

EmiLee moved out of her husband's arms, and went to stand by her son at the window. Mature far beyond his seventeen years, her eyes flowed over him, and her heart warmed. He was so like her eldest son, Austin Guy, who had left home long ago to seek a life as a Shakespearean actor. Weeks had passed with no word, and when they began their search, it was as if her son had simply vanished. As she studied James, her heart ached for the lost son, but swelled with pride and maternal love for this tall, handsome boy -- no, he was a seventeen-year-old man, she corrected herself. She wagged her head, for he was so like his brother, and generous to a fault. His deep blue eyes turned tense in his desire for justice, and beneath the broad chest beat a heart of compassion. Slowly, she turned and looked out the window.

James had seen his mother's look and knew she was relenting. "Look, Mother," he said. "She's about the same age as our Jane. Are they really so different?"

"I'll thank you not to compare a slave's child to mine, young man," she snapped. A flush immediately feathered across her features at the hastily spoken words. But James dismissed them, feeling confident in the impending victory. He had seen his mother's face soften, and he knew she was clinging to the last shreds of dignity in her surrender, for she knew full well that she had already lost this battle.

James took the moment to drive home his point. "She's just an unfortunate little girl with no say in the matter. She didn't ask to be dealt this hand that fate has handed her. How can we turn her away?"

"Oh, all right, James. Enough! It seems you and your father have already made up your minds. But, mind you -- the first sign of trouble among our slaves and she is gone!"

James planted a kiss on her cheek. "Thank you, Mother. I knew you could not be so uncharitable as to turn her away." And he slipped out the door, leaving his father to smooth the last of his mother's ruffled feathers.

He met Mammy Ticey standing guard in the hallway. Her eyes were round and wide. "Missus fit to be tied?" she asked.

Smiling, James hugged the old woman whose ample proportions filled his arms. "Mother is fine," he reported. "She's agreed to allow them to stay."

"Well, I do declare!" breathed Mammy Ticey.

"Now, will you find someone to get old Aunt Sallie so she can help them get settled in?"

Old Aunt Sallie surveyed Beulah's young daughter whose skin was as fair as the massa's child. She shook her grizzled head. "Gonna be trouble with that 'un," she muttered.

"Tilda's a good chile," Beulah said quietly, drawing herself up straight, her arm slipping protectively around Tilda's thin shoulders, determined to defend her child to this old woman who seemed to be in charge of the black folks affairs.

Old Aunt Sallie peered up at the woman through faded, dim-sighted eyes. "No need to git 'fensive," she stated.

Changing the subject, Beulah asked, "How dey treat folks 'round here?"

"Depends on how yo' does yo' work," the old woman answered in a quick, sharp tone.

Beulah looked thoughtfully at the old woman, whose eyes grew round with apprehension as they swung warily from side to side. Beulah feared she might be missing something. "I don't hear no overseer yellin', or anyone screamin' from the lash o' the whip," she murmured in quiet undertones, falling into step behind the ancient black woman.

"No whuppin' done here no mo'," Aunt Sallie told her, "not since Massa Andrew's pappy died. Old Massa wasn't like Massa Andrew." The old woman grew silent a moment, thinking back to the days of her youth. Days that were filled with hard work and the lash of the whip if one fell behind. She waggled her head again, peering up at Beulah. "Massa Andrew don't hold with no whuppin'. We's lucky here at Stafford Hall Plantation. Over at Willow Manor," she jerked her head to the side, indicating the next plantation, "dey ain't so lucky." She pointed a bony finger at Tilda. "Yo' make sure yo' an' yor chile does the work dey gives yo', and yo'll do jus' fine. Yo' give Massa an' Missus trouble and yo' be sent up de river. Yo' listen to ole Aunt Sallie, chilluns. Dis is a good place to be. Don't take no chances bein' sent somewhere else. Lots of places out dere ain't a good place to be." She drew a deep breath as though her long speech had winded her, then turned abruptly and went up the path.

Beulah and Tilda followed the old woman's hunched figure to the cabin that would be their new home.

"Go ahead and git settled in, then yo' two git on up to de great house. Mammy Ticey waitin' fo' yo'. She tell yo' what yo' duties be." Abruptly, Aunt Sallie turned her scrawny back on them and walked back to her own small cabin, disappearing inside.

It was early morning, but already the slaves were in the fields tending to their day's work. Tilda could hear them singing softly, their voices drifting across the wide expanse. She knew their hoes would be striking the ground at exactly the same time, each of them moving in time to the chant that kept them working rhythmically. She stopped, turning her attention to a fat bumblebee buzzing industriously among the green leaves of the boxwoods lining the path beyond the slave quarters up to the manor. The bright sun beat hotly down on the two in the path. Beulah nudged her daughter along the path to the back entrance of the great house.

Life at Stafford Hall was much the same as at any other southern plantation except that Andrew Hamilton ran his estate with a firm but kind hand. He believed that happy, contented people were reasonably happy, contented workers. With that perception of running a successful estate, he strove to keep that balance, thus insuring the smooth operation of his plantation. More lenient than other plantation owners, Andrew allowed his slaves a certain amount of leisure. They often held small, festive gatherings, and met at a cabin for religious meetings on Sunday.

The slaves owned by Benjamin and Alice Witherspoon of Willow Manor Plantation were allowed little freedom. Benjamin was harsh and oftentimes cruel in Andrew's estimation. However, the slaves from both plantations occasionally met in a clearing in the woods owned by Stafford Hall, which lay between the two properties. While this fact was known to those at Stafford Hall, they felt it necessary to keep it to themselves.

The clearing lay in close proximity to Stafford Hall, and on a quiet summer evening, one could hear voices singing and music filling the air. The muted sounds of stamping feet pounding the earth in pagan-like dances, accompanied the strains of banjos, fiddles and drums. Simon, who had been born on Stafford plantation, led the festivities with an innate love for the fiddle, which he had begun playing at an early age.

EmiLee's days were filled from dawn to dusk with the many duties necessary in running the house and domestic end of an estate as large as Stafford Hall. She supervised the planning of the meals, saw to the candlemaking and soapmaking, as well as the spinning and weaving, and the making of the clothing for the slaves. With the assistance of old Aunt Sallie, she was nurse to the slaves for minor ailments. A doctor was always called in for more serious illnesses. She was a gracious hostess, opening her home to a bevy of diverse visitors who arrived just as frequently by water as they did by land.

Beulah and Tilda soon grew accustomed to life under their new master. Beulah felt that God -- and Marsa James -- had smiled on them, for she was given duties in the kitchen quarters, and Tilda ran errands and was learning to spin and sew. Beulah tried hard to please her new mistress, for she was well aware that Tilda received privileges that other children in the slave quarters did not. She knew it was because young Marsa James stood up to his mother. Although Missus EmiLee was not unkind to Tilda, Beulah could see it in her face that she did not approve of her son's high-handedness where Tilda was concerned. Wes was another child of the same circumstances and was a slave on the plantation. The son of a previous owner, he was dark-skinned like his mother and showed none of the white blood of the planter. He was treated the same as the other slaves, which made it all the more important to Beulah that she please her mistress in every way. She knew from experience that if Missus EmiLee wanted to overrule her son, she could, and was thankful her mistress often looked the other way.

Tilda was soon drawn into the circle of the other plantation children who, while initially curious of her soft cloud of long dark hair and fair skin, accepted her as just another slave like themselves. Wes was about Tilda's age but he worked in the fields with his mother and her husband, Mose. He was a slow, somewhat lazy boy who would much rather lay on the hay in the barn, than play with the other children. Ivy, a few years older than Tilda, was beginning to cast an eye toward the young male slaves. She worked in the laundry with her mother and lived just two cabins down from Beulah. Mingo was a different story. He was a tall, strapping young boy who carried his belligerence on his shoulders, and anger on his face. Mingo lived farther away in a group of cabins near the fields where he and his family worked.

As soon as Beulah got settled into the vacant cabin, old Aunt Sallie told her she could raise some chickens, and put out a garden on a small plot of ground near the cabin, to add to the rations of cornmeal and pork or beef that all the slaves received on a weekly basis.

"Catch all de fish yo' wants at the river," the old woman told her. "An' if'en yo' wants to sell some o' yor veg'tables and eggs to the store in town, Massa don't care. Long as yo' don't let it interfere with yo' other jobs."

Beulah could not believe her good luck to be sold to a plantation such as this. Her mind was whirling with the possibilities that were imaginable by selling eggs, vegetables, even fish from Marsa's river. She might even be able to save enough money to buy Tilda's freedom. Her heartbeat quickened and her mind raced with the thought. She would bake her ginger cookies. Ol' Missus from her last plantation had orders every week from her friends. Not a week went by that Beulah hadn't baked hundreds of those cookies. Beulah wagged her head. 'Course old Missus never gave her no money. She kept it all for herself. A smile spread over Beulah's features. The Lawd sure was smilin' on dem when he sent young Marsa James their way!

With this last thought, Beulah's glanced flowed over the cabins that stretched in a double row beyond her. She saw a cluster of older slave women watching babies and small children while their parents worked in the fields. The little girls cradled corncob dolls dressed in scraps of cloth handsewn by the women, and the little boys played in the the dirt outside the cabin with blocks of wood cut into many different shapes and sizes. She could hear the cry of a small baby or two, which sent two of the women inside the cabin to tend them.

Beulah had been to a campfire meeting last night, invited by old Aunt Sallie who told her they gathered for storytelling and a chance to visit. Before the night was over, the talk had turned to freedom, and their hopes of "'scapin' to the No'th." But Beulah had stayed silent, holding her daughter next to her. She didn't want to go No'th. She agreed with old Aunt Sallie, who had told them when they first arrived, "This plantation is a good place to be."

A faded brown ribbon road meandered downhill, gently winding from the back of the estate to the land's end, which stopped abruptly at the edge of the Potomac. Slave children of all ages enjoyed running down the "rolling road" to watch as the Negro men rolled huge casks of cured tobacco to the wharf, where the hogsheads and huge bales of cotton were picked up and delivered to a waiting ship that would take them north, to England and other foreign ports. The ships that picked up the tobacco and bales of cotton brought, in exchange, bolts of silks, satins, velvets, coffee, and spices.

Beyond the wharf, in a clearing surrounded on three sides by tall trees, was a stone gristmill powered by a nearby pond. Its massive waterwheel, turning on wooden gears, powered its millstones, grinding corn, wheat, barley, and oats grown on the plantation.

Tilda stood with the other children watching, hopping from one barefoot to the other, as the men rolled the huge hogsheads down to the wharf. She saw John Avery, Stafford Hall's clerk, making notations in his large accounting book, which he allowed no one to touch. She had seen him many times when she played outside beyond daylight, sitting on a high chair at his desk, working by lamplight.

The book looked almost too large for his thin frame, but he clutched it to his chest, peering over small, wire-frame eyeglasses at the children who had gathered to see the casks rolled aboard the small vessel waiting to take it to a ship anchored in the harbor of the Potomac. And though the slave children rarely got the opportunity to see the contents of the crates and boxes that were brought ashore, he knew it still excited them to watch them being unloaded. His dove-gray eyes fell on Tilda, and shyly, she smiled up at him. He returned the smile, feeling an ache in his heart for the girl fate had betrayed so wretchedly. He thought she was almost too beautiful.

John Avery was, many years ago, an indentured servant from England who came at a young age to work for Andrew's father, Palmer Hamilton. He was under bond to stay for seven years to repay a debt. Being conscientious and having formed a lasting and loyal friendship with the Hamiltons of Stafford Hall, he had remained as a hired clerk after Palmer's death, working for Andrew and EmiLee Hamilton. A quiet, gentle little man, John Avery lived in rooms above the office space where he spent his days, and often long into the evening, tending to all matters pertaining to the plantation.

The children stayed on the bank until the last crate had been hauled up to the estate. Only when the final one was out of sight did they disperse, running and skipping, some singing as they went, in their separate directions. John Avery watched them go with a slow waggle of his head.

One evening, after dark, Tilda and Ivy crouched behind the boxwoods, watching the flickering lamplight and dancing figures of the guests attending the party at the big house. They whispered in hushed and excited tones as the carriages arrived, and the ladies alighted in their colorful gowns of silk and satin. Their eyes grew large as they watched from their wonderful vantage point, the white folks eating dainty morsels served from silver trays by white-suited slaves. The faint tinkle of crystal reached their ears, and it sounded like fairy music to Tilda. She watched with delight as they danced, their skirts swirling in a palette of pinks and blues and greens. The men wore fine suits and broad ties, keeping in perfect step with the ladies in their dainty leather slippers.

Once, Tilda saw Mister James dancing with a young girl with blond curls piled on top of her head and a cascade of long ringlets hanging down the back. She wore a deep-pink gown with small rosebuds sewn onto the overskirt that was gathered up to show just a hint of white lace beneath. Tilda frowned. Her young heart did a curious flip when she saw Mister James smiling down into the upturned face of the girl he held in his arms. She was so beautiful. But that thought only made the frown deepen. As Tilda continued to watch, bits of conversation and laughter floated out to them captured by the summer night breeze.

Some of the dancers had climbed the stairs to the platform stretching across the rooftop between the four chimneys clustered on each end of the rooftop. The chimneys were joined by white wooden balusters which made a small enclosure within the four brick structures. It also entered onto the balcony-like platform at the top of the house. It was high above the buzz of mosquitoes and enabled the guests to take advantage of cool breezes. The chimney cluster enclosures were also a private place for the younger couples to slip away to escape the eagle eyes of their elders.

At the end of the house nearest the boxwood gardens, Ivy pointed out a couple concealed in the shadows of the chimney cluster. They were wrapped in a firm embrace, their lips pressed gently together. Ivy watched with wide eyes. Tilda cared not for the kissing scene that so excited Ivy. She was more interested in watching the dancers floating round the room, and perhaps to catch yet another glimpse of Mister James. A rustle behind them caused Tilda to turn away from the festive atmosphere.

"What yo' two think you's doin'?" Beulah demanded, making both girls jump. "Git over here, Tilda! You, too, Ivy! Git on home!" Beulah said sternly. She caught up Tilda by the nape of her cotton dress. "Marsa catch yo' spyin' on dem white folks, and yo' git whupped!" she declared, dragging the little girl off.

But Tilda wasn't concerned about "gittin'

whupped." She had learned from her first day that Massa Andrew never allowed no one to whup his slaves. They might be punished in other ways, but he never struck them with a whip like she had seen done on her other plantation. Tilda liked this plantation. She never wanted to leave it, or Mister James Hamilton. She put her small hands over her mouth, stifling a giggle at that admission, which had been in her young heart since the first day she met him.

2

Hide thyself as it were for a little moment,
until the indignation be overpast.

Isaiah

*T*he warmth of the summer day lay on the land in a blend of deep greens and vivid shades of floral pastels, all of it topped by a cloudless, bright blue sky. In the side yard, like a canopy of delicate lace, the dogwood trees hovered, their branches barely moving as a lazy breeze sighed through them. Tilda sat beneath the lace canopy playing with a crudely made rag doll. The sound of a horse walking over the hard-packed dirt road caused her to look in that direction. A smile spread across her face at the sight of James astride the black horse. He waved and she leaped to her feet and ran to him.

James reined in the horse, reached into his breast pocket, and withdrew a peppermint stick. He leaned down, handing it to Tilda as she approached. "How are you today, Tilda?" he asked.

"Fine, Suh," she answered softly, accepting the peppermint stick in wide-eyed awe to be the recipient of such a wonderful treat.

James derived great pleasure from bringing the little girl an apple or peach or small piece of candy. It was such a small gesture in the bleakness of her world. "I did not see you playing with the others yesterday," he said quietly.

She lowered her head, avoiding his eyes and offering no reply.

A frown creased James' forehead. "Is something wrong, Tilda?" His senses seemed so sensitive to the moods and thoughts of this unusual child.

"Dey's laughin' at my hair," she began softly. Her brow knitted and she spoke with sharp decisiveness, "Maybe I get it cut off."

James slid off his horse, and bent to the child. His hand caressed her softly curling, full cloud of black hair. "Your hair is beautiful, Tilda. You mustn't listen to the children who tease you." He lifted her chin in his hand. "You must not think of cutting it."

"But dey say it ugly -- "

"Stop talking like the slaves, Tilda," James insisted, correcting her speech as he often did whenever he spoke with the little girl.

Her dark eyes searched his face. "What's it matter how I talk, Mister James? Mama says I am a slave, that I always will be, but Mingo says I don't belong nowhere, that I ain't," she hesitated, peeping up at James, before correcting her speech. "He says I'm not either black or white. That I'm just hangin' in the air, and don't belong nowhere." Her last words caught in her throat.

"Well, Mingo's wrong. You mustn't listen to him, Tilda," James told her gently. "Right now, you belong here, and I will see that you are taken care of, but one day you will be free. I promise you that. You must learn to speak properly. It will help you when that time comes. Trust me, Tilda. Pay no attention to what Mingo says. Now tell me," he asked, "where were you yesterday?"

Shuffling her bare feet on the ground, she replied slowly, "I was at my secret place."

"A secret place, huh?"

She nodded, speaking in a hushed voice as though fearing her secret would take flight, like the mockingbird she'd seen venture from its nest yesterday trilling a melody for all to hear. "Nobody knows about it except me," she said. "I was going to tell Jane. She's my friend. She's nice to me." She blinked long lashes that feathered like tiny bird wings. Then shyly conceded softly, "You're my friend, too."

James smiled. "When I was a boy," he told her confidentially, "I had a secret place, too."

"You did?"

He nodded.

"Were there lots of flowers?"

"Lots of flowers," he said emphatically.

"And clover that's so soft on your bare feet, just like the rugs in the great house?"

Again James nodded. "Yes. I remember a carpet of wildflowers and a wall of honeysuckle vines that smelled so sweet. And," he continued to the wide-eyed little girl, "when I pushed those wild honeysuckle vines aside, there was a cut out place in the rock that made a perfect hideaway. It was my favorite spot."

Tilda caught her breath at the familiar description. She smiled, her eyes holding his. "It was your secret place, too?" she whispered.

He nodded. "It was my secret place, too," he repeated.

Tilda's smile grew wider, pleased that she shared something as wonderful as a secret place with Mister James.

A commotion in the yard beyond the house caused them to turn. Andrew was striding ahead of Mingo, who was accompanied by a slave girl in her early twenties with close cropped hair and a twisted foot that caused her to limp. She was singing in broken speech and refusing to allow Mingo to touch her.

"Who is that?" Tilda asked, hearing James click his tongue, as he shook his head ruefully.

"Dora from over at Willow Manor. She wanders off sometimes," James told her.

"She acts funny. Is she sick?"

"Only in her mind," James replied.

Tilda stared. She'd never seen a crazy person before.

"Don't stare, Tilda," James admonished. "She is to be pitied. She can't help what she is. Besides that," he said sadly, "she will be severely disciplined if they discover she is gone. That's why we try to get her back home before she is missed."

Andrew approached his son. "She's come wandering in from across the fields again," he explained to James. "I've told Mingo to take her back, but she won't go with him, and if he takes her arm or touches her, she screeches like a banshee." His exasperated glance fell on Tilda. "Perhaps Tilda could go with them?"

James started to protest, but clamped his mouth shut.

Tilda edged up to Dora. "Hi. I'm Tilda. Do you want me to take you home?"

Dora's black eyes briefly drilled into Tilda's, then darted over her small figure. Her squarish hand came up to stroke Tilda's hair. "Oooh," she murmured.

Tilda took her hand. "Come on, Dora. Come with me," she said gently.

They fell into step beside Mingo and hurried up the lane where they entered into the woods. Tilda broke the peppermint stick into thirds, handing one piece to Dora and one to Mingo. As the peppermint flavor melted in Dora's mouth, a smile spread over the tortured features. Gaining comfort from the kindness, she moved with childlike trust closer to Tilda, her crippled foot dragging awkwardly.

"Where yo' get dat candy?" Mingo demanded.

"Massa James give it to me," saidTilda.

"Massa James, hummp," he snorted. "He treats yo' different. Acts like yo' ain't no slave."

"Massa James say I ain't always gonna be a slave. He say I gonna be free someday," Tilda flung back, slipping easily into the familiar dialect.

"You stupid if yo' believes dat," Mingo snapped. "Cause we is all slaves and dat's all we's ever gonna be. Yo' better stay away from dem white folks at the great house. Deys makin' yo' brain as soft as Dora's. Yo' ain't never gonna be free, Tilda," he said firmly. "The sooner you gets dat through yo' head, the better off you's gonna' be. Yo' ain't black, dat's fo' sho'," he said, marking his last words with slow emphasis, "but you *is* a slave."

"What makes you think you know more than Massa James?" snapped Tilda, tossing her head. She refused to listen to Mingo any longer and hurried Dora ahead.

They emerged from the woods beyond the tall pillared front of Willow Manor. The rough hewn log cabins housing the slaves were located in the clearing below the house. The slaves were gathered in a cluster, their faces stricken with fear. It was apparent Dora was already discovered missing. Orem Lemly, a big brute of a man with broad shoulders and ham-like hands, held the position of overseer. When he snarled, which was often, his face contorted into a dog-like grimace of cruelty. The slaves knew he was mean to the soul. When he brandished the whip with a look of pleasure on his face, there was not a person who didn't believe he would use it. He flicked it menacingly, snapping it overhead. The sound sent chills up the spine of every man, woman and child.

He confronted the group, demanding, "Which one of you let dumb Dora run off again?"

Waiting for no reply, he turned to a tall, thin woman who quaked with fear at the piercing eyes drilling into her over a bulbous nose. Her turban wrapped head shook uncontrollably. "You weren't watching her, were you Mandy?" Orem Lemly snarled. "You're the one who let her run off again, aren't you?"

"No, Suh," she whimpered. "Missus sent me off to fetch young Frankie there, Suh."

She pointed to her mistress's youngest son, six- year-old Frankie, who stood watching them tremble beneath the glare of the nasty overseer. His young features were alight with excitement and a perverse enjoyment at their misery.

"Don't blame it on the boy, wench!" Orem yelled, raising the whip.

"No, Suh, please!" the woman begged, falling to her

knees. "Mandy couldn't be two places at once."

"Don't sass me, nigger!" And the whip came down. Mandy's scream ripped the air.

"There's old dumb Dora," Frankie called out to the overseer.

Orem Lemly turned to where the boy pointed. "Who the hell are you?" he demanded, his flashing eyes settling on the trio standing at the edge of the path, staring.

"Dey's from over at Stafford Hall," answered a strapping, shirtless man at the center of the group, who hoped to gain favor by answering the overseer's question. His bare, ebony-skinned back gleamed with sweat in the sunlight.

But the overseer turned on him. "Who the hell asked you? Shut up 'til you're spoken to!" The whip cracked through the air, popping with a sickening sound against the back of the black who had spoken. His moan crawled with piercing arrows over every slave in the frightened cluster. They shivered in fear of the man wielding the whip, watching with black eyes as he turned away from them to the three who came out of the woods. Orem's steely gaze flicked over Mingo and Tilda. With one long stride, he came abreast of them, reached out with that ham-like fist and snatched Dora from the false security she had felt with Tilda.

"I'll teach you to run off, you dumb nigger!"

Despite her mental deficiency, Dora knew what was coming, for she covered her head with her arms, and began to screech even before the whip met its mark. The first blow knocked her to the ground. Incensed by her relentless screeching, the man brought the whip whistling through the air, striking her again and again.

Amid it all, Frankie's voice cheered the overseer on. He chanted a taunting verse over and over, hopping up and down.

> *"Old dumb Dora,*
> *dumb as a stick.*
> *If she can't stay home,*
> *she's gonna get whipped."*

Dora's moans and high-pitched screeching filled the air. Mingo and Tilda stood as if rooted to the spot, staring wide-eyed.

Suddenly aware that they were still there, the overseer turned on them. "What the hell are you two starin' at?" he yelled.

Mingo reached out to Tilda, who stood frozen in her steps.

"Go on! Get out of here!" the man yelled. "Get back to your plantation where you belong! And take that half white bitch with you!" The whip whistled through the air, emphasizing his words.

Mingo ran, his long-legged stride carrying him toward the woods. At first, Tilda backed away for several feet, then when she saw the whip rise again, she turned and began to run. Tilda heard the whip sing a shrill note through the air. It hit her shoulder, ripping her dress and tearing the soft flesh beneath. A bolt of searing pain knocked Tilda to her knees. A cold shudder jabbed through her body, accompanied by a terrified scream bubbling unbidden past her lips. She struggled to her feet, running to escape the fiery thrust of the lash again soaring behind her. She ran as fast as she could, crashing through the woods, panic-stricken when a branch dipped down at her, tearing at her hair and arms. With renewed terror, breathlessly, she ran and ran.

It was long past the dinner hour when James returned home. He whistled a tune as he loped up the stairs to the wide front door. Mammy Ticey threw open the door before he reached the top step, her face drawn, and her eyes strangely clouded. It was a look that struck fear in James' heart.

He stopped abruptly, his eyes meeting hers. "What is it, Mammy Ticey? Mother? Father?"

She shook her head. "No, Jimmie-James. They is both all right. It's Tilda. She -- "

"Tilda?" James grew white, though he tried to quell his emotions. "What has happened?"

"She . . . she," the old woman faltered. "She got hurt when she took Dora over to Willow Manor today."

"Hurt? Hurt how?"

"Now Jimmie-James, you's got to be calm. I knows how yo' feels about dese things, 'specially that little chile, but yo' can't go runnin' off, smokin' 'tween de ears," Mammy Ticey said sternly.

"Mammy," he said sharply, "stop telling me what I can't do and tell me, what has happened to Tilda?"

"Well," she rolled a deep pink tongue around thick lips, striving for a way to tell him gently.

But the delay only frustrated James, and he demanded, "For God's sake, Mammy, tell me what has happened!"

She stepped back at the sharpness of his voice. "Well, it seem Orem Lemly, the overseer, was a lashin' out at those po' black folks over dere, an'," she faltered, "an' he done hit dat po' chile."

"Tilda? He struck Tilda?" James gritted the words in a slow, clipped tone that scared the stalwart Mammy Ticey, who quickly stepped aside as he took the last of the steps in two long strides, pushing through the front door. "How bad is she hurt?"

Mammy Ticey shook her head. "Don't know, honeychile."

James turned back to the door. "I'm going to Beulah's cabin."

"She ain't dere," came softly from behind him.

He turned back. "What do you mean she's not there? Where is she?"

"Don't know. Beulah's waitin' to talk to you. Wants yo' to help her find Tilda."

"Find her? No one knows where she is?"

Mammy Ticey shook her head.

"Where was Mingo? Wasn't he with her?"

"He runned when de overseer yelled at 'em, but Tilda was behind him and got struck with the whip."

James felt his muscles grow taut and Mammy Ticey saw his eyes grow ice cold. "So no one knows how badly she's hurt?" he asked quietly, striving to control his anger.

42

Again, Mammy Ticey shook her head.

"Have they searched for her?"

"Master Andrew got some of de men together and dey looked fo' a long time, but couldn't find her."

"Fetch me a lantern, Mammy," James said.

"Where is yo' goin' Jimmie-James?" the old woman asked fearfully.

"Don't worry, Mammy," he said kindly. "Send word to Beulah for me. Tell her I'll bring Tilda home. I think I know where she is."

Carrying the lantern, James' hurried gait took him round the outskirts of the tobacco field to the edge of the woods where a bed of wildflowers spread in twilight drenched splendor. He paid no attention to the riotous array of bright colors poised momentarily in the lantern light. His heart raced as his anger persisted. Tilda was such a fragile, delicate girl, and once again, he cursed her fate.

The sweet scent of the honeysuckle blossoms that twined round the vines, assailed his senses long before he reached the spot where he believed Tilda had gone to hide from a world whose cruelty she did not understand. He reached the vine-covered, carved-out rock Tilda had called her secret place, and which had once served as his retreat. He knew she was in there. Every instinct told him he would find her there.

Slowly, he pushed back the full curtain of vines and held up the lantern. In the scintillating light, he saw the small figure crouched in the furthermost corner of the cave. The forlorn image of her cowering against the cold rock brought an instantaneous pain to James' heart. The sight of her in such a desolate curled up position, like she was trying to withdraw from the world, to hide within herself, made his heart ache.

"Tilda?" he said softly, moving inside and setting aside the lantern.

She looked up with terror-filled eyes red from weeping, saw him and with a jerking sob, scrambled to her feet and ran to him.

His arms closed about her in much the same manner

as he would have done Jane, but his heart knew this was different. And once again, he wondered what it was about this little girl that had captured his heart, lingered like a taunt in his brain, and tormented his soul.

Tilda clung to him, burying her face against his jacket, sobbing uncontrollably. Holding her, his fingers encountered the torn dress, and they shook when they felt the open flesh that still oozed with the warmth of her blood.

She whimpered, shifting her shoulder from beneath his touch.

James lifted the lantern, holding it high. The gash was deep and ragged. He let the lamp fall with a jarring thud that echoed in the lower regions of his stomach. "Oh, God, Tilda," he moaned, sinking to the ground with her.

The reality of the savage act swept over him with sickening force. He cradled her in his arms, numb with a burning anger. "I'm so sorry, I'm so sorry," he whispered.

When he calmed, he rose with her still in his arms. "I'm taking you home," he said softly. "Your mother is worried and we need to take care of this."

She made no answer, simply locked her arms about him, and pressed her face against his chest.

He carried her through the field of flowers, retracing his steps, until he reached the cluster of slave quarters. Beulah, standing at the door, watching, came running toward him when James called out to her.

"Tilda, baby," her mother cried, reaching for the child. "She okay, Marsa James?"

"She'll be all right, Beulah," he answered, not relinquishing the child. He carried her inside, speaking over his shoulder. "Get me some warm water, and ask Aunt Sallie for some ointment," he said, placing Tilda gently on the wooden bed that had a thin blanket pulled over the mattress of straw.

By the time the water was warm, old Aunt Sallie arrived. She stood at the foot of the bed looking down on the child. James began to remove Tilda's dress, nudging it gently from the dried blood near the ragged gash. Beulah came forward with the pan of warm water. When James reached to take the cloth from her, he saw tears streaming down her face. He wanted to console her, but couldn't, for his own emotions were filled with rage.

Intending to take over the ministrations, old Aunt Sallie moved around to the side of the bed and bent to take the cloth and pan of water, but James stopped her with a quietly spoken, "I'll do it."

Old Aunt Sallie's black eyes met Beulah's, but neither dared to speak.

James cleansed the wound gently and thoroughly and applied a soothing coat of an herbal balm. When he finished, he leaned over Tilda, smoothing her hair back from her forehead with his fingertips. "Rest now," he whispered.

When he rose, Tilda reached out and caught his hand. He looked down at her, expecting her to say something, but she merely stared at him with huge brown eyes. A smile tilted her finely drawn lips upward. James smiled down on her, turned, and strode across the room and out the door.

The night was still, and every person on Stafford Hall Plantation heard the pounding of hooves thundering down the lane toward Willow Manor, echoing portentously in the moonlight.

James rode directly up to the overseer's cottage, leaped from his horse, ran up the steps, and pounded hard on the door.

Orem snatched open the door, disgruntled at being disturbed at the late hour. "What the hell do you want?" he growled.

Without an answer, James' fist shot out, grasping the man by his shirt front. He pulled him through the door, dragging him down the porch steps to the ground, whereupon he began to pummel the man relentlessly.

Orem raised to his knees, holding one beefy hand over his bloody face. "You son of a bitch! You broke my damn nose!"

"And I'll break your damn neck if you ever lay

another hand on one of my slaves," James threw back at him. "You're damn lucky that's all I've done. If I had my way, I'd take the whip to your good for nothing hide."

"I intend to talk to Mr. Witherspoon about this," the man shouted.

"Don't bother," James returned. "I'll tell him myself!" And he strode away toward the manor, leaving the man lying in the dirt.

At the home of Benjamin and Alice Witherspoon, James rapped sharply. A servant answered the irate knock. "I want to see Mr. Witherspoon," James demanded.

"Yes, Suh. Yes, Mistuh Hamilton. Come in," the servant said, standing back to allow him to enter. "Mistuh Witherspoon in de library. I'll tell him you is here."

"Never mind," James said, striding past the startled servant. "I'll announce myself."

His knuckles rapped once on the library door before he pushed it open and strode inside with a step as firm as his jaw.

Benjamin Witherspoon looked up in surprise at having a visitor so late at night. "James. Is something wrong?"

"Your overseer struck one of my people today," James answered bluntly.

"What had he done?" asked Benjamin, chewing on a fat cigar.

"Not he -- her. A nine-year-old girl. And she had done nothing more than bring home your Dora who had wandered away. We've brought her home several times, Benjamin. I must admit, I am surprised at the authority you allow that callous bastard, Lemly."

"He's a good overseer," replied the man.

"Well," James said dryly, "cruelty is not something I look for in a good overseer. This little girl will be scarred for life, and I resent the manner in which this incident was handled."

Benjamin Witherspoon rose, striding toward James. "This is the first I've heard of it, and if that is the case, then of course, you are absolutely right. I apologize, and

I will see to it that Lemly is reprimanded."

James shook his head. "Not good enough. I want him fired," he said firmly.

The man shook his head. "I can't do that. I have no one to replace him."

But James remained insistent.

After a lengthy interim, Benjamin heaved a sigh. "All right, I must admit he has been a bit hard on the slaves of late." He put his hand on James' shoulder. "I'll see that it's done in the morning."

James nodded his head tersely, turned sharply on his heel, and walked out of the room.

Later that night, when James slipped silently into the house, he did not know that awaiting his return, Mammy Ticey hid behind the heavy portieres draping the doorway.

Thankful to see him safely home, she shook her head, bewildered with the thoughts that jumped around inside it. "Dear Lawd," she prayed silently, "what has happened to my Jimmie-James?" Fearing she knew the answer, she pushed the impossible thought back into the far-reaching regions of her mind, unwilling to admit it even to herself. Her old heart fluttered tremulously with foreboding as she watched him climb the stairs to his bedroom.

The next day both plantations buzzed with the news that Orem Lemly had been fired from Willow Manor, but not before young Massa James of Stafford Hall had beaten him up and broken his nose, they reported. The slaves relished the details and the story grew each time it passed from one to another. For several nights following the incident, the party in the woods grew loud in celebration.

The joy was short-lived, however for within the next week, Benjamin Witherspoon hired a new overseer at Willow Manor. Devlin Wilcott was as cruel as his predecessor, and his actions soon earned him the name of "Devil" Wilcott. Once again, the slaves of Willow Manor lived in fear.

The incident was soon forgotten as new concerns arose with the new overseer. However, the slaves of Willow Manor, determined to gain a tiny bit of respite from their daily ordeals, continued their practice of sneaking away to the gatherings in the woods whenever they thought it safe.

Plantation life was never silent, the work unending. By the time the harvesting of one crop began preparations were well under way for the next year's planting. There was always an abundance of chores to keep even the youngest child busy. Crops that must be harvested and put up for the long winter months were soon keeping everyone busy. The cold, dragging days of winter lay just around the corner.

Snow lay on the ground as James climbed into the sleigh en route to take Abigail Johnston for an afternoon outing. He saw several of the slave children sledding on a nearby hill and heard their gleeful laughter and shouting as they tumbled about in the freshly fallen snow. His eyes searched among the children for Tilda, but he didn't see her. He shrugged it off, and climbed up into the carriage.

Two days later, Andrew strode down to the slave quarters in search of Sophie, who worked in the kitchen quarters, and Jake, who was a sawyer in the mill. Neither had been to work for several days.

He encountered old Aunt Sallie just entering Sophie's cabin.

"Something wrong with Sophie?" he asked her, peering inside to the bed in the single room.

"She feelin' po'ly today, Marse. I gib her some herb med'cine," said the old woman. "Jake's been sick, too, but he better today. Sophie should be all right 'nother day or two."

Andrew's glance fell over the woman on the bed, for he was aware the scalawags feigned illness on occasion to keep from working. However, the woman did appear fitful, and so he conceded, "All right, Aunt Sallie, do you need anything for her?"

"No, Marse," Aunt Sallie shook her head. "My med'cine's good. She be okay soon."

Andrew smiled inwardly, knowing the old woman used a combination of African incantations and herbs to heal the slaves. He turned to go, then looked back. "Everyone else all right?"

"All 'cept Tilda. She been sick fo' a week now."

"I'll stop by Beulah's and check on her," Andrew said, as he left the small cabin.

At Beulah's cabin, he found a feverish Tilda tossing and turning on the double bedstead she shared with her mother. He spoke briefly to Beulah, as he touched the girl's fevered brow.

"Aunt Sallie been giving her medicine?"

Tilda's mother nodded. "Don't seem to help. She don't seem to be much better, Suh."

"I'll get Mrs. Hamilton to take a look at her," Andrew said gently.

"Thank you, Suh," Beulah replied.

En route to the manor, Andrew met James just returning home. He waved, and James waited for his father to catch up to him.

"It's cold out. Where have you been?"

"Over at the slave quarters. Sophie and Jake have been sick. I went to check on them."

"They all right?"

"They are better now, but Tilda is pretty sick. I want your mother to take a look at her," Andrew told him. "She's running a fever and been sick for more than a week."

James started toward the cabin.

"Where are you going?" his father asked. Futile to ask, he thought, hurrying to catch up to his son who loped onward without a word.

James marched to Beulah's cabin, rapped once, calling out, "Beulah, may I come in?"

The door opened immediately. "Yas, Suh, Marsa James."

James strode past her to the bed where Tilda lay. Gathering the blanket around her, he lifted her in his arms. He spoke quietly to Beulah, "Pack whatever you need and come up to the house. You'll be staying there a few days. Mother can care for Tilda easier at the house. Mammy Ticey will be there to help."

He strode across the floor and out the door past his father.

He heard Beulah's softly uttered, "Yas, Marsa James, thank yo', Marsa James."

Andrew strode ahead of his son. He had started to reprimand him, to call attention to the example he was setting to the other slaves, but some inner voice stopped him. At that moment, he was acutely aware of his own shortcomings and wished for the thousandth time that he had the courage to do exactly as his son had done. He clamped his mouth shut. At the entrance to the manor, Andrew held the door open so that James could enter with the girl in his arms. He carried Tilda upstairs to a small back room.

EmiLee came running up the stairs. "James Robert Hamilton, what on earth do you think you're doing?" his mother demanded.

"She cannot survive in that cabin," James answered. "It is too cold, and she is too delicate. She will stay here with her mother until she is well," he said firmly.

His father had pulled out the trundle bed beneath the big bed, and James settled Tilda onto it.

His mother watched, open-mouthed. Finally, she said, "James, this is just not done. She is a nigra. A slave."

"She is as white as you or I," James retorted. "It is not her fault to be born part black, part white." His deep blue eyes beseeched his mother. "She is a child, Mother," he entreated. "A child who is very sick. Where is the compassion you have administered to so many others? Why do you persist in treating Tilda differently?"

"Because, James," his mother answered quietly, "*you* insist on treating her much too differently from the other plantation children."

"She *is* different, Mother. Can't you see that?"

Andrew, quiet until now, laid his hand on his wife's arm. "Listen to him," he urged.

She saw the look in his eyes, and drawing a deep sigh, she conceded, "All right, James. Attend to your other chores. Mammy and I will see that the child is cared

50

for."

James planted a kiss on EmiLee's forehead. "Thank you, Mother," he said softly.

Beulah and Tilda stayed in the great house for nearly three weeks. And in that time, James often climbed the stairs to the little room at the end of the hall. He'd stand in the shadows of the wide hallway, watching, listening, making sure that Tilda was progressing. After she began to regain her strength, he often saw Jane reading from a storybook to her, sharing her dolls as they participated in a tea party, and laughing like little girls do. Smiling to himself, James would slip silently back down the stairs.

3

I am going to seek a grand perhaps;
draw the curtain, the farce is played.
                   Rabelais

*P*ink skirts rustling, Jane swept into the room in search of Tilda. Most of Tilda's work was of a domestic nature, usually within the house, though on occasion she helped her mother in the kitchen dependency. Today, however, Jane found her at the spinning wheel in a small room on the second floor.

Ever since that long-ago day when Tilda had been ill and spent several weeks in the great house, she and Jane had remained good friends. She refused to allow Tilda to call her Miss Jane, unless in the company of other slaves, even though she thought it hypocritical. However, it was not because of herself that she did it, it was to spare Tilda any repercussions from the slave quarters. It was already well known to the others that Master James treated Tilda as an equal rather than a slave. Over the years, the slaves had become so used to young Master James' concern for the white slave that it now went relatively unnoticed.

"There you are!" Jane called out cheerily. "Tilda,

you simply must come and help me with my costume for the masquerade ball."

"It just arrived from Philadelphia yesterday. What is the matter with it?" Tilda asked. She never used Negro dialect around Jane, who was more adamant than James about her using proper speech. She drilled Tilda at times with determined rigidity.

"Just come look at it," Jane implored winningly.

With an indulgent shake of her head, Tilda rose. She found it hard to deny her young mistress anything, remembering all the long days when, as a little girl sick with pneumonia, Jane had slipped into her room and shared her dolls, read her stories that had made her eyes grow round with wonder, and reached out to her in genuine friendship.

She followed Jane down the hall to her room. When they entered, Tilda saw the masquerade gown spread out upon the coverlet draping the high four-poster bed. Her eyes grew large at the sight of the apricot-colored silk that was trimmed in white lace with gold trimmings set inside the rows of white lace.

Tilda strode to the bed, her fingers caressing the beautiful fabric. "Oh, Jane," she breathed. "This is so beautiful."

"It's a Marie Antoinette costume," Jane said. "See the wig," she pointed to the headdress on a stand on the dresser.

"Oh, my goodness," Tilda said, staring at the enormously high white wig intertwined with beads and lace that matched the dress. A small black hat, trimmed in tall feathered plummage that curled in every direction, was pinned to the mass of curls. Nestled among the white and gold feathers were two plumes dyed to match the apricot gown.

Tilda's small hands covered her mouth in awe. "It's so beautiful."

"Yes, it is," Jane agreed, "but I can't wear it."

Tilda cast a glance at her. "Why not?"

"It doesn't fit," she replied simply.

"Maybe we can fix it," Tilda suggested.

"I don't want you to fix it," Jane said, impatiently. "I want you to make me this." Her slender finger pointed to a picture in the current copy of *Godey's Lady's Book*.

Tilda peered over Jane's shoulder to see a sapphire velvet gown with plunging neckline, puffed sleeves, and yards and yards of lace trimming sleeves, bodice, and a wide swath that circled the full bottom of the skirt.

"It's from Paris," Jane told her. "The very latest in fashion. It's perfect for me, and I like it. I want to go as a Godey's Fashion Doll." At seventeen, Jane had grown into a tall, striking blond. She was willow slim and moved with grace and elegance.

"I don't know, Jane, if I can make this dress."

"Of course, you can," Jane said enthusiastically.

But Tilda shook her head with uncertainty.

"Remember when we were little and we left my doll, Miss Miranda, outside, and her dress got all muddy and was ruined. When I discovered her, I started to cry, and you told me you would make her another dress. Mother gave us some scraps of fabric and you made that beautiful dress with a cloak and muff."

"But, Jane," Tilda protested, "that was a doll."

"So what? You just make this dress bigger." She grinned. "Come on, Tilda, please."

"Well," Tilda drawled, thoughtfully. "Do you have the material?"

"There's lots in one of those crates in storage. Let's go look." She grabbed Tilda by the hand and hauled her to the door.

When they returned to Jane's room, their arms were loaded with bolts of fabric and rolls of white lace in different widths and styles.

Jane laid her bundles on the floor, hurriedly scooped up the Marie Antoinette dress on the bed, and draped it over a silk-cushioned chaise lounge. Retrieving her discarded bundles, she put them on the bed, then unloaded Tilda's arms.

Tilda stood back a moment, glancing from the material to Jane and back again, as though envisioning the gown in her own mind. She bent and picked up the roll of sapphire material and held it up to Jane. "This will look lovely with your fair skin and blond hair."

"It's my favorite color," Jane said absently, pushing the bolt away. "Tilda, first, I want to tell you something."

Jane's demeanor and the serious note in her voice made Tilda raise questioning eyes to her mistress.

"I didn't order the Marie Antoinette dress for myself," she said quietly. "Can't you see I'm much too tall for such a short gown?"

"I heard you ask your mother to order it for you," Tilda said softly.

Jane nodded. "I know. But I didn't say for me. I told her it was for a friend from school who would be meeting me here for the party."

Jane's eyes flowed over Tilda's slight figure. She felt a deep sadness about her, feeling that life had been unfair to Tilda. It made it more important to her to treat Tilda as a friend and equal. It also made her conscious of how precarious life is. Any of them could just as easily have found themselves in such circumstances. Softly, she said, "I was ordering it for you."

The bolt of fabric slipped from Tilda's hands. "What do you mean?"

"I mean," Jane said firmly, "I want you to go to the masquerade ball and wear that costume."

"Me?" Tilda squeaked.

"It will be perfect on you. I had to guess, but I think it will fit you with some minor adjustments."

"Why?" Tilda whispered.

"Because," Jane began, and her voice grew serious again, "you deserve some fun in your life. You know," Jane said softly, "none of us in this family thinks of you as a slave, Tilda. Sometimes I feel so angry about you -- your circumstances. It just isn't fair," she said adamantly. "Please say you'll go." Then she added with a sly sideways glance, "James will be there."

Tilda peeped up at that, but couldn't disguise the faint blush that stole across her features.

"James doesn't know," her young mistress was

quick to say, "but I know he will be happy about it. And you musn't tell him, Tilda. Promise me you won't tell him."

Tilda was shaking her head, caught up in the unexpected thrill.

"This must be our secret. I'm going to tell everyone that I've invited a friend. You can be our mystery guest." She put her finger to her pink lips. "Let me see," she said, "you have to have a new name. Something no one will recognize." Her brow puckered in thought. "Victoria," she said. "Victoria Meade. That suits you." She waved a finger at her. "And we'll tell them you're a friend from school."

"Jane, I don't think we should do this," Tilda said from the bed where she had plunked down among the fabrics and lace in sheer astonishment. "Master Andrew and Missus will be awfully angry -- "

"Now you hush, Tilda," Jane demanded. "Nobody is going to be angry. Besides, if they find out, I'll handle Mama, and Daddy lets James get by with anything," she replied confidently. "Now, come on," she said, reaching for the Marie Antoinette gown, "let's try this on."

"Who is this Marie Antoinette?" Tilda asked as Jane helped her remove her own clothes and slipped the gown over her head. "Was she a slave, too?"

Jane laughed shortly. "No, Tilda. She was the Queen of France. She was married to Louis XVI."

"A queen?" Tilda drawled out thoughtfully.

Jane shook her head, frowning. "Don't look so bemused. It wasn't a good marriage."

"Why not?"

Jane shrugged. "I don't know, but he had her killed."

Tilda looked shocked.

Jane nodded. "He had her head cut off at the guillotine."

"What is a guillotine?"

"A razor-sharp contraption that cut peoples heads off," Jane answered in an oversimplifying manner.

Tilda shuddered, looking down at the dress, as

though it carried a curse.

Laughter bubbled past Jane's lips. "Forget that part of it," she said. "You will look absolutely beautiful in this costume. With a nip or two at the waist, it will fit you perfectly. Every young man at the ball will be asking you to dance."

Tilda frowned.

"What is the matter?"

"I can't dance," Tilda answered solemnly. "Leastways, not like white folks."

Jane frowned. "Well," she said after a moment's thought, "we'll just have to find time to teach you." She glanced up, demanding, "Now what are you frowning about?"

"I'm afraid no one is going to believe I'm a friend of yours when they see these hands." She held out work-worn hands that no amount of old Aunt Sallie's salves could keep soft and callous-free.

"Nonsense," Jane said. "I thought of that, too. You can wear a pair of my gloves, and no one will know." She smiled, proud of herself for thinking of everything.

"Miss Jane," Tilda said, overwhelmed and forgetting for a moment that it was not necessary to address Jane in such a way, "how will I ever thank you for doing this for me?"

"By not calling me Miss Jane," she answered somberly. "And for goodness sake, don't forget and do that at the party." Then she smiled. "And also by making this gown for me in time for the ball," she said spritely. Then as though speaking her thoughts out loud, she murmured, "I just can't wait for Adam Ward to see me in it."

"Who is Adam Ward?" Tilda asked, noting Jane's flushed face and the faraway look in her eyes.

"He lives over at Pope's Creek, on Calvert Hall Plantation. Oh, Tilda," she whispered, "wait 'til you see him. He has black wavy hair and eyes as green as a summer meadow. I met him at a party last summer, and . . . and," she faltered. "I just can't seem to forget him," she said simply.

Tilda smiled. Jane probably didn't think she could understand how she felt about this young man. But then, again, maybe she did, since she had confided in her. After all, hadn't Jane concocted this unbelievable opportunity for Tilda to be at a party with Mister James? And hadn't she provided a gown that was beyond her wildest dreams. Tilda thought her heart would burst with the wonder of it.

Jane's eyes had suddenly gathered fire. "And I'll tell you one thing, Tilda, Margaret Witherspoon had better keep her claws off of Adam! She is so disgustingly forward!"

Her eyes met Tilda's and they both erupted into laughter at the spontaneous outburst.

Tilda worked long, painstaking hours creating the ball gown for Jane. She wanted it to be everything her young mistress expected and more. It was the only way she could repay the kindness shown.

Later in the week during a fitting session, Tilda asked casually, "Do you know what James will be wearing to the party?"

With a sly grin, Jane nodded. "He was trying to be so secretive, but I slipped into his room while he was out."

Tilda waited, not realizing she was holding her breath.

"He'll be dressed as a highwayman," Jane said, a distinctive note of triumph in her voice. "He's wearing a black suit and cloak, a white shirt with a bunch of lace flowing down the front, and a black mask."

Tilda closed her eyes, trying to conjure up an image of James in the costume.

"I have to admit, he'll look exciting in it," his sister confided.

"Do you know what Adam will be wearing?"

She shook her head. "I don't want to know."

Tilda looked surprised. "Why not?"

"Because I want him to find me," she answered softly. "I want him to seek me out."

With the girlish chatter, the stitching and hemming that kept Tilda busy, and the numerous other daily duties, Jane still managed to find time to teach her the basic steps of ballroom dancing.

"Remember to smile a lot, and apologize if you don't do it correctly. Men love to be gallant and forgiving. You must get here to the house early that morning, because we have a lot to do. Mammy Ticey will help you bathe, and we'll help each other dress -- with Mammy's help, of course."

"Does Mammy Ticey know?" Tilda asked, feeling her heart skip a beat.

"Not yet." Then seeing Tilda's worried look, she said, "Don't worry about Mammy. She may appear gruff, but she wouldn't deny me anything." Jane grinned. "And just in case she does, I'll tell her James begged me to invite you. She'd do anything for James," she said smugly.

"I'm scared, Jane," Tilda whispered. "All this lying. My Mama always said, if I don't do right here, I would be sold and sent away." Her dark eyes filled with fear. "I never want to leave here," she whispered.

"Don't you ever worry about that for one instant," Jane scolded. "Why, you're like family, Tilda. Nobody is going to send you anywhere." She slipped her arm around the girl's shoulders. "Besides, this is just fun, Tilda. Youthful pranks. Nobody's going to be angry. Trust me."

Preparations continued and the time drew near. Tilda knew she could not put it off any longer. She had to tell her mother.

Beulah was not happy when she heard about it. "I's afraid fo' you, Tilda," she whispered. "The white blood of yor daddy is goin' crazy in yor veins, and it's gonna get yo' in trouble," she pronounced in an agitated manner.

"Jane said it will be all right."

"Miss Jane is jus' a chile," Beulah said sharply. "This is fun to her, but you, chile," she wagged her head sorrowfully. "I is tryin to save enough to buy yor freedom, but it's slow, Baby. You has to learn to be a slave, Tilda," she said sadly, "'cause fo' now that is what you is. Going to this party with the white folks ain't gonna change it."

Tilda started to cry. "I thought you might be happy for me, Mama."

"Honeychile, I is happy that Marsa James looks out fo' you, and that Miss Jane thinks she is bein' good to you by invitin' you to this party, but, baby," she put her arms around Tilda, "my heart is shakin' in fear."

Tilda reached up to her mother, trying to console her, as well as convince her that she would be all right. "No one will know it, Mama. I'll go to the great house just like I was going to work in the morning. Everyone will think I'm just helping Miss Jane. Please, Mama," she whispered imploringly, "please let me go."

Beulah had moved away and now held her head in her hands. "I know how you feels, Tilda," she whispered softly. She raised her head, looking steadfastly at her daughter. "Don't think I don't know. I loved yor daddy, and he truly cared 'bout me. But look at us. Didn't make no difference, did it?"

She took a step toward her daughter, reaching up to caress her hair, as she looked down into her young face. "Don't think I don't know how yo' feels 'bout young Marsa James," she said softly, unable to suppress a deeply troubled sigh. "Don't yo' see, Tilda. It's worse fo' you cause you looks white. But deep down, baby, it ain't gonna make no difference," she said with finality.

Another sob escaped Tilda. "Mama, please, just this once, let me go, and I promise I'll never ask you to let me do anything like this again. Just one night," she begged, "a night when no one will ever know that it's me. No one will ever recognize me with the mask. Please," she whispered fervently.

A ragged sigh clawed its way up from the pit of Beulah's stomach, and though her heart scorned the judgment of her decision, she whispered softly, "All right, chile, go."

Tilda threw her arms around her mother's neck. "Oh, thank you, Mama. I'll be careful. I promise. Please don't worry."

But Beulah's heart had already begun a vicious fluttering that left her nearly breathless with fear for her daughter.

James was standing at the window on the second floor looking down onto the gardens. He shifted to get a better view of the path, for he could see Tilda strolling along, the sun making her hair shine like a raven's wing. She wore a simple white cotton dress that flowed gently around her slim ankles. He smiled, noting she was barefoot. She paused and he watched as she bent to smell a flower before continuing on her way. His gaze followed her until she was gone from his sight.

Tilda could hardly wait to get to the great house the morning of the party. There were still some finishing touches she must do to Jane's gown. It was a beautiful gown, and Tilda was proud of the outcome. Jane was beside herself with excitement, and bragged to everyone about Tilda's handiwork.

Guests had already started to arrive and those who had traveled great distances had already been shown rooms in the left wing. The house was decorated in festive attire from top to bottom, and the servants were bustling under the sharp surveillance of EmiLee's all-seeing eyes and strict orders. Beulah and the other women in the kitchen dependency had been working for a week preparing foods and baking pastries and cookies. Since early morning, a whole pig had been roasting on a spit in the huge kitchen fireplace.

Rummaging in her jewelry box, Jane said for the thousandth time, "Tilda, don't forget your name is Victoria Meade."

Tilda looked up from where she was fussing with a bit of lace on the freshly pressed ballgown. "You have told me so many times, it's not likely I'll forget."

Mammy Ticey came bustling through the door, lamenting, "I ain't never heard o' such a thing in all my bawn days."

Jane caught Tilda's glance, and grinned. "Now, Mammy, you know deep down in your heart, you're tickled to death over the prospects of Tilda going to the ball," Jane admonished the woman good-naturedly.

The woman's broad face twisted into a scowl. "Don't matter how I feels or what I thinks! I's tellin' yo', we is all gonna git in trouble!"

"No, we're not," Jane assured her, even though she'd had to do that for the last two days, ever since she'd told the old Mammy of her plan.

"When I tol' them boys to fetch all them pails o' warm water up here, they thought I was crazy," Mammy Ticey stated indignantly.

"It's your imagination, Mammy," Jane told her. "And even if it isn't," she said firmly, "it's none of their business how much water I order for my bath."

"Then tell me, Missy, just what I should say to Missus if she questions it?" Mammy huffed.

"She won't," Jane replied confidently. "We have too many guests to keep track of the number of pails of warm water ordered. Besides, you must remember, Mother thinks I have a friend from school joining me. 'Twould be only natural that I need extra water so that she can freshen up," Jane replied somewhat smugly.

"Hummph," the old woman snorted. "Been sassy from the day yo' was bawn!" she muttered, waddling out of the room.

Jane returned to the contents of her jewelry box. "Ah, here they are."

Tilda looked up. "What were you looking for?"

"These sapphire earrings." She held them up for her to see. "Mother gave them to me. They belonged to her mother. Don't you think they will be perfect with the dress?"

Tilda nodded, thinking the teardrop earrings, surrounded by small diamonds, would have been perfect with any dress.

Jane turned back to the jewelry box, picking up a triple strand of choker pearls and a pair of matching pearl earrings. She handed them to Tilda. "I want you to wear these tonight. They will set off your gown."

Tilda drew back. "No, Jane, I couldn't."

"Nonsense. Of course, you can. I want to loan them to you, just for tonight." She lifted Tilda's hand and put them in it, closing her palm over the gems.

Staring down at the lustrous pearls, Tilda whispered, "I have never worn anything so lovely."

"You deserve so much more, Tilda," Jane said softly, then turned abruptly saying, "Come on, let's finish up. Mammy Ticey will be back soon to help us bathe."

Shortly afterwards, Mammy Ticey came sailing down the hall, her huge girth filling the doorway, as she gave instructions to the servants who were carrying huge pails of steaming water. When the tub was filled, she sent them on their way, bustling around to prepare the bath exactly the way she knew Miss Jane liked it. While she worked, she fretted about the consequences she feared were impending.

"I do declare," Mammy Ticey fumed, waggling her head, "Massa and Missus gonna skin us all fo' this!"

"Mammy, will you stop worrying?" Jane begged. "I'll tell Mother you knew nothing about it."

"Don't molly-coddle me, chile," old Mammy said, scowling at the young girl. "Don't nothin' 'scape old Mammy Ticey 'round heah. I'll handle the Missus, yo' just get on with yo' bathin', so's I can help Tilda," she demanded.

Jane caught Tilda's glance and quickly clamped the washcloth to her face to stifle the giggle.

When it was Tilda's turn to bathe, Jane insisted she use some of her scented bath salts that filled the room with the lovely fragrance of lilacs. Tilda had never enjoyed such a leisurely, pampered bath. Mammy Ticey was as kind to her as she was to Jane, treating her as if she had been born to the manor.

Nearly two hours passed before the girls stood in their costumes.

Jane waved a hand in Tilda's direction. "Mammy Ticey," she said, "I want you to meet a friend of mine, Victoria Meade. She'll be spending the evening with us."

Tilda giggled behind her gloved hand.

"Shake hands, Tilda," Jane directed, "and say, 'so nice to meet you'."

Tilda repeated the words like a parrot.

"For goodness sakes, Tilda," Jane admonished, with a roll of her eyes, "say it like you mean it."

"Sorry," Tilda mumbled, repeating the words again with more vigor.

"Now, come over here and look at yourself," Jane said, urging her toward the full-length mirror in the doors of the armoire.

Tilda stared at her reflection. The looking glass threw back an image that she didn't recognize. The apricot-colored ballgown, trimmed in white lace, molded Tilda's tiny waist. The neckline of the bodice was cut just low enough to show a hint of bosom, pressed high, as was the fashion. Tilda's black hair was covered with the tall white wig that swept smoothly back from her brow and had large puffy curls down to her shoulders, across the crown, and down the back. Pinned to the wig was the small black hat with the dyed feathers that matched the colors in her gown. Around Tilda's slender throat was the pearl choker necklace and on her earlobes were the pearl droplets. A smile spread across Tilda's face. It wasn't only the outside that looked pretty. Tilda felt pretty from the skin out, for Jane had seen to it that she had just the right garments beneath the gown. A delicate flush feathered over her features, remembering Jane's gentle manner in presenting them to her.

She turned to Jane. "How can I ever thank you?" she asked softly.

"By having a good time," Jane replied.

Mammy Ticey had swept Jane's long blond hair up into a twist at the back leaving wispy tendrils to curl at will on the sides and at the nape of her neck. The sapphire velvet gown hugged her figure at the waist before spreading out into a mass of midnight blue, swirled with matching lace around the bottom of the skirt. The plunging neckline showed off her translucent skin, while subtly drawing attention to the gentle swell of her bosom.

Her throat and earlobes perfectly displayed the sapphire and diamond jewelry.

"Ready, Victoria?" Jane asked, picking up her mask that Tilda had trimmed in narrow lace to match the color of her gown.

Tilda nodded, lifting her own black lace-lavished mask and slipping it on over the tall headdress. She turned to Jane, suddenly frightened of the charade she was about to play out. "Are you sure no one will be able to recognize me?"

"Never in a million years," Jane assured her. "Remember now, be mysterious," she cautioned in a low voice. "Don't answer too many questions. Steer them away from yourself."

"I'll remember," Tilda said, following Jane out the door.

"Lawd have mercy," Mammy Ticey murmured behind them. The words sounded like a prayer.

4

. . . and the mask is torn off, reality remains.

Lucretius

*"L*et's get down the stairs as quickly as possible and mingle," Jane suggested softly, between barely moving lips, "so we don't draw too much attention to ourselves."

Tilda didn't answer. Her heart was beating so hard beneath the tight bodice, she could hardly breathe.

It didn't matter anyway. Several people looked up as they moved lightly down the curve of the wide staircase. Tilda saw Simon far across the room making his fiddle seem alive, as his hand glided the bow over taut strings. His eyes encountered the pair on the stairs, and for a moment Tilda feared that he might be the one who would recognize her, but his black-eyed gaze swept quickly over them as he concentrated on his music. Tilda caught her breath, trying to still the rapid staccato of her heart.

A sea of faces stared up at them, and a comment or two floated upward about their costumes and who might be wearing them. Tilda glanced briefly at Jane, but she only smiled calmly, thus giving Tilda courage to continue down the stairs at a seemly gait. The girls were greeted at the landing by two gentleman requesting the honor of dancing with them.

Jane smiled at Tilda.

Tilda, trying to gain courage from that look, placed her gloved hand in the outstretched palm of the man standing in attendance before her, allowing him to sweep her away into the center of the ballroom.

While they danced, he asked, "Would you tell me your name?"

"Really, Sir," she answered with a coquettish tilt of her head, "this is a masquerade party, with mysterious faces behind the masks. And it is so early in the evening. Now you wouldn't want me to spoil your fun by telling you who I am so quickly, would you?" She peered coyly up at him, just as she'd seen Jane and Ivy do, and was amazed at how adroitly she'd sidestepped his question. And even more amazed that he had accepted it and seemed delighted with her response.

She was soon caught up in the arms of a persistent young man who told her his name was Carter Stively. He was, however, insisting she reveal her identity to him.

"But Sir," she began, "the evening is young. The unmasking is not until midnight."

He danced her to the sidelines, pressed her firmly against the wall, and whispered provocatively in her ear, "To hell with rules! I must know who you are! Look, I'll take mine off first," and he stripped the mask from his face. Then reaching up, his fingers searched for the ties that were lost in the white curls of her high headdress.

Tilda moved, trying to dodge his groping fingers.

"Carter," Jane demanded, striding up to them. "Are you making a nuisance of yourself?"

"Go away, Jane," he answered absently.

"This is a friend of mine from school, and you are being obnoxious and ungentlemanly," Jane snapped.

"I just wanted to know her name," he countered.

"Come, Victoria," Jane said, ignoring the man, as she took Tilda's arm. "I want to introduce you to someone." And she guided Tilda away, leaving Carter gaping after them.

"Who is he?" Tilda asked.

"Carter Stively, and he's a first-class bore. So

pompous and conceited. I never did like him. He likes Abigail Johnston but right now she's chasing James."

Tilda threw a quick look her way. "James? Does he like her?" she asked softly.

Hesitancy kept her momentarily silent, but then Jane admitted, "Yes, I think he does."

Tilda felt a curious pain in her heart.

"There she is, over there," Jane whispered, indicating the girl across the room in the costume of a dance hall woman. Blond hair was piled high on her head with a cascade of curls rippling down the back. On her cheek she had painted a brown beauty mark.

"She's pretty," Tilda murmured.

Jane shrugged.

"Where is James?"

"I don't know. I haven't seen him yet. But come on," she said, "I want you to meet Adam."

Tilda searched her face. "Did he find you just as you wanted him to?"

Jane's smile told her that he had, even before she whispered, "Yes, he found me almost immediately."

She moved with Tilda around the room to a far corner where a dark-haired man dressed as Daniel Boone, frontiersman, stood watching them approach.

Tilda knew as soon as she saw the emerald-green eyes, peering unwaveringly at them through the brown leather mask, that this was Adam Ward, the man that had stolen Jane's heart.

"Adam," Jane said, "this is my friend Victoria Meade. Victoria," she said turning to Tilda, "this is Adam Ward."

After a moment of polite talk, Adam asked Tilda if she would excuse them while he danced with Jane.

"Of course," she replied, moving out of their way to stand by the wall.

With a courteous smile, Adam drew Jane onto the dance floor.

Leaning back against the wall, Tilda watched them circle the floor. Slowly, her gaze moved around the room. Watching the wealthy planters from the nearby plantations and their wives, sons, and daughters mingling in the party atmosphere, Tilda was suddenly struck by the fact that all of them were totally unaware who she was. There was no doubt in her mind, that there would be many who would be affronted if they knew a slave joined in their festivities, spoke familiarly, and dared to dance with their sons. For a moment, she was angry, and then sadness began in the lower regions of her stomach, flowed all the way to her heart, and surrounded it in a vise-like grip. The strangling tightness closed slowly, surely, squeezing away the joy of the evening, leaving her life bare and empty as it would always be. She knew that was a certainty to which she must become accustomed, and all because of the circumstances of her birth.

Her dark eyes, peering through the black mask, roved over the crowd once more, stopping abruptly when they encountered James Hamilton, the highwayman, leaning against the mantle across the room. For a long moment, his eyes held hers, staring staunchly through the black mask. With an effort, Tilda pulled away. Her pulse raced and she drew a deep breath to regain her composure.

Her downcast eyes first saw the tips of his shiny black boots. Then they traveled up the length of him, skimming over the black suit to his face, above a snowy white cascade of frothy lace and hidden partially by the mask. A dark cloak draped around his broad shoulders. She thought it added to the mysterious persona of his masquerade costume. He smiled. The partially concealing mask made little difference. She would have known him anywhere.

"So you are my sister Jane's friend," he stated quietly.

Tilda nodded. Well, she thought, thankful he had worded it in just such a manner, at least she had not had to tell him an out-and-out lie. Something deep within her rebelled at the thought of lying to James.

"Let me see," James continued, his brow furrowed, "I believe Jane said her friend's name was Victoria."

Again Tilda nodded, flinching inwardly at that tiny lie.

"Well, Victoria," he said softly, "I am pleased that my sister invited you." He bent slightly, lifting her gloved hand, and kissed her fingertips.

Tilda felt faint, trying desperately to quell the joyful emotions welling within her.

"Would you dance with me?" he asked softly.

Tilda shook her head, murmuring, "I . . . I don't dance very well." She drew a deep breath, which caused her bosom to rise even higher, knowing she would surely faint were he to hold her in his arms.

"We'll stake out a little corner for ourselves," he said conspiratorially, "where no one will bother us, and if we step on each other's toes, we'll just smile and ignore it. But, quite frankly," he said with conviction, "I think we'll dance beautifully together." He smiled down on her; one dark brow quirked above the black mask in expectation of her agreeable answer.

Tilda searched frantically for the proper thing to say, but could think of nothing. James took her silence for agreement and taking her hand in his, led her to the nearest corner. His arm slipped around her and his hand held hers firmly. Remembering the dainty little steps that Jane had taught her, she slowly allowed her footsteps to match his and they moved lithely, making a small circle within the corner. Tilda was glad that she hadn't fainted, but she had no time to worry further about it, for she had to concentrate to keep her steps in time with his.

"See," he whispered against her ear, "I told you we would dance beautifully together."

She didn't look up. She was too fearful if he gazed directly into her face, into the depths of her eyes, he would recognize her.

He bent down to her, and in doing so, the lace of his cravat tickled her face. "When I first saw you," he said quietly, "you looked sad. What were you thinking?"

Surprised that he had been aware of her feelings, she glanced up quickly, then just as swiftly averted her eyes. "It was nothing," she murmured.

He shook his head. "I don't believe that. Something touched your heart so strongly, it echoed in your eyes."

And this time she did gaze up at him, unflinching, and with a long, lingering look.

Softly, he said, "Perhaps sometime you will tell me." And without another word, he gathered her closer, where he could feel her heart beating like the wings of a caged bird, and silently swept her into a slightly broader circle.

In the few moments before Simon launched into another song, James made no move to relinquish her. He kept his hand on her arm, until he heard the first note fill the air, then gathered her to him once more, and began the measured steps that kept them within their small corner.

Tilda saw Abigail approaching them with Carter in tow. The girl stopped at such a point that it made it impossible for the dancing couple to continue. Politely, James stopped.

"I do declare, James Hamilton," Abigail pouted prettily, "but if I didn't know better, I'd say you were ignoring me."

"Not so, my dear," James replied. "You did seem engaged with Carter."

"Well, I'm not at the moment," she answered, moving close enough to twine her finger into the lace of his cravat. "I must say, James dear, you make a handsome and exciting highwayman." She peered up at him, fluttering incredibly long lashes. "Are you," she purred, "stealing anything besides hearts?"

"A gentleman, even a highwayman, never tells," he replied, quirking an eyebrow at her.

She laughed, tugging at his arm. "Dance with me now," she begged. "Carter wants to dance with Jane's friend, Victoria."

At the mention of his name, Carter took Tilda's arm possessively. "No one as beautiful as you should be kept in this stuffy corner. I'm surprised at you, James," Carter looked down his autocratic nose at him and led Tilda away.

Tilda spent the next half hour listening to Carter talk of himself and his plantation that was, according to him, one of the largest in the South. "There is not anything in this world I couldn't buy," he finished pompously.

When she finally slipped away from him, she sought refuge in the maze of the boxwood gardens. As she left the ballroom, she noted that Jane stayed close to Adam's side, no doubt to keep Margaret Witherspoon from snatching him away. She had seen the girl hovering nearby. Tilda smiled to herself, sure that Jane could handle Margaret.

Smoothing her skirts so as not to catch the delicate lace on the metal curly-cues of the iron garden bench, she sat where she could look toward the house. Beneath the light of the moon, she peered up at the rooftop. There were no couples melting into the shadows of the chimney clusters at the top of the house, seeking privacy and a cool breeze. The night air was too chilly. A small shiver ran over her, and Tilda wondered if she should go back inside. The party was not as much fun as she had expected. Except for the dance with James, it had been an uncomfortable strain. But she couldn't waste the moment. She'd never have another opportunity to be this close to him again.

She went back up the brick walk, skirting round the front porch to a smaller one on the side of the house. Standing in the shadows, to the side of a long window that opened into the ballroom, she searched the crowd for James' tall, dark figure.

He was nowhere in sight, and with a heavy sigh lifting her shoulders, she turned away. It was then she saw him, beyond her in the yard, leaning nonchalantly against the trunk of a wide-spreading tree. Unmoving, he leaned there, watching her with a pensive look behind the shield of the mask. She wondered how long he had been there. The white lace of his cravat fluttered in the night breeze, standing out like a bright beacon beneath the light of the moon. His black cloak flowed around him, lending a mysterious aura to his aloof presence. Stoically he stood there, staring at her in an unsettling way through the holes in the black mask.

He raised his hand, holding it out to her. "Come

here," he said softly. His words winged their way across the short expanse.

Tilda moved, as if in a trance, across the porch, lifting her skirts as she went down the steps toward him. When she drew near, without a word, he reached for her gloved hand, lifted it to his lips and kissed it, much as he had in the ballroom. Only this time, his lips lingered as his eyes sought hers holding them possessively.

Once again, she trembled with the wonder of it despite the fear lying like a heavy weight in her mind of what he would say if he found out. She hated to deceive him, yet she couldn't stop herself from continuing with the masquerade.

"Are you tired of the party?" he asked, drawing her out of her silence.

She shrugged.

"Sometimes they can be quite a bore," he pronounced. "Will Jane be looking for you?"

"No. She is with Adam."

"Well, then," he said lightly, "would you take a walk with me?"

Wondering if she dared to walk with the master, Tilda looked back over her shoulder at the house illuminated with ornate lamps, and ringing with voices and music.

"It will be all right," he assured her. "No one will miss us."

A tiny voice inside Tilda cautioned her not to continue the charade. She started to offer an excuse.

"Please," he coaxed winningly before she could refuse. "Let's walk in the garden. It's a beautiful night." His hand indicated the bold round moon hovering above their heads. "The moon will light our path."

Tilda smiled, unable to think of anything except being with James. "All right," she heard herself whisper.

They strolled back down the brick walk, passing one or two other couples. Tilda's full skirt brushed his legs as she walked beside him. Even that minute contact seemed intimate to her.

Beyond the boxwoods, they stepped into a small

clearing surrounded by tall white oaks. The moonlight streaked through the branches and caught them in silvery beams.

James stopped abruptly. Tilda, halting her footsteps, turned to look silently up at him.

Tenaciously, his eyes held hers as if connected by an invisible thread. She detected a strange light in his eyes that the half mask was unable to conceal. Holding his glance, her eyes were questioning.

For a brief moment, James rubbed his hand over his chin in a thoughtful motion. Then he placed his hands on her shoulders. "You are so beautiful," he whispered. "I -- I would like so much to kiss you."

His words were spoken so softly and sincerely that Tilda knew she would cherish them forever. But they struck pain in her heart. The masquerade must end. She could not allow James to kiss someone he thought was Jane's friend, a stranger named Victoria and a person he thought was white. Should he ever find out, he would be embarrassed and furious. She gave no conscious thought to her own feelings in the matter. It was simply unthinkable for James to kiss a slave under such pretenses. If it should happen, he would certainly not have to ask.

Tilda felt sick to her stomach and was suddenly weary of this charade. "Please, no. I -- I don't think -- " Her words trailed off, stumbling through a catch in her throat.

Immediately, James was apologetic. "I'm sorry. Please forgive me."

She looked down, away from him. How could she stand looking into those eyes as blue as the heavens and not tell him how she felt about him? How she wished her life was different, that she had the right to walk by James' side, without fear, without hurting him.

"You're doing it again," James said softly.

She glanced back up at him, puzzled. "Doing what?" she asked.

"That sad look that begins in your heart and echoes in your eyes," he answered gently. "Do you want to tell me about it?"

She shook her head.

A deep sigh rumbled up from his chest. They walked on for a short distance until they were in the center of the clearing. In the stillness of the moonlight, they heard the music from the house drifting over the gardens to the canopy of trees over their heads.

James turned, holding out his hand to her. "Come, Tilda. Dance with me in the moonlight."

Tilda stood stock still, staring at him aghast. "You knew it was me?" she breathed.

"Of course, I knew," he said quietly.

"When?" she whispered, still overcome with this new development.

"From the first moment I saw you across the room, when you were looking so sad."

"Are you angry?" she ventured.

"No. I could tell by Jane's smug attitude these last couple of weeks that she was up to something."

"Don't be mad at her," she said hurriedly. "She was only trying to be nice to me."

"Mad? Never! I shall be eternally grateful." He looked down into her upturned face. "Didn't you realize that I knew?"

She shook her head. "I felt terrible that I was deceiving you."

"Is that why you wouldn't tell me what was making you so sad?"

She nodded, explaining, "It was because I didn't belong there, would never belong, and I knew that the others, even though they were nice to me then, would be angry if they knew who I really was."

James nodded. "I thought it was something like that." Then, as though preoccupied, he turned abruptly, striding to the edge of the clearing where he clutched a limb jutting out over his head from the broad tree trunk. His head was bent beneath the overhanging bough, and Tilda could see his shoulders move beneath the folds of the cloak as his hands twisted the limb agitatedly.

"Tilda?" he asked quietly, his voice edged with

emotion. "Why wouldn't you let me kiss you?"

Tilda crossed the clearing to stand behind him, her heart skipping breathlessly within her breast. "Because," she answered softly, "I was afraid you would be angry if you found out it was me and not Victoria. I . . . I thought you would be offended by asking a slave for a . . ." her words trailed off into an uncomfortable murmur, " . . . a kiss."

He turned slowly, surveying her. "And now?" he asked quietly. "Now that you know that I knew all along who I was asking? What would you say now, Tilda?"

"I would say yes," she whispered. She took one step forward.

His arms reached out, and he swirled his cloak about her, gathering her to his hard frame, and kissed her gently, without hint of the passion that had been building up for many years. Instead, it was delicately sweet, with the whisper softness of an angel's wing.

When he held her back from him, he peered down into her face with a tenderness that startled Tilda.

"Shall we have that dance now, Miss Tilda?" he said gently, sweeping her back into his arms. Their footsteps whispered a sonata that echoed in their hearts as they circled round the clearing beneath the shimmering moonlight, keeping perfect step to the music drifting out to them from the manor.

5

The woods are lovely, dark and deep,
But I have promises to keep.
                        Robert Frost

*D*uring the course of the following year Jane married Adam Ward and moved to Calvert Hall Plantation on Pope's Creek. James began seriously courting Abigail Johnston.

On one of those days when the stifling heat of a late summer sun dried the land, sapped one's strength, and lulled the spirit into a lazy lethargy, James stood on the porch, his eyes scanning his surroundings. Slowly, he removed his hat and blotted at his brow with a handkerchief. As though searching, his eyes continued to rove over the landscape. A light reflected in the depths of the blue eyes when he saw Tilda's lithe, barefoot figure on the path beyond the boxwood gardens. He shifted his weight, proceeding down the steps with an air of indifference as he moved toward her approaching figure. He walked slowly to give her sufficient time to gain the brick walk. As she did so, he strode toward her and paused briefly just as they would have passed.

He made a casual comment about the weather, as he would have done with anyone. James felt it necessary to maintain a certain amount of decorum for propriety's sake, as well as Tilda's. For a moment, he allowed his gaze to scan the perimeter. He mopped at his brow once again. Before he replaced his hat, he held it out from him, as though inspecting the inside. It was a conscious effort to conceal his lowered voice when he murmured, "Tonight. At the secret place. I need to talk to you."

"It sho' is a hot day, Mister James," Tilda said, as though replying to a casual comment about the weather.

James replaced his hat and strode on down the walk. Tilda continued on her way as well, allowing no emotion to show on her face.

Late that night, using the moon to light her way, Tilda moved stealthily toward the small cave. She crouched in the darkness waiting for James, wondering what was so urgent that he could not tell her on the path. In the dark confines of the carved-out overhanging lip, she heard many noises, some real, some imagined. Most of the sounds came from the nocturnal animals whose habitat she had invaded.

She waited, and waited, first walking back and forth, then standing outside watching the black path for his tall shape. But her eyes grew weary of staring into the black space, and she became jittery of what lay beyond the cave in the darkness of the woods. She went back inside, curled into the corner, and continued to wait.

The night sounds lulled her into a dream state as she leaned against the rock wall, remembering when she had first discovered the cave in those early days at Stafford Hall.

Tilda was so engrossed in her reverie that she didn't hear James' footsteps approaching. Nor did she hear a twig snap or the rustle of a leaf. Not until she saw the swaying, scintillating light of the lantern in front of the thickly woven honeysuckle curtain did she know he had arrived. Somewhat apprehensively, she rose as he entered.

"Tilda," he said, setting down the lantern. "Thank you for coming."

"Is something wrong, Mister James?" she asked, her

voice reflecting her fear.

He didn't answer, but strode across the floor, much as she had done earlier, rubbing his hand across his chin, pacing like a caged animal.

She went over to him and timidly touched his arm.

He looked down on her as his hand came across to cover hers, pressing it against his arm. "No one knows you came?"

She shook her head.

"I need your help, Tilda," he said softly. "I couldn't think of a way to do this alone."

"What, Mister James? You know I would do anything for you."

"I know, and that is what scares me. This could be dangerous."

"What?" she asked again softly.

Still holding her hand, he pulled her to the ground, where he sank down and leaned against the far wall. Tilda knelt in front of him, looking up with wide, questioning eyes, leaning against his drawn up knees.

James' eyes held hers in the soft glow of the lantern light. "Tilda?" he asked softly, "have you ever heard of Harriet Tubman?"

She nodded. "The slaves call her Moses, 'cause she leads people out of slavery into freedom."

"Yes. That is right," James nodded. "Do you know that she has many people helping her, both black and white?"

"I 'spose so," she replied thoughtfully. "Couldn't help so many people by herself."

James made no reply, seeming to be in deep thought.

Tilda looked up into his face. "You know her?" she whispered, even though she felt she already knew the answer.

"I know her," James answered simply. His eyes met Tilda's, but his next words, even though spoken softly seemed to fill the small space. "I'm meeting with her tomorrow night."

James heard the sharp intake of breath that she tried

unsuccessfully to stifle.

"There are many who help her operate what they call an underground railroad," he said. "We pass slaves from one safe place to another, until they reach the North. Those safe places are called stations. Helpers are called conductors. Harriet Tubman is a conductor. She has led many slaves to freedom."

Tilda swallowed hard, and asked softly, "Are you a conductor, too?"

"Yes," he answered quietly.

Tilda nodded, feeling a wonderful sensation of satisfaction in her heart. She looked up. "What is it you want me to do?" she asked in hushed tones.

"There is a child, a little boy about three years old," he told her. "I'm going to take him away from his master's plantation. I helped his father to escape last year. His mother has died, and the child is to be sold in a few days. We cannot wait. If I don't act now, I may not be able to get to him. Harriet is meeting me tomorrow night. I'm to deliver the child to her. She will see he gets to his father." He paused, casting a slow glance over Tilda. "I need your help in caring for the boy until she arrives."

"Of course, I'll do that," she said quickly.

"Don't give me your answer yet. There is more." He looked down into her upturned face, then tossed his head irritably. "Oh, God, Tilda. I hate to ask this of you. It . . . It just doesn't seem fair."

She reached up one slender hand and stroked his jaw. "Ask me," she said firmly.

"I need you to go with me to the plantation. The child is only three. He will not understand that I am there to help him. If he cries --" He left the sentence unfinished.

"I will go with you," she said softly, "and I will keep the child quiet so that his -- and our -- enemies are not made aware of what we are doing."

"The last is the worst," James said. "You must hide with the child beneath a pile of hay on the buckboard," he said apologetically. He paused, allowing his words to sink in.

"I am not afraid of the dark," she assured him,

ignoring the indignity, of which James was aware, of having to hide in the hay like a rodent.

"It is not the dark that will hurt you, Tilda," James replied seriously. "There are many spies out there and if the child is recognized --" He stopped. His thoughts did not bear putting into words. He cupped her face in his hands, speaking down to her, his face very close to hers. "You must understand, Tilda, that this is very dangerous. If we are unsuccessful, there will be many who will want to hang me. Of course, I will protect you as long as I can. But it is entirely possible that they will kill me. So please, don't be afraid to say no to my request." He watched her thoughtfully for a moment. "Even," he added quietly, "with your white skin they would not be kind to you. Especially if someone knows that your mother is black. It would only add to your trouble. Do you understand me?" he asked earnestly.

The implication was not lost on Tilda, and she nodded, silent for a time, remembering several years ago when she had come around the corner of one of the cabins and heard some of the women talking in an excited manner. Hearing the name Lizzie Stratton, she had paused to listen. Lizzie, a free mulatto, though not as white as Tilda, had a white father and a mother who was a slave. Because of this, Tilda felt a bond with Lizzie. As a child, Tilda had often delivered Beulah's ginger cookies to Lizzie's home. Lizzie's father was a wealthy planter. Before he died, he had given Lizzie her freedom papers and a piece of property with a small house on it. Lizzie lived there alone. Tilda often heard whispers circulating the plantation that she was suspected of helping slaves escape. While her father lived, she went about her activities without any trouble, but after his death, there were some planters who, suspecting her involvement, made it their business to catch her. And they finally did. Lizzie had been raped repeatedly and then hung. The words had stunned Tilda, and she had run away, unable to listen to the horrifying details of Lizzie Stratton's death. The slave quarters had buzzed for days.

Tilda had been silent for so long that James repeated

his question, giving her a little shake. "Do you understand the dangers, Tilda?"

Solemnly, she answered him. "Perfectly," she said. "But don't worry about me. If anything happens to you," she added matter of factly, "I would not want to live anyway."

Tilda felt his fingers tighten on her shoulders at her words. "I did not want to ask you," he confessed, "but I felt I could trust no one else."

"I'm glad you did," she said softly. "I feel the same as you, there are some things worth the risk. Now," she went on briskly, "tell me what to do."

James smiled. "Uncle Abrams will bring the buckboard around tomorrow. Come up to the house and get in the buckboard with him. Bring a small container of ash. You will need to put it on your face after you are away from the house. With the approaching dusk, no one will be able to detect your white skin beneath the ash. You can pretend to be his granddaughter if you are stopped." James caught her cloud of dark hair in his hands, allowing its silkiness to slip through his fingers. "You must tie a bandanna around your head like your mother does. Nothing must give you away. If you are stopped, let Uncle Abrams do the talking. He will know what to say. After we get the child, you must ride under the hay until we are well away from the plantation. Uncle Abrams will know where to meet me. I will bring you and the child here by horseback." He paused, looking at her solemnly. "If you want to change your mind, do it now," he said. "Once we begin, there is no turning back."

She shook her head adamantly. "I will not change my mind." She paused, holding his eyes with her own. "I cannot tell you," she said softly, "how happy it makes me that you asked my help."

"There was no one else I felt I could trust, except Mammy Ticey, and she is too old for such matters."

"What is the child's name?" Tilda asked.

James smiled. "Joscephus. He's a cute little boy. He should be with his father." He glanced down at her. "He deserves a better life. We have to give him that chance."

"We will," she said firmly.

"Tilda?"

She glanced up at him, hearing that serious note in his voice again.

"If you want to go, as well, I can make arrangements for you."

Her brow creased. "Go? Where?"

"Up north." He cupped her face again, speaking so fervently she sensed she could feel his heart beating. Involuntarily, her fingertips touched his shirt front. "I can't give you the life you deserve here, Tilda. We both know that. But up north you can be free and live a different kind of life."

He raised his fingertips to her lips, to still the protest he knew had sprung there. "Think about it tonight," he whispered. "There is a whole new world waiting for you, Tilda, a world beyond this plantation."

"We both know there is no world for me if you are not in it," she said quietly.

A deep sigh dragged from him. "Don't make your decision now," he said gently. "Give yourself some time to think about it. If you want to go, you must travel lightly. Pack only what you will need and bring it here tomorrow. You will have no time to go back to your mother's once we get here."

He waited for her to respond, but she remained silent. James did not want to know what she was thinking. He didn't want to know until the last minute that she was going to walk out of his life. He wanted her to go, for her sake. He wanted her to stay, for his own. His heart was at odds with his good sense, and he pushed the feelings away with resolute determination.

"Come on," he said, pulling her to her feet. "We will have a long night tomorrow. You must get some rest."

They left the security of the small cave, melting into the wooded shadows that, caught by the glow of the lantern, cast spectral shapes around them.

James saw Tilda to the edge of the clearing near the slave cabins and waited until she hurried up the worn dirt path and disappeared inside Beulah's cabin. Then he skirted round the back way to the drive of Stafford Hall, loped up the broad front steps with a lighter step to his gait, flung open the front door and closed it softly behind him.

In late afternoon, Tilda glanced out the window of the room where she had been sewing and saw the buckboard pull up at the side of the house. Quickly, she put away the fabric she had been working on and ran down the back stairs and out of the house. She moved hurriedly toward her mother's cabin, aware Uncle Abrams was watching her from veiled eyes that appeared indifferent.

She picked up a shawl where she had wrapped a bandanna and a small tin of ashes the night before while her mother slept. "I have to go on an errand for the Missus," she told Beulah nonchalantly. "Uncle Abrams is driving me. Got to take some material to Jane over at Pope's Creek. It will be late, Mama, so don't wait up for me."

She dropped a kiss on Beulah's forehead and hurried out the door.

Uncle Abrams was painstakingly inspecting the wheels of the buckboard while he waited, busying his eyes and his hands in the event anyone was watching their movements. Tilda climbed up into the wagon and waited for him to join her. She noticed, instead of the dark suit and white shirt worn when driving the carriage, he was wearing work clothes of the sort he wore around the plantation. Presently, he climbed into the driver's seat, clicked his tongue to the horses, and settled back for their journey. He spoke not a word to her until they were a good distance from the house.

At that point, he pulled the buckboard over to the roadside beneath the branches of some low spreading trees. "Git yo'self fixed up, girl," he said softly. "We meet someone, yo' lets me do the talkin'."

Tilda nodded, remembering James' instructions from the night before.

Quickly, she wrapped the bandanna around her hair, making sure to hide every strand. She opened the tin of ashes and spread the blacken ashes onto her palms and rubbed them on her face all the way to the roots of her hair. Her arms were already covered with the full-length sleeves of her gray cotton dress. When she had her face completely blackened, she rubbed the ash over the backs of her hands, then turned to Uncle Abrams for inspection.

"Am I covered sufficiently?" she asked.

His black eyes drilled into hers. "If yo' is askin' me, does yo' got 'nuff, then the answer is yas," he replied sharply, reminding her that if she was going to look like a slave, she must talk like one.

Tilda smiled shyly. "Sorry, Granpappy," she said, slipping into the pretense as James had suggested. "I reckon that ol' hot sun's 'bout made me half-witted."

The old man returned a grin, whistling through his teeth to the horses, and the wagon pulled forward again.

They traveled for a long time, meeting no one except a stray dog that turned and followed them for some distance before giving up and turning back the way it had come. The sun began to set, and Tilda had grown weary, a fact she tried to hide from the wiry old man beside her. A few miles back, he'd had her unwrap a cloth containing cornbread and two apples. Tilda had eaten her share without comment, thankful for the cold cornbread that, dry as it was, silenced the rumbling in her stomach. The apple was ripe and juicy and she made it last as long as she could.

Finally, they turned from the main road to a worn path in the woods. "Dis where yo' gets out, girl," Uncle Abrams said.

Unbidden, Tilda's heart began to pound. She turned frightened eyes his way, nonetheless holding his look steadily and unwavering.

"Yo' be all right," he said gently. "Go on into de woods. Massa James will meet yo'."

She nodded, swallowing over the lump that had gathered in her throat, and climbed down over the side.

"Tilda?"

She looked up at the old man. "Yo' is doin' a good thing. I's proud of yo', girl," he said softly.

Tilda smiled up at him. "Thanks, Granpappy. I loves yo', too, an' I's goin' to see yo' real soon."

He smiled, clicked to the horses, and pulled away from the roadside without looking back.

Tilda stepped into the lee of a tree, watching him leave. She ventured forward, down the path that was slowly becoming cloaked in twilight.

She stayed on the path until she heard a horse approaching. She ducked into the bushes, gathering the greenery around her. She peered through the foliage at the bend in the path. Her heart pounded as hard as the horse's hooves striking the hard-packed earth. It was not long before the rider came into view and Tilda breathed a sigh of relief.

She stepped out into the path. James slid from the horse, and strode to meet her, his black cloak swirling around his ankles.

"Are you all right?" he whispered, as though fearing the trees had ears.

Tilda nodded, gesturing to her turban-wrapped hair and ash-blackened skin. "You knew me. Is this all right?"

He smiled. "It would take more than a bandanna and black ashes for me not to recognize you, Tilda."

She was suddenly reminded of her Marie Antoinette costume in which she felt so different and totally disguised, and yet, he had still known her. She shook away the heightened sense of pleasure that swept over her, asking, "What do we do now?"

"Go get Joscephus," he replied, swinging back up into the saddle. With a swift movement, he reached down and lifted Tilda up in front of him. "We're going to the plantation where Joscephus lives. I'll point out the cabin, then I want you to go down into the slave quarters and bring the child back."

He said it like there would be nothing to it, but Tilda knew his air of nonchalance was not intended to sound that way.

"Does anyone know I'll be coming for him?" she

asked softly.

"If by that you mean, do I have a friend down there who is helping us?" He shook his head solemnly. "Sorry. It's safer that way. Someone is going to be punished as it is when they find the boy is missing." James shook his head, sadness clouding his eyes. "And it'll be because of me."

Tilda's heart ached for him. She turned within the circle of his arms that held the reins. Looking up into his face, she said gently, "Just one at a time, Mister James. That's all you can do."

At the edge of the woods beyond the small group of cabins, they dismounted and James pointed out the cabin where she would find the boy.

Tilda started forward.

James reached out, catching her arm.

She turned back, eyes questioning.

"Be careful," he said.

She smiled, nodding.

"I'll be right here waiting for you," he assured her. "Try not to linger. We must move as quickly as possible."

Again, she nodded. For a moment her eyes held his, then she turned abruptly and walked out of the woods toward the back of the cabins.

Dusk was falling and there was no one around. She heard a dog bark in the distance, but paid it no mind. Stealthily, she slipped up to the back of the cabin James had indicated and peered through a wide crack in the wall. A woman sat on the dirt floor playing with a little boy. Tilda smiled. Joscephus. She noted the gentleness in the woman's manner toward the child. While she watched, the woman leaned over and kissed the little boy. His small hand came up to pat her face, and she kissed it as well.

With that small gesture, Tilda knew what she must do. It was obvious the woman loved the little boy, and Tilda felt certain she would not call out to alert the overseer of the child's abduction. Tilda also knew the woman would be whipped for punishment if she did not.

Having felt the bite of the lash, Tilda felt an intense emotion about saving her from that fate.

Tilda caught up a rock, skirted around to the door, and boldly entered the one-room shack, announcing to the startled woman, "I have a message from Moses. She wants to take Joscephus tonight."

The woman's wide-eyed look flashed over Tilda as she gathered the boy to her bosom. "They gonna sell him up the river," she said sadly, holding his small body to her.

"No, they're not. I'm delivering him to Moses, who is taking him to his daddy," Tilda explained quickly, secure in the knowledge that there was not a slave alive who did not know who Moses was, and what she meant to a slave.

A smile spread over the woman's features. "His pappy? Joscephus goin' to his pappy?" she asked joyfully.

Tilda nodded. "Will you let me take him?" she asked gently.

"I sho' will," she said, handing the child out to her.

Reluctantly, Tilda showed her the rock. "They will whip you when they find him gone," she said slowly, "but if I knock you out, then it will appear that you could not do anything to stop it. Let them think someone stole up on you out of the dark, knocked you unconscious, and took the child." Tilda waited for the woman to understand what she was saying.

"Who is yo'?" she whispered.

"Someone who has felt the lash of the whip. I want to spare you that pain."

"You gonna take care of Joscephus?" she asked.

"Yes," Tilda answered quietly.

With a slow, thoughtful nod, the woman turned her back.

Tilda drew a deep breath, watching the woman's shoulders rise and tense, steeling herself for the blow. "I'm sorry," Tilda whispered, raising the rock.

Whirling, she caught the little boy by his hand. "Come on, Joscephus. We have to hurry."

She pulled him quickly through the door, not able to focus on the inert figure lying on the dirt floor. Tears streamed down Tilda's face. She had never raised a hand in violence to anyone in her entire life. She walked the child as fast as he could make his short legs go. At the back of the last cabin, she picked him up and ran as fast as she could to the woods where James waited.

He met her as she crashed through the brush to the path, already astride the horse. He bent down, grasping her under the arms, and swung her and the child up in front of him. Tilda leaned back against him, her breast heaving and great sobs escaping from between clenched teeth. James spurred the horse back up the path. Tilda was cognizant of hooves that sounded muted. It was a strange sound that should have resounded like thunder as they galloped through woods already blanketed in semidarkness.

When James realized that Tilda was crying, he bent his head next to hers. "Tilda? What is it? Tell me."

She looked up at him, clutching Joscephus who watched them both in wide-eyed wonder. "I had to hit her," she said. "I had to do it hard enough to knock her out, so they would believe she had no part in it."

"You were wise to do that."

She felt his breath feathering across her wet cheek and tried hard to stop the little gasps that accompanied her sobs.

"I know it is difficult," he said in a quiet attempt to console her, "but you must remember that a headache for a day is much better then the pain endured to scar a back for a lifetime."

He gave her a little jostle. "Come on, Tilda. We've done what we set out to do. You got little Joscephus out of there, and he'll soon be on his way to his daddy."

Happy with that thought, Tilda smiled through her tears, hugging the little boy to her breast.

At the end of the path Uncle Abrams waited for them. He stood by the wagon, his black eyes piercing the growing darkness of the woods. When he saw the child, his mouth spread into a broad grin. "Praise de Lawd!"

they heard him mutter, as he hurried forward to take the child from Tilda.

After they dismounted, Tilda noted the hooves of James' horse had been covered in leather, which had served to mute their hoofbeats. She was amazed at the small details James had attended to, small things so important to the success of this race to freedom.

She turned her attention to Joscephus, telling him they were going to play a game. They were going to pretend to be tiny mice and hide in the hay. They would see who could stay quiet the longest. Fishing into her pocket, she withdrew a peppermint stick, one that James had given her weeks ago. She held it up for Joscephus to see. "If you are very quiet, and don't make a sound until I tell you, I will give you this candy."

The little boy's eyes widened with the prospect of such a treat. Uncle Abrams lifted him into the wagon. James scrambled up behind him and turned to pull Tilda aboard. She settled the boy on the floorboards, then lay down next to him, turning him on his side to face her. She glanced up once at James. With a curse, he stripped off his cloak and laid it over them, covering their faces.

"Keep this end up," he instructed Tilda. "We'll leave an opening here at this end so you will have air." She felt him touch her head in a caressing movement. Minutes later, she and the child were covered with straw.

It was not long before the swaying of the wagon lulled the child to sleep. Tilda wondered how the boy could sleep. It seemed they hit so many bumps in the rutted roads that her bones felt as if they would break.

Tilda lost track of time, but she was certain it must be quite dark out by now. She wondered when Uncle Abrams would allow them to get out. She lay there listening to the night sounds, when she suddenly heard Uncle Abrams whisper, "Steady, Tilda. Jus' stay nice and quiet."

She heard the sound of a horse approaching, and someone shouted, "Who is there?"

"Jus' me, Suh," Uncle Abrams called out.

Tilda was aware the rider had moved up alongside

the buckboard. She placed a shaking hand over Joscephus' mouth in case he wakened and cried out.

"What you doin' on the road this late at night, nigger?" the voice demanded.

"I's been over to Popes Creek. Wheel done got broke, Suh, took me a long time to fix it."

"Who's your master?"

"Massa Hamilton from ober Stafford Hall," drawled Uncle Abrams. "He be worried 'bout me. I ain't neber late, so I's better be gittin' along."

"What you got in back that wagon?"

"Jus' hay, Suh."

"You sure you ain't got no runaways hidin' in there?" the voice asked half in jest.

Tilda heard Uncle Abrams laugh shortly, as if they shared a good joke. "Oh, no, Suh. Massa skin me alive if I picked up any runaways. He say they scalawags, an' nothin' but trouble," he lamented, shaking his old head from side to side.

She heard the rider approach the back of the buckboard. Tilda's heart beat rapidly.

"Maybe," the man drawled, "I should shoot into that hay just to make sure." He paused, watching the old driver slyly. "Would you mind if I do that?" he asked, drawing his gun.

"Well, Suh," Uncle Abrams said slowly, "don't reckon it'd make no difference to me, but Massa'd probably be fire-hot mad if someone went ta shootin' holes in his buckboard."

The rider laughed. "Reckon you'd be right," he said, riding back to the front. He waved the gun, saying, "Git on out of here, nigger!" Then raising the gun, he fired into the air. The horses bolted and the wagon sprang forward with jarring force.

The gunshot rang in Tilda's ears. Had he shot Uncle Abrams? She didn't dare call out. She could hear the man's laughter echoing behind them, and then she heard Uncle Abrams trying to soothe the horses. Thankfully, she closed her eyes, trying to still the erratic beating of her heart.

Above the thunder of the horse's hooves, she heard the old man caution, even as he fought to quiet the spooked animals, "Stay put, girl. Everything's all right."

Much later, she felt the wagon come to a halt. She lay still, holding Joscephus in her arms when he began to stir. She heard Uncle Abrams climbing down from the driver's seat. He scrambled aboard, pulling at the straw. "Come on, girl," he said. "Git out and stretch yor legs. We's close 'nuff to home now, that yo' can ride up front."

Tilda rose up from the mound of hay with Joscephus in her arms. She gulped at the fresh air, drawing deep breaths before setting the child aside. She turned and flung her arms around old Uncle Abrams neck, nearly knocking the old battered hat from his head, and hugged him tightly.

The old man was startled. "What dat fo'?" he asked in surprise.

"If it hadn't been for you, that man would have shot us back there," she answered.

"Naw," he shook his grizzled head. "Sorry white trash like that jus' tries to scare yo'. Jus' gotta keep yor wits, an' outsmart 'em!" he declared. "Now come on, girl. Let's git goin'. Massa James will be a'waitin' fo' us."

And Master James was waiting for them when they arrived at the pre-determined place. Joscephus was happily sucking on the peppermint stick Tilda had given him, as Uncle Abrams pulled the wagon off the roadside. Despite the darkness that cloaked them in shadows, Tilda saw the horse and rider before the wagon came to a halt.

James slid from his mount and strode toward them. "Have any problems?" he asked, reaching for the little boy.

Tilda's eyes met Uncle Abrams.

"Nuthin' we couldn't handle, Massa James," the old man answered.

They left Uncle Abrams to return to the plantation, while they rode off through the woods to circle round to the small cave. Joscephus had finished his peppermint stick and was asleep again by the time they reached the cave. James carried him inside. Tilda followed, carrying James' cloak. She spread it on the ground and he laid the sleeping child on it.

Tilda drew a long sigh as James rose. Her eyes met his. "We did it," she whispered jubilantly.

Silently, James reached out, enclosing her in his arms. He held her thusly a long moment. Moving back, he withdrew a handkerchief from his pocket and wiped it over her face trying to brush away the tear-streaked black ash. James pulled the bandanna from her head, letting the silky waves cascade down around her shoulders. A piece of hay still clung stubbornly, and he reached out, picking it up between his thumb and forefinger, and tossed it to the ground.

A dull thumping noise sounded just outside the cave. "She's here," James said.

He stepped around Tilda, pushing aside the curtain of honeysuckle. A woman, leaning on a thick stick and dressed like a man, entered. Though she wore a crumpled, broad-brim leather hat on her head, it did not hide the ragged scar on her forehead.

Harriet Tubman scanned the interior with a sharp eye. "We got to be goin'," she said softly. "Not safe to linger." She looked at James. "How many parcels we got?"

With a heavy heart, James replied, "Two."

From the darkness over their shoulders came one softly spoken word. "One," Tilda whispered.

James looked up sharply. "Tilda -- " he began.

But Tilda ignored him, and bent to pick up the sleeping child. She handed him to Harriet. "I hope you get Joscephus to his daddy."

"Don't worry," Harriet Tubman said, "I never ran my train off the track, and I never lost a passenger."

Tilda smiled.

The woman hurried out the opening with her small burden. James followed.

When he returned, he stood just inside the entrance of the cave, looking at Tilda, as though searching for words.

Finally, she asked quietly, "Did you want me to go?"

"It would mean a better life for you," he replied.

"Did you," she repeated pointedly, "want me to go?" He shook his head. "No," he murmured softly.

"The only life I want is right here with you," Tilda said fervently.

James covered the short expanse between them with one stride. He drew Tilda into his arms, looking down into her face. "Our lives are so separate and yet seem so intertwined," he whispered. "You know -- we both know -- that I love you, and it drives me insane that I can do nothing about it." His words were as frustrated as the agitated movements of his head.

While her heart sang to hear him speak words she never expected to hear, great sadness filled her. Her eyes ran over his face, and one hand came up to stroke his jaw. "It is the black blood of my mother flowing in my veins that makes me a slave. But the white blood of my father pumps in my heart, as well, and it is with my heart that I love you." Her eyes clouded and she paused a moment before saying solemnly, "The only way I can stop loving you, James, is for my heart to stop beating."

She had forgotten and spoke his first name, using it as naturally as though she had always done so. James, though keenly aware of it, made no mention of it. And it was, from that day forward, that she called him by his given name when speaking directly to him.

"This world we live in seems destined to taunt us. While I cannot deny the way I feel about you, Tilda, I could never tell it to the world. And it hurts that I can't offer you more."

"Being a slave, I know I can never be anything more to you," she said with a shrug of despair, "but I cannot change the way I feel."

"I do not think of you as a slave, Tilda," James interjected gently. "Surely, you know that."

She nodded solemnly. "I know," she assured him, though there was a painful spot in her heart that would never heal. Reality was all that ever mattered, it seemed.

Feelings were of little consequence.

"I know it is selfish of me," he said quietly, "but I am glad you did not want to leave, and I hope you never change the way you feel."

"I will carry it with me through eternity," she murmured.

He gathered her close to him, holding her tightly. Leaning back within the circle of his arms, she looked up wistfully and their lips brushed -- holding a tenderness only they could know.

Outside the small, secret sacredness of her world, a hoot owl broke the silence of the night.

6

From hope and fear set free.
Algernon Swinburne

*A*ndrew strolled down the rolling road en route to the mill. Gabe, Ivy's young son, was coming from the river, carrying a string of fish.

"Mawnin', Massa," the boy greeted cheerily.

"Good morning, Gabe," Andrew replied, stopping to inspect his catch. "Good fishing today, eh?"

"Yas, Suh." He rolled his black eyes. "Massa like some fish fo' his suppa?" the lad asked.

Andrew smiled to himself. He often bought fish, caught on his own property, from the young slave children who were patient enough to catch them and wily enough to approach him to sell them.

"Yes, Gabe," Andrew said, "I believe the Missus would be proud to have some of that fine catch."

The black face beamed. He selected several of the glistening fish, and handed them up to his master.

"Would you take them up to the house for me?" Andrew asked.

"Sho' will, Massa," the boy answered jovially. "My mammy gonna cook the rest o' dese fo' us. She'll be plumb tickled when she see how fine dey is." He was shaking his head in pride, watching slyly for his master's hand to reach into his pocket.

It was a game they played, Gabe pretending surprise at the coin, and Andrew pretending not to know that he expected it.

The boy skipped off up the road. Andrew watched with a grin before he continued on his way to look in on the operations at the mill.

That afternoon Uncle Abrams saddled Andrew's horse and stood waiting in the drive, nuzzling the horse's nose and speaking softly. The door opened and the old colored man saw Andrew pause to speak to EmiLee before striding down the porch steps. With a nod to Uncle Abrams, he swung up into the saddle and rode off down the lane, en route to Willow Manor to attend a planters meeting. There had been reports of slave uprisings at some of the nearby plantations, and the stories were causing the planters great concern.

Meanwhile, at Willow Manor, Dora sloshed through the mud of the hog pen, filling the troughs with slop from the large pails she carried from the kitchen quarters. Her crippled foot made it difficult to maintain her balance.

From the side yard, Frankie, the Witherspoons son, caught sight of Dora coming from the kitchen area carrying heavy buckets. He shouted profanities at her, ordering her to get moving or he'd have the overseer help her. He laughed at the hunched figure moving awkwardly, dragging the crippled foot. She appeared to crouch even more under his jeering threats.

Dora had endured insults from the boy when they began as a childish thing. Now, however, the taunts had grown through the years to become more vicious as Frankie approached his teenage years. He was extremely cruel to Dora, one time knocking her down in the hog pen and laughing raucously as she struggled to regain her footing. Her silence and efforts to disregard him only served to make the taunting more ruthless. Frankie caused her no end of grief with his callous, and often brutal pranks. Dora's back had felt the lash of the whip so many times in her young life that it had become almost a weekly occurrence. She ambled through each day, flinching every time the overseer drew near.

Frankie came up to the fence, still shouting insults. Dora turned her back on him, ignoring him as she moved with her crippled gait outside the pen to the gate where she had left two large buckets of hog slop. As she bent to pick up a bucket of slop, Frankie kicked it with his booted foot, knocking over the pail with its foul-smelling contents. Slow-witted though she was, she was not so dull of comprehension that she didn't understand he intended this as yet another way to cause her trouble with the overseer, as well as the master and missus.

She turned away, concentrating on feeding the hogs, before cleaning up the mess Frankie had made. A frown creased her plain features, but she kept her eyes turned away from the mess on the ground at her feet. As she bent to pick up the full pail, she saw Frankie's foot raise again. She flung out one squarish hand, grabbed him by the hair with amazing strength and dragged him down. Before the first yell was completely out of his mouth, she had submerged his head in the bucket of slop. Calmly she held him there, watching until he stopped struggling. She released the limp body, and rose from her crouched position. Shaking her head from side to side, she mumbled, "No mo' trouble now."

Frankie's single scream had brought Mandy down the path to investigate. She arrived just as Dora released Frankie's inert form. She saw Dora rise from her crouched position, and dust her hands together as though she had just completed a messy job.

"Dora!" Mandy yelled. "What yo' done now?" She ran to the fence, throwing her hands up over her face when she saw Frankie's head submerged in the bucket. Her screams brought the overseer and several nearby slaves running.

Someone ran to the house, yelling for Benjamin Witherspoon. Within seconds, pandemonium broke out in the yard.

Benjamin came running down the steps, heading toward the hog pens, directed there by a slave. By the time Benjamin found his son, Alice Witherspoon, summoned from the parlor by the wailing of a slave, hurried toward them. She stopped, staring at her husband's shaking shoulders as he clutched their son to his bosom.

Absorbing the scene, she swayed. Mandy reached out to her, but Alice drew herself up sharply with a long ragged breath and shrugged off the slave's hand. Her eyes turned steely as she approached her husband and the limp form of her son.

Benjamin's clouded eyes met his wife's.

"Who has done this?" she asked woodenly.

Benjamin looked up at the overseer, hovering nearby.

Devil Wilcott flung a hasty look around. The slaves turned as a unit and looked at Dora, standing to one side and watching them in a confused state. Wilcott signaled two of the others to detain her though she showed no resistance.

"Take her to the barn," he snapped, turning back to Benjamin. "How many lashes, Sir?" he asked.

"None," Alice snapped sharply before her husband could answer.

Benjamin looked up at his wife in surprise.

Alice did not meet his look. Quietly, she said, "Hang her."

"Alice --" Benjamin began. He looked down at the body he held in his arms. He didn't look up. "Do it! Hang her."

Alice turned abruptly and hurried up the path to the house. Without a word to anyone, she climbed the stairs to her bedroom, went to the long window overlooking the backyard and stood there waiting, watching. Her face, while drawn, showed no emotion. That would come when the deed was done. Then she could collapse on her bed and mourn the son who had a wayward streak she had never been able to curb.

Down in the yard, Dora was hauled forward and thrown on the back of a buckboard parked beneath a tree. She stood docilely, staring down into the many black faces as they tied her hands behind her. Not one pair of black eyes dared shed a tear. Dora's eyes grew wide. She wondered why everyone had gathered to stare at her. When Devil Wilcott slipped the rope over her head, her eyes closed. Through the dense fogginess in her brain, she finally understood. For a moment, her eyes looked quite sane, and in the next instant grew wide in terror. The overseer climbed over into the seat and with a crack of the whip, sent the horses forward with a jarring movement, leaving Dora to dangle grotesquely, the crippled foot twisted at an awkward angle.

When Andrew returned home from the postponed meeting, he gravely described the incident that had taken place at Willow Manor.

By the following morning, the story had traveled far by way of the planters who had ridden to the estate for the meeting. The details were embellished upon with graphic clarity as the tale was repeated. It was a sobering theme, one that struck deep in the heart of master, slave, black and white. Yet, below the surface, there was an underlying degree of satisfaction that in some bizarre and inhumane way, justice had been done on both sides. But to James Hamilton it was a sad day, for he felt responsible. "It's my fault," he had lamented to Tilda. "I should have gotten her out of there. I knew how callous and brutal Frankie was to her."

"Don't blame yourself," Tilda pleaded. "You can't save all of us, James."

News of a different sort drifted in like the wind to cause hurried discussion among the slaves and give them hope that someone was, indeed, leading them out of slavery and into the promised land -- the North.

7

And then there crept
A little noiseless noise among the leaves,
Born of the very sigh that silence heaves.
                                        John Keats

*I*t was a sultry day in late August when the Negroes working in the fields saw a slave coffle winding up the lane of Stafford Hall. Even though the coffle was a familiar sight on the dusty roads, the workers paused to watch it pass. Chained together in a double line, they trudged along, encouraged by the slave trader on horseback and his long leather whip.

At the front entrance of the manor house, the slave trader was greeted by a cautious Mammy Ticey.

Mammy Ticey knew what the man wanted, but in her scorn of him and his kind, she hedged, deliberately making the bearded, scruffy slaver ill at ease. "What yo' want?" she demanded sharply.

The slaver confronted her hostility with a mumbled curse. "I want to speak to your master."

"He busy," Mammy replied shortly.

"Your mistress, then," the trader suggested.

"She busy, too," the old woman said haughtily.

Before the man could raise his voice, Andrew came onto the porch, his eyes flowing over the man on horseback, and the long line of black cargo shackled together. To the longtime servant, he said, "I'll handle this, Mammy." He addressed the trader. "What do you want?"

"Water from your pump and a place to rest."

Andrew nodded. "You may use the well near the large barn, but don't bother my people. Stay out of the way and keep your Negroes together."

The man nodded. "Yes, sir. I will. I thank you for your hospitality."

Grouped beneath the boughs of full-branched trees, the slaves began to take turns drinking from gourd dippers plunged eagerly into the bucket of cold well water. The slaver sat opposite, casting a calculating eye over his cargo and the plantation.

It was not long before Uncle Abrams came scurrying to the back entrance of the great house. "Fetch Massa Andrew!" he said to the house servant that answered his call. "Tell him he gotta come quick!" He dipped his grizzled head toward the young girl still standing there, "What yo' waitin' fo', gal? Git on and get the Massa!" he demanded, greatly agitated.

Old Uncle Abrams was striding up and down the porch when Andrew came to the door.

"What is it, Uncle Abrams?" Andrew asked.

"Gotta come, Suh," he said, a look of relief flashing over his dark features that his master had responded immediately to his message. "That trashy white slaver is a'beatin' one of them po' niggers. He got him trussed like a Sunday turkey, and jus' a'lashin' 'im." He loped down the steps with a gait that belied his years, throwing a harried look over his shoulder, to make sure Andrew was following.

"What did the man do?" Andrew inquired, lengthening his stride to keep up with the old man.

"His name Jubal. He didn't get no drink, an' when he ask, that slaver done tol' him to shut up, and then he tied his hands together, forced him into a squat, and run a stick in front of his elbows and 'hind his knees. That po' nigger helpless, Suh, when he tied in a buck," Uncle Abrams lamented. "That slaver beatin' him bloody."

By the time they reached the barn, Andrew striding beside Uncle Abrams and the overseer right behind them, Jubal was lying on his side, unable to move or escape the lashing blows of the whip. His shirt was in tatters and his back was furrowed with open wounds.

Andrew broke into a run catching the brawny arm of the slaver before he could bring the whip down in another searing blow.

"What the hell you think you're doin'?" the slaver demanded.

"There will be no whipping on this plantation," Andrew informed him rigidly.

"Until this nigger is sold, he is mine to discipline," the slaver retorted, his face growing very red with anger at the interference.

Flinging a quick look at the prostrate man, Andrew shook his head. "I understand he only asked for a drink of water."

"He's defiant, and high-handed," the slave trader snarled. "He's been giving me trouble all along."

Andrew ran a steely-eyed look of repugnance over the slaver. "No man will be denied water on this plantation," he said. Quietly, he spoke to Uncle Abrams, "Untie the man and let him drink." His sharp blue gaze defied the slave trader to object, and the overseer moved with a firm step to Andrew's side, gun in hand.

While Uncle Abrams administered to the unfortunate man's needs, Andrew stood staunchly, his eyes drilling into the slaver's, silently daring him to make a move to stop his order.

When Uncle Abrams finished, he rose with a heavy, remorseful heart that fluctuated between sadness and jubilation. Slowly, he joined Andrew, who told the slave trader firmly, "You have a half hour, then I expect you to be on your way."

Through glaring eyes, slitted with malice and anger, the slaver watched Andrew's stalwart back as he proceeded up the walk.

Later, Andrew met James returning from an outing with Abigail Johnston. Helping her alight from the carriage, James inquired of his father about the group of people beneath the trees near the barn. The slaves were not so weary that the handsome couple did not spark a bit of interest in their black eyes.

Andrew related the incident to his son, saying, "It is time for them to go. I must go down and make sure he leaves as I instructed."

"I'll go, Father," James offered. "Abigail? Would you mind going with Father into the house? This will just take a few minutes."

Abigail tossed her head, directing a flirtatious glance at Andrew as she slipped her arm through his. "It's deplorable how your son brushes a young lady aside," she said.

Andrew patted her gloved hand. "I just don't know about this younger generation," he intoned gravely shaking his head with mock severity.

James heard his father and Abigail laughing together as they entered the house. Uncle Abrams had climbed into the carriage to return it to the stables, and James turned toward the barn.

Approaching the group, he saw the coffle was standing in a double line, preparing to leave. His glance fell on the last man in line. It would have been difficult for James to miss the bloody, tattered shirt, and the recently scarred back. He felt his insides pitch in revulsion. For just a second, his eyes met Jubal's. James dragged his gaze away, forcing his attention to the slaver standing beside his horse, looking thoughtfully at Beulah's cabin.

As James approached, the slaver nodded a greeting. "I am James Hamilton," he told him. "I assume you are preparing to leave as my father requested?"

Scratching at his scruffy beard, the man ignored James' question, asking bluntly, "The wench I saw go in that cabin," he pointed to Beulah's, "she a quadroon?"

James didn't reply.

"Born here?" he asked, assuming she was the planter's daughter.

"No," James replied curtly, wanting to knock the knowing look from the man's face, "and I don't think it is any of your business."

"I ain't never seen such a bunch of snobby people. Yo'all sure think you're better than everyone else, don't you?" the man drawled. "You act like you're above me, but let me tell you, young man, you ain't no different from me," he said. "We're all in the same business, we just do it differently."

"I think it is time for you to leave," James said curtly.

But the slaver continued as though he had not heard, saying, "Back to the quadroon. You want to trade her for Jubal, since your old man seems so concerned about his welfare?"

"No."

"I could fetch you a pretty good price for one as comely as that," he offered.

"No," James replied firmly.

"Well, I'll buy her outright then," the slaver persisted. "Want to talk to your father? I'll make him a good offer."

James' clenched his fists at his side. "There is no need to talk to my father," he bit off.

"Well, maybe we'll just let your daddy have a say," the slaver intoned, seeing Andrew heading their way.

James turned.

Having seen his son's disquieting manner from the side window of the study, Andrew proceeded to the clearing where James faced the slaver squarely. Drawing level, he asked, "What is the problem?"

"He wants to buy Tilda," informed James.

"She isn't for sale."

"I have a buyer for light-skinned Negroes. This gal looks white. I could get you a good price," he said to Andrew. And when the man continued to refuse, the slaver nodded his head in a knowing manner. "I see. I suspect, " he drawled insultingly, flinging a look at James, "that he has his own plans for her."

James stepped forward, but was restrained by his

father's firm hand.

"She is not for sale," snapped Andrew, "nor are any of my people. Now I suggest you get on your way . My patience with you has just reached its end!"

The slaver swung onto his horse, yelling at the shackled blacks. He flipped the tip of his hat in a mocking salute, and drove the slaves at a fast gait, urging them onward with curses and a crack of the whip.

Andrew returned to the house. Jame stood watching the caravan until they were down the road. He went to find Uncle Abrams. He sent the old man to follow them at a safe distance and find out where they made camp. He knew they would get off the road and into the woods by nightfall. By noon the next day, they would have reached town and the auction block. He had little time to waste.

Later that night James met with Tilda at the cave.

"Did you find them?" she asked.

"Yes. Uncle Abrams followed them to a woods north of here. I must act quickly. I wish I could take them all, but there are too many. Jubal is the one we must concentrate on." He ran his fingers through his black hair in an agitated motion. "If I can get him back here, can you stay with him until I can make arrangements with the next station?"

Tilda nodded. "Of course. Whatever you need me to do."

James smiled at her, though he did so absently and Tilda knew his mind was on the imminent rescue. "I have to get him to someplace farther away," he said. "This slaver won't end his search quickly, and I can't take the chance of endangering the lives and identities of our close helpers." As an afterthought, he inquired, "Jubal has some pretty bad lashes on his back. Can you take care of them?"

"Yes," Tilda said softly. "I'll get some salve from Aunt Sallie."

"Good," he answered, distracted. Then, "I'd better be on my way." He reached out to push aside the curtain of honeysuckle that filled the small space with its perfumed fragrance.

"James," Tilda called softly from behind him.

He turned back.

"Thank you for once again saving me," she said softly.

"You heard?"

She nodded.

James strode back into the small enclosure and took her into his arms. He held her close to him, whispering against the waves of dark hair, "I'm so sorry, Tilda. It's a terrible world we live in," he said sadly. His arms gathered her more tightly. "Somehow, this madness has to stop."

"It's already too late for us, James," Tilda murmured wistfully.

Long after they left, the melancholy atmosphere lingered in the darkness like a fog, hovering with smothering tendencies in the small enclosure.

That night Jubal disappeared from the woods where the slaver and those he owned slept. Not a sound was made to alert the slave trader. It was as if Jubal had disappeared into the heavy mist of the early morning.

A search was conducted at neighboring plantations where it was thought the man might be hiding -- or was being hidden -- but no trace was ever found.

The plantation slaves whispered that "he got spirited away by Moses." And they walked away into the fields with rapt expressions on their dark faces. They sang louder as they worked, and the refraining chorus of "Hallelujah" rang across the land and echoed in the treetops.

8

Coldly, sadly descends
The autumn evening. The field
Strewn with its dark yellow drifts
Of withered leaves, and the elms,
Fade into dimness apace.
                    Matthew Arnold

*L*ate in the fall EmiLee died in her sleep. Her death was so unexpected it threw the plantation into a stunned sense of disbelief. Jane arrived home to a grief-stricken household. James worried about his father. Andrew became withdrawn, blaming himself for not knowing that his wife's health had rapidly deteriorated. She had given him no clue that she had a heart condition. The doctor advised there was nothing he could have done, that her heart was weak and simply gave out. The knowledge did not assuage Andrew's guilt or desolation.

A long procession followed the horse-drawn wagon pulling EmiLee Hamilton's coffin up the gently rolling, green knoll to the cemetery. A black wrought iron fence enclosed the grave sites. The Potomac flowed in the distance. The tall oaks stood guard at the entrance. A chill breeze wafted through the tree-tops, sighing in accompaniment to the tears of grief as the clergyman read from the Bible.

A dismal pall settled over the plantation. On the eve of the funeral, Andrew locked the doors of his study. Jane returned home with her husband, Adam, and their two children. James paced the floor of his bedroom, knowing that time was the only healer, yet the pain in his heart drove him restively.

As the moon rose high, he went to the window, looking out into the shadowy night. Down at the slave quarters the cabins sat bathed in moonlight. He had seen Tilda only briefly that day. She stood in the back with the other slaves, next to her mother, weeping softly. He'd wanted to go to her and console her but of course, he could not leave Abigail's side. Once again, James cursed the circumstances that kept them on separate sides of the divided world in which they lived.

Broodingly, he looked down onto the small cabin, wishing he could see her, to talk to her. He needed her and that thought burned in him so intensely that with a curse, he caught up a cape to ward against the chill evening, and slipped quietly down the stairs.

Like a shadow, he moved among the boxwoods. He was halfway to Beulah's cabin, when the cool wind in his face brought him to a halt and he abruptly sat on an iron garden seat. Some masculine force inside him, a male instinct as old as the universe, burned in his body. That elusive second-nature told him that if he met her tonight, he would not be content with seeing her, would not stop at just holding her. James knew he would want more. He also knew she would give, selflessly, whatever she sensed he desired. That thought held him. He could not do that to Tilda. To do so would be to treat her like a slave. To make demands that she felt she had no right to refuse was not the way he wanted Tilda. He rose from the bench and lumbered back up the boxwood walk.

He did not know that Tilda stood outside in the shadows of the cabin. Sensing he was coming to her, she waited with a breathless feeling, her heart stuttering in limbo, as it always did whenever he was near. She saw his tall figure hurrying her way and watched silently as he sat pensively on the garden bench. Suddenly, he rose and went back the way he had come. Her brow furrowed. What had caused him to change his mind? A chill stole over her as she drew the cloak around her and went back into the cabin.

One early winter's eve the slaves gathered around a campfire in the center of the clearing near their cabins. With muted voices they huddled in close camaraderie, telling tales of yesterday and voicing hopes of a tomorrow when they would be free.

"Tell us 'bout yo' granny and the red cloth, Aunt Sallie?" someone asked.

"She done tol' that a million times," another protested. "Ain't no truf to it."

"Is too," Aunt Sallie declared. "Yo' young'uns don't know nothin' 'bout nothin'," she lamented with an aggravated toss of her wise old head.

"Aunt Sallie's right," Uncle Abrams said quietly. "Times used to be powerful diffrunt den dey is now. What we is, we has done to ourselves," he stated firmly.

"Ain't our fault we is slaves," Mingo snapped huffily. "It's the white folks that keep us in shackles."

"You don't know what yo' is talkin' 'bout," Uncle Abrams told him sharply. "We is lucky here at Stafford Hall."

Mingo swore. "Yo' call not bein' free, lucky?"

"Yo' know why yo' ain't free, boy?" old Uncle Abrams asked him with an angry fire in his dark eyes that they were unaccustomed to seeing.

"'Cause o' dem white folks."

"Yo' quick to blame, boy, but yo' don't know the whole truf."

"What yo' mean?" Mingo asked quarrelsomely.

"My grandpappy used to tell me that back in Africa, the tribal chiefs made war on another tribe, jus' fo' the purpose of capturing 'smany peoples as possible." He peered down hard at Mingo. "Yo' knows what he wanted with 'em?"

Mingo shook his head.

"He wanted 'em to sell to the white slave traders.

'Cause dey give him tobacco, an' guns, an' ammunition, an' liquor. Yeah, dat's right," he said, shaking his head up and down. "Dey give him anything he want fo' his black brother. So you see," he finished sadly, "ain't all the white folks fault. We is jus' as much to blame," he drawled, his voice trailing off.

There was a heavy silence before someone asked old Aunt Sallie again for the story of her granny and the red cloth.

Old Aunt Sallie moved to and fro in the old rocking chair that someone had carried out for her. The cushions were worn, and the paint had long since peeled away, but she sat rocking in the chair every night until evening shadows fell and she grew sleepy. She was so quiet now that they thought she had fallen asleep, but she was only gathering her thoughts to repeat, once again, the story she had told so many times.

She smacked her lips together as she did when she was thinking. "My old granny said," she began, "that many years ago in Africa, a big ship came to the shore. 'Course no one had ever seen such a thing befo', and natur'ly dey's all curious. One day, someone seed a piece o' red cloth on de ground. Didn't have no red cloth dere, yo' know, an' it sho' was purty, and so someone picked it up, an' den dey followed along 'til dey finds another piece. Dey keeps movin' along, followin' de path o' dat bright cloth, 'til dey gets to de river where de big ship is. Dem black folks jus' kept followin' dat bright red cloth all de way up into dat big ship. When dey had 'smany peoples on boa'd 'sdey wanted, de gate was chained up and couldn't no one get back. And that, chilluns, is how come my granny left Africa an' come here." Aunt Sallie smacked her gums together in emphasis, and leaned back in her rocker with her eyes closed, as if the long speech had winded her.

"Still wish we wasn't slaves," a voice lamented.

"Ain't our fault what happened in Africa," another snapped viciously.

"It jus' da way it is," Aunt Sallie told them. Then her voice softened, "But times is changin', chilluns."

"Don't see much changin fo' us," someone stated.

"Yo' listen to me, chilluns," old Aunt Sallie said, sitting up sharply. "Times *is* a changin'," she announced firmly. "I's lived most a hundred years now and things is already diffrunt. Soon we all be free," she said softly.

"We all be dead fo' we is free," Mingo said angrily.

But Aunt Sallie shook her head stubbornly. "Not me, chile. I ain't gonna die 'til I is free," she said firmly. "'Cause iffn I does, I's gonna be powerful mad at the Lawd when I sees him!"

Dusk was beginning to gather as Tilda came from the big house where she had been sewing on a dress Jane had asked her to make. She encountered John Avery, the recordkeeper, out for an evening's stroll.

"Good evening, Tilda," he greeted.

"Evening, Mr. Avery," Tilda returned.

"Out for a walk?" he asked, his tone conversational.

"I'm making a gown for Jane. I've been stitching all day. Thought I'd go down the rolling road to the landing. I like the soft murmur of the river."

"Nice night for a walk," he acknowledged, and watched as she moved past him toward the barn at the side of the road.

John Avery had always been concerned about Tilda. He felt she, and many like her, had a particularly tough cross to bear. But Tilda, having much of her father's blood in her veins, managed to hold herself aloof from her slave status. She expected nothing and was therefore not disappointed. John Avery was congnizant of James' actions toward her but he did not fault him for it, rather he was happy there was someone who cared enough to elevate the girl's meager existence. What he did not know, and could only guess at, was the seriousness of the relationship.

Tilda had moved beyond his range of vision. He had seen her approaching the barn. He looked for her again when she should have reached the corner, but she was nowhere in sight. He dismissed it, and started to move on.

Moments later, as Tilda stepped in front of the barn doors, an arm shot out, pulling her inside. The thick hand on her mouth stifled her scream.

When she saw Mingo, she shoved his hands away from her. "What you doin'?" she demanded.

"I is tired o' seein' yo' pinin' after Massa James," he stated.

"You don't know nothin', Mingo," she snapped, glaring at him.

"That what yo' thinks," he declared. "I knows you slip around meetin' the massa."

"You knows nothin' of the sort," Tilda hedged, not sure how much he did know. Her heart tripped a beat as she stood defiantly, denying his words.

"You too uppity, girl," Mingo hissed. "I hates the way yo' keeps yo'self above the rest o' us." He suddenly grabbed her by the shoulders, shaking her. "You thinks yo' is like dem white folks? You not!" he spat. "Don't matter how white yo' is, you nigger jus' like the rest o' us. Yo' ain't got no right to care 'bout the massa noway," he flared angrily. "Time yo' understand yo' gotta' settle fo' yo' own kind." He pulled her toward him, trying to kiss her.

Tilda struggled, using all her strength to push him away. "Leave me alone, Mingo, or I'll scream."

"Scream all yo' want," he said, unperturbed. "Ain't nobody gonna hear yo' down here." With work-hardened arms, he pulled her toward him with a strength that made her gasp. One hand fondled her breast, while he tried to pull aside her clothing.

"Mingo, stop," she implored, pushing at his rock-hard body.

"Bet yo' don't say no to Massa James, does yo', Tilda?" he gritted, shaking her again.

Tilda reached out, raking Mingo's face with her fingernails.

He swore and slapped her so hard she fell to the floor. Mingo fell on her. Terrified, she struggled against him, but he struck her again, knocking her head back against the floorboards. For a moment, Tilda lay stunned.

It was just long enough for Mingo to shove her skirts up above her thighs. In anticipation, his heavy body was already pumping against her as he struggled with his own clothing.

Tilda fought, begging him to stop. Tears of anguish streamed down her face.

Suddenly, she felt the weight of his body jerked away from hers.

John Avery landed a blow to Mingo's jaw that sent him careening backward. But Mingo recovered quickly, bouncing up, swearing at the clerk, and striking him a resounding blow. They rolled in the dust-covered floor, and finally, regaining his footing, John Avery grabbed a pitchfork and started toward Mingo. Seeing the rage on the accountant's face, Mingo backed away, turned and fled outside.

John Avery flung the pitchfork aside and bent to Tilda. "Did he -- " he began.

She shook her head, unable to meet his eyes. "He . . . he didn't --" She couldn't bring herself to finish. "Thank you for stopping him," she whispered.

The clerk helped her to her feet, holding his hand over a bloody nose. "I'm going to the house to report this to Mr. Hamilton. Mingo cannot get away with this."

Tilda was silent.

"Do you want to go with me?"

She shook her head.

John Avery took a step toward the doorway, then turned back. "Are you sure you're all right?"

She nodded. But in her heart she knew she would never be all right. Because she was a slave, she had no right to be insulted. As a slave she was nothing. As a slave, she did not matter. Tilda felt as if her soul had been crushed.

Reluctantly, John Avery left her and retraced his steps to the house. He entered without knocking, holding a handkerchief to his nose. "Where is Mr. Hamilton?" he asked Mammy Ticey.

"He in the library, Suh," she replied, her brow raised in concern as her dark-eyed gaze fell on the bloody handkerchief he held to his face.

He hurried down the hall to the room where the door stood ajar. John Avery did not bother to wait to be asked inside. He walked in, greeting them abruptly, "Andrew. James."

"What happened, John?" Andrew asked, rising from the wing chair where he had been talking to James across a small table. Andrew noted the drawn features and disheveled clothing.

"Mingo," John replied quietly. "He attacked Tilda."

James leaped to his feet, dropping a book he had been holding.

"Tilda was out walking. Mingo must have been watching her. He dragged her into the barn. I --" he hesitated.

"Where is Mingo?" Andrew asked.

"He ran off after we fought."

"And Tilda?"

"In the barn. She didn't want to come with me."

James stepped in front of his father, heading to the door.

John reached out, detaining him as he drew near. He hesitated, meeting the younger man's eyes. Pointedly he said, "He didn't succeed."

James went immediately to the barn, but did not find Tilda there. At Beulah's, he found only a worried mother who had already heard of the attack. Retracing his steps to the house, he lit a lantern and hurried outside, hoping that he would find Tilda where she had gone to hide so many years ago.

Meanwhile, Andrew had gone with John Avery and the overseer to the slave quarters in search of Mingo. They found him in Ivy's cabin. There was no need to question either of them. Andrew knew Mingo would lie to save his own hide and Ivy would lie because she loved him.

Mingo's attemped assault filled Andrew with anger. He was aware that he must take immediate disciplinary action to forestall further conduct of such a contemptible nature. He ordered every slave roused and into the clearing. Two of the older men held Mingo whose wide eyes watched Andrew warily.

"I cannot -- and will not -- tolerate this type of behavior on this place. It saddens me greatly to have to do this, but I cannot overlook such a deplorable action." Andrew drew a deep breath. "Take him to the barn. I want him publicly lashed."

A gasp rippled among the slaves. Many of them had never before seen a man whipped.

For the first time in twenty years, one of Stafford Hall's slaves was tied to the post and lashed. When it was over, Ivy stepped out of the crowd to tend to Mingo's wounds.

Carrying the lantern, James hurried past the tobacco field, eroute to the vine-covered cave. He could hear Mingo's screams echoing across the night skies. He held no sympathy for Mingo, and ignored the cries as he hastened on his way.

He paused at the cave entrance, steeling himself for a weeping and desolate Tilda. When he entered, Tilda looked up and the look in her eyes sent a chill over him. Silently, he set the lantern down and went over to sit beside her. He didn't try to touch her. Some intangible something was keeping him at a distance.

"Are you all right?" he inquired shortly.

She didn't answer.

James took a deep breath, berating himself for the stupidity of the question.

After a while, staring straight ahead, she spoke, breaking the silence that hovered like a cloud. "He said I was a nigger, that I have no right to care for you."

"Tilda -- you can't listen to him," James began.

She continued to stare straight ahead, continuing as though he had not spoken. "He's right you know. Guess I always knew it. White skin don't make no difference, does it, Massa James?"

"Tilda, stop it! Stop talking like a slave," he demanded.

She laughed shortly. "But Massa, I is a slave." She turned to him and James grabbed her by the shoulders, shaking her.

"I won't tolerate this type of behavior from you, Tilda," James said firmly, despite the anger bubbling up in him when he saw the bruise on her face. "You are above this."

Suddenly she crumpled beneath his touch, and burrowing her face in his chest, wept, "I hate who I am -- what I am. Part black, part white, not belonging in the slave's world or the planters. Mingo felt he could insult me like that because I am a slave -- because I have no rights. I'm not supposed to feel, to care. I am nothing -- nothing!"

"Listen to me, Tilda," James said, lifting her tear-stained face up to him. "You can't change what you are, but you can rise above it."

She shook her head. "Mingo says I am too uppity. Says I got to learn to settle for one of my own." She looked up at him. "What is my own, James?" Distraught, confused emotion filled her eyes, her face and her voice as she asked the perplexing question.

"Well," James said quitely, "you told me once that the white blood of your father made your heart beat and that it was with your heart that you love me."

"That is true," she sniffed, not understanding what point he was making.

"Then, don't you see?" he said gently. "You have settled for one of your own."

Wanting desperately to believe his words, a watery smile slowly crossed her features.

"The sad part of it is that, much as I love you, I cannot marry you. And you should marry, Tilda. You should have many children around you."

She shook her head adamantly. "No. To bring children into this world where they would not belong any more than I do would be cruel. As long as I know that you love me, James, it is all I will ever want."

After a period of silence, James said, "Father had Mingo whipped."

The knowledge brought her no comfort. "I'm sorry," she murmured. "Mingo is a very angry man. He resents me. In a way, we're alike. We want so much more than we will ever be able to have."

James made no response for he had no words that would comfort her.

His arms suddenly tightened around her, and she saw a wistful seriousness laying like a mask on his features.

"What is it, James?" she asked. "What has made you so sad?"

His lips brushed the top of her head before he spoke. "Tilda," his voice came low, "I can still make arrangements to get you to the North if you have changed your mind."

She shook her head vigorously.

A long sigh rose up from him. "God," he groaned. "I wish I had the courage to make you go."

"Sending me away, James, does not solve anything. Even in the North, I will still be black coffee with a spoonful of cream stirred in."

"Tilda?" He turned her to look up at him. "Suppose we went away together? We could make a life for ourselves up North."

"No," she said firmly.

He glanced down at her in surprise. "I thought you would be pleased to know that I am willing to leave behind everything to be with you."

"This is your family home, James. Your heritage. I could not take that away from you. You have all that I can never have," she said earnestly, "I could never ask you to give it up." She shook her head. "No. We will stay here and face whatever we must. I will remain here at Stafford Hall where I can be with you. Now, please," she touched his face with her fingertips, "don't talk anymore about the north, and promise me, you'll never try to do what you would think of as noble and send me away. To make such a sacrifice on your part," she said gravely, "would only sacrifice us both."

He didn't answer.

"Promise me, James," she insisted.

And after a moment, he murmured, "I promise."

They grew silent, sitting on the ground of the small enclosure, holding each other.

After a while, Tilda ventured timidly, "This -- that Mingo tried to do -- " She hesitated, choosing her words carefully. "Everyone knows that Ivy has bedded more men than most of us can count. But, I have never laid with a man." She did not look up at him as she asked, "Did you know that, James? That no man has ever bedded me?"

"I was sure of it," he answered quietly.

"Mingo thinks that you have bed me."

James made no response and she went on, "Did you ever want to lay with me, James?" she asked softly.

"Many times," he answered honestly.

"Why didn't you?" she inquired curiously, and this time cast a quick look up at him.

"Because to do so would have been to treat you like a slave. I did not want you like that."

"But I would have let you -- " she began.

"Exactly," James snapped. "You see, Tilda, you think of yourself as a slave when it comes to pleasing me." Enunciating every word, he said slowly, "You are not a slave to me, Tilda. You are my equal." He grasped her shoulders, shaking her. "Do you understand? My equal."

He released her, but words were still bubbling from his mouth. "I don't want just sex from you," he snapped. "Lovemaking between a man and a woman is meant to be more than just satisfying a desire. You have to think with your heart, not just the rage in your body. You would have given yourself to me because you think of me with your black blood -- as your massa!" He spat out the word. "If and when you ever give yourself to me, Tilda, it must be with your heart and most of all because you want to," he tapped her shoulder gently with his fingertip, "and not because you think you have to."

James suddenly stood, needled and frustrated by his own words. He stood with one arm pressed against the overhanging lip of the cave, staring at the wall of dried honeysuckle. He heard a soft rustling behind him, but he didn't turn.

"James -- "

His name came softly to him from over his shoulder. He turned. Tilda had pulled the torn dress from her shoulders and let it slide to the ground. She was barefoot, as she so often was, and she stood delicately among the cotton folds of her discarded dress. The lantern light played over her body like a musician's hands played over violin strings. James stood quietly, absorbing her beauty through his senses and reveling in the sculpt marble perfection of her body.

"Lay with me, James," she whispered. "Make love to me just as we both have always wanted." She held out her hand. A gentle smile curved her lips upward. Slowly, she took one step toward him. "Please," she whispered, "I am asking you with my heart."

His eyes held hers for a long interim before he accepted her hand. He closed the space between them quickly, caught her up against his body, his lips trailing from her temple to her neck. Breathlessly, he stepped back, removed his cloak and spread it on the earthen floor. He turned to Tilda and swung her up into his arms, cradling her to him.

Against her soft hair, he murmured, "This is not the way I had hoped it would be. You should be loved on a bed of silks and velvets."

"I don't care where it is," she whispered, "as long as it is you making love to me."

James laid her down on the coarse wool cloak, and lowered himself down to meet her.

9

And sings a solitary song
That whistles in the wind.
Wordsworth

*I*n the summer of 1860, James arranged to meet Tilda at their secret place. He was already there when she arrived. As she entered honeysuckle perfume wafted through the dank interior. Tilda's heart trembled when she saw him.

He came forward immediately, drawing her inside with both hands. Without speaking, he gathered her to him, holding her close. She could feel his heart beating against her cheek. The silence seemed threatening.

She looked up. "James, you're scaring me. What is wrong?"

"I have asked Abigail to marry me," he said reluctantly.

Tilda's heart skipped, and she struggled to speak. "When?" The solitary word was all she could manage.

"Two months from now."

She absorbed the announcement in silence. It was something Tilda had been dreading for a long time for she knew it would happen eventually. Her heart ached as never before.

"I have no choice," he said, his voice broken.

"Stafford Hall needs a mistress. We both know we can have no formal life together, but even with this marriage, I will not allow things to change between us." His fingers beneath her chin tipped her head up to him. "You must believe that, Tilda. No matter what, I will always love you."

Tilda knew she must be content with that, but the pain cut deeply and once again she cursed her fate. When James left, and she was alone, she crumpled into a desolate heap and cried angry tears of frustration.

That night James rode off. When the moon appeared as a small boat rocking in the heavens, he returned home and he was very drunk. Though she would never have admitted it to him, Mammy Ticey was waiting up for his return. Crooning softly, as he leaned heavily against her, she helped him to bed.

James left for Philadelphia on business and had been gone for two weeks. His absence was like a dark cloud hovering over Tilda's head. She did not like him being away from her, and kept herself busy to keep from thinking about him. That sufficed during the daytime. At night, it was different. She yearned to see him, to touch him, to have him hold her as he did in the cave when they made love. Her body yearned for his touch, and her heart ached for sight of him.

He returned late at night. Tilda heard the soft nicker of the horses, and heard the carriage wheels rumble over the dirt drive. She wanted to run to him, to welcome him home. But she knew she could not. Instead, she rose from the bed beside her sleeping mother and slipped quietly to the doorway, watching the front porch. A smile brightened her features when she saw his tall figure lope up the steps. As usual, Mammy Ticey stood at the wide doorway, waiting for him with open arms. How she envied the adoring old woman.

The next day, James sat in the study, pensively looking down at a small box he held in his hands. Lumbering down the hall, Mammy Ticey looked in and saw him.

She came into the room. "What you doin', Jimmie-James?"

James looked up with a slight shrug of his shoulders.

"You all right?" she asked quickly. "You sad 'bout somethin'?"

"I am, Mammy Ticey," he said.

She came closer to the desk, looking at him more closely. "Yassuh, I 'spose you is."

James watched her for a moment, then twisted the small box around for her to see. "I bought this while in Philadelphia, Mammy," he said softly.

Mammy glanced down. "Oh, chile, dat is beautiful," she said appreciatively, lifting the delicately carved cameo, set in gold filigree, out of the velvet box. The necklace chain dangled over her broad hand. "It sho' is pretty," she said, admiring the beauty of the hand-cut stone. "Miss Abigail sho' gonna like this," she enthused.

"It's not for Miss Abigail," James said.

"What you mean?" The old mammy jerked her head up. "Who it for?" she demanded brusquely.

"It's for Tilda," James informed with a touch of defiance in his voice.

"Oh, good Lawd!" Mammy breathed, her black eyes wide.

James abruptly stood and went across the room to lean against the fireplace mantle.

Mammy Ticey followed him, facing him staunchly. "What you think you is doin', chile?" she asked.

James looked down at her, his mouth forming a tight, straight line. Stubbornly, he didn't answer.

"It ain't right, Jimmie-James," Mammy said softly, "an' you knows it."

"She is as white as I am," he protested.

But Mammy Ticey shook her gray head. "Don't matter, honeychile. Almost white don't count fo' nothin' an' you knows that, too. She is still black. She is a slave and always will be."

"Her father is white," James retorted.

"Don't matter who her daddy is. It's who her mammy is that counts," the old woman snapped adamantly.

When he made no reply, Mammy Ticey turned to look up into his face, and her heart trembled. For the first time since her Jimmie-James was a little boy, she saw tears running down his cheeks. "Dear Lawd!" she breathed. "You really loves her!"

His silence told her what she had refused to acknowledge before. Her Jimmie-James had gone and lost his heart to a love that could never be.

That afternoon James rode out on his horse to skirt round the plantation and back to the small cave where he knew Tilda waited. Common sense told him he should have waited until nightfall, but he could not wait any longer to see her. While he was in Philadelphia, he had heard her voice in the wind that whispered down the cobblestoned streets, had seen her face in every reflective surface, and felt the softness of her supple limbs in every sense of his being.

He spurred the horse, anxious to see her, to hold her. And to give her the cameo, a token of his love. Within a short distance of the cave, he tied the horse to a low branch of a tree, and went on foot up the path to the cave. Tilda heard his footsteps, and met him at the green and white curtain of honeysuckle. She held the vines back, her eyes eagerly searching for him. She smiled when she saw him. James ran and caught her up in his arms, hugging her tightly .

"I missed you so," Tilda murmured.

"I feel like I have been away from you for an eternity," James confided.

When Tilda started to draw him into the confines of the small cave, he whispered against the waves of her dark hair, "Come, ride with me."

"Where?" she asked softly.

"Anywhere. We need to be away from here," he replied, leading her to where he had tethered the horse.

He swung astride and reached down to lift her up in

front of him. She put her arms about him, resting her head against his chest.

They rode swiftly as though racing with the wind. James wanted privacy, so they rode for an hour away from the plantation.

They passed a field where slaves worked and Tilda glanced up. He understood her knowing look. It didn't matter where they went, they could never get away from reminders of that which kept them apart.

They turned onto a worn path that meandered its way off the main road that snaked its way, undulating like the back of a dragon, into a small community. The path was flanked by woods and far into its midst they stopped. James tethered the horse, and hand in hand they walked in comfortable silence. Not far along, they came to a small stream. Across the shallow strip of water was a clearing.

"Shall we cross over?" James asked, indicating a crooked line of rocks that provided stepping-stones to the other side.

Tilda smiled. "Yes, lets," she said, heading eagerly toward the edge of the brook.

The first stone was some distance from the stream's edge. With his long-legged stride, James had no difficulty making the jump to reach it. Leaping to the next one, he turned back to her on the bank. "Can you reach it?" he asked, holding his hands out to her.

Tilda nodded confidently, poised on the edge momentarily, then leaped, clutching her skirts in her arms. She landed with a jarring thud, let her skirt fall and grabbed for James' outstretched hands. His fingers closed around hers but her frantic movements caused him to lose his footing, and they both wobbled precariously. Tilda shrieked in a mixture of exhilaration and expectation of falling into the knee-deep water at any moment.

Laughing, James regained his more surefooted stance and in the process steadied her. Like frolicking children, laughing and leaping from one stepping stone to the next, they reached the other side. James caught her hand in his and pulled her down onto the soft carpet of green grass.

He cupped her face in his hands. "I know that I have obligations to the plantation, but I have been unable to get you off my mind. I know my decision has upset you. I do not mean to hurt you, Tilda."

Tilda covered his hands with her own, knowing he referred to his marriage to Abigail. "I know that, James," she told him softly. "It does hurt," she admitted honestly, "but I know it has to be." She raised her hands to his face, caressing it gently. "I have always known we can never have a life together but that does not mean I did not have my dreams."

"Don't think I do not know what it is to dream, Tilda," James said with quiet vehemence. "I have dreams in my heart that I know can never be, but I keep them there just the same, peek at them occasionally, wonder at their beauty, and wish I could make them real." As he spoke, he gathered her to his chest. "My dreams haunt me at night, Tilda. They mock me in the most agonizing way." His lips brushed her temple. "They make me wonder why I should be allowed to find someone as perfect as you are, someone I feel a soulmate to." Absently, his lips touched her temple again. "But always, in the harsh light of day, I am flagrantly denied all the illusions and the promises of those same dreams." He fell silent.

Tilda wanted desperately to comfort him, but she didn't know how, didn't know the right words, and so she raised from his embrace to put her arms about him, holding him close to her breast. She heard the soft flapping of a bird's wings as it flew from one tree branch to another and the gurgle of the brook as it splashed over the rocks.

James held her away from him, looking down into her face. "While I was in Philadelphia," he told her softly, "I found a gift for you, a small token of my love." He dug into his breast pocket, withdrawing the small velvet box containing the cameo. He held it out to her.

Tilda accepted the small box, but her eyes clung to James'.

"Go on, open it," he said.

She flipped back the top, exposing the gold encased cameo lying on a bed of silk. Tilda covered her mouth with her hand. "Oh, James. This is so beautiful. I --" Overwhelmed, further speech eluded her.

James lifted it from the box, opened the tiny gold clasp and draped it around her neck. It rested just below the small hollow of her throat, where the pulse throbbed.

"I want you to wear it, Tilda, a small keepsake to remind you of my love," James whispered.

A cascade of tears coursed in twin rivulets down Tilda's cheeks. Her hand closed around the cameo as though fearing it would disappear. She moved back into James' arms without a word, crying softly. The thought that James felt so strongly of her wreaked havoc on her emotions.

It wasn't the thought of owning something so exquisite. It was true that some favored slaves, for many different reasons, did receive gifts of jewelry and other items from their master or mistress. But never had Tilda ever entertained the notion of receiving anything from James. She was so deeply touched by this expression of his love, that no words could possibly tell him how very much the gesture meant to her. She could only lean against him while holding him.

James set her aside and stood, pulling her up as well. "We must be getting back," he said softly.

They crossed the meandering stream, mastering the technique of leaping from one stepping-stone to another with more ease than they had exhibited earlier. On the bank, James took her hand and they retraced their steps back to the path in the woods to his horse.

They reached the plantation and rode to the cave where James would leave her.

"I don't know how to thank you for the cameo, James, except to tell you I will always wear it, and I will always love you."

James kissed her lightly. "There are so many things I wish I could give you and do for you, but," he left the sentence unfinished, shrugging his shoulders.

"It is your love that is more important than anything

else," she whispered, lifting the cameo and tucking it inside the bodice of her dress. The feel of the metal touching her skin gave her pleasure in knowing that James' token of love lay near her heart. Thinking that James may wonder why she had put it out of sight, she said, "There is no need to invite questions from others about where I got it, or how. It will be part of our secret."

"Probably just as well," James murmured.

After a moment's ponderance, Tilda said, "Except for my mother. I'd like her to know. Would you mind if I show it to her?" She didn't explain her mother's fear but sensed James understood.

"Show her if you like," he replied.

Tilda picked her way through the field of wildflowers and skirted around the field of cotton reaching the plantation manor house long before James came riding up the road.

Tilda prepared for bed, washing with cold water from a pitcher on a shelf. She slipped a cotton shift over her head. She had sewn bits of delicate lace that the Missus had given her around the scoop neck bodice of the night shift. The cameo rested on her breast in full view and Tilda waited in silence for her mother to notice it.

Beulah had seen it almost immediately, but she held her tongue waiting for an explanation. When none was forthcoming, she asked point-blank, "Where you get dat? From Miss Jane?" Her last words were hopeful.

Tilda shook her head.

Beulah waited, but Tilda did not respond. Closing her eyes, Beulah nodded her head in silent cognizance and began to stride with agitated movements across the cabin floor.

Tilda interrupted her disconcerted pacing. "No one knows," she told her. "Except you, no one will ever know."

"What dat s'pose to mean?" her mother demanded. "Dat makes it all right, jus' cause no one knows?"

"Just what is so wrong about it?" Tilda returned sharply.

"What is wrong with it, chile?" Beulah repeated in

exasperation. "Don't you see?" Her mother shook her head. "It ain't the present, Tilda. It who give it."

Tilda made no comment.

"What matters," Beulah continued, "is dat it's from the Massa."

"I'm not the first person --"

"Slave," corrected Beulah, interrupting bluntly. "Yo' is a slave, Tilda!"

Tilda nodded, swallowing hard. "All right," she agreed, "slave. I am not the first slave to get a present from the master," she finished quietly.

"This ain't jus' a present to a slave from the massa," Beulah said, shaking her head. "It's mo' den dat, an' you knows it."

"James cares about me," Tilda said softly.

Her mother's head came up abruptly when she spoke his name without the preceding "master".

"I is scared fo' you, Tilda," she said breathlessly. "No matter how you feels, you is not like dem. You has no right to call him dat."

A deep sigh dragged from Tilda's midriff. "I'm sorry, mama. I did not mean to call him that in front of you. It -- it just slipped out."

"And what if it slips out in front of someone else?" her mother demanded. "What den?"

"It won't," she answered in a subdued voice.

But Beulah's head wagged in consternation. "Don't you understand, chile," she implored. "You is not one o' dem."

"So everyone keeps telling me," Tilda snapped. "I don't belong here, I don't belong there. It's like Mingo told me when I was a little girl. He said that I was just hanging in the air, not belonging anyplace, and he was right," she finished bitterly.

Beulah crossed the small expanse to her daughter's side. She put her arms around her. "I is so sorry, Tilda. I knows dis is all my fault, but what's done is done. You has got to be careful, chile. I's so afraid you is gonna get hurt." She caressed Tilda's head with a loving hand. "I is sorry," she repeated, "but I is yo' mammy, and that makes you black."

Tilda looked up, her eyes full of tears. "But I love James," she whispered.

"It can only lead to trouble, chile," her mother answered sorrowfully.

"James cares about me, too," she added earnestly. "For who I am, not what I am."

"Don't matter," Beulah said matter-of-factly. "You can't love Massa James."

Tilda nestled in her mother's arms in stubborn silence. She did love him, would always love him, and she knew she couldn't change that anymore than she could change being a slave.

Two months later, as planned, James brought Abigail home as his bride. Tilda turned a blind eye and a deaf ear to the joyful atmosphere and the slaves' celebration of Stafford Hall having a mistress again.

10

It looked as if a night of dark intent
Was coming, and not only a night, an age.
                                    Robert Frost

*T*hings were beginning to change in the South.
There were more and more reports of slave uprisings, and
even greater talk of war between the states. Economic
differences were rapidly driving the north and south apart.
Unlike the North, a region dominated by cities and
manufacturing industries, the South was a territory of
great tracts of farmlands and plantations.

In a large section of the lower southern states, cotton
was produced in two or three thousand acres or more on
most plantations. The cotton gin, which separated cotton
fibers from the seeds, made it enormously profitable to
raise the product with slave labor. However, while
feeding the demand for raw cotton, the South had placed
itself in a precariously unsound economical position by
depending overwhelmingly on this crop.

Otherwise responsible southerners felt that cotton
was so great a benefit to the world that it justified
slavery. The North was just as adamant about the moral
and social ramifications of enslavement. All of these
factors gradually urged the North and South toward
irreconcilable differences.

With the Northern states increasingly expressing their anti-slavery, initial stirrings of war often crept into the planters' conversations. It was becoming an unstable and worrisome time for large plantation owners. There were rumors daily of slaves escaping to the North and freedom. While still cloaked in mystery, the Underground Railroad had become proficient in hiding its cargo and delivering it safely in the North. All of these issues combined caused a great deal of unrest for the planters.

Andrew, James, and John Avery were in the library going over the accounting ledgers when a commotion in the hall caused all three to look up. Uncle Abrams' voice was a jumble of excitement. They heard Mammy Ticey murmur fearfully, "Oh, good Lawd."

"I's got to see Massa right away." Uncle Abrams' hastily spoken words floated into the room. "Cain't wait. Got to get 'im."

James strode across the room and flung open the door. "What is it, Uncle Abrams?" he asked, noting Mammy's hands clasped apprehensively to her mouth.

The old colored man moved past James, his eyes seeking Andrew. "Trouble at Willow Manor, Suh," he said with an air of urgency. "Bad trouble."

"What kind of trouble?" Andrew asked.

"The wust," the old man replied with a grim shake of his head. "Slave revolt, Suh."

"How do you know this?" Andrew questioned, moving toward the man he'd known since a child.

"Charlotte -- she a house servant at Witherspoon's Plantation -- done runned all de way ober here and tol' me."

"Where is Charlotte?"

"She runned off. She scared out o' her senses, I reckon. " The old head wagged grimly.

"She say dey's got knives, an' clubs, axes, and eben some guns," Uncle Abrams reported, his eyes wide in disbelief. "Dey's planning to attack jus' fo' dark, so's dey can hide in de woods. She say yo' better come help the Massa and Missus, 'cause dere's a lot of mad niggers ober dere."

Andrew opened a tall cupboard in the wall paneling and withdrew a revolver and rifle.

"I'll go with you, Father," James said, crossing the room.

"Someone needs to stay here," Andrew replied quickly, "to keep our people calm."

When James started to protest, Uncle Abrams said, "You go on, Suh. I's stay here with Massa James. Slaves won't gib yo' no trouble. Dey be all right. Dey listen to me," he finished quietly.

Andrew's eyes rested on the old man who had lived his whole life at Stafford Hall. "Thank you. I know you will help my son keep order."

"I'll go with you," John Avery spoke up.

Andrew handed him a rifle. "Uncle Abrams? Would you get someone to saddle up our horses?"

"I do it fo' you, Suh," he said briskly, leaving the room quickly.

Within minutes, Andrew and John Avery were saddled and ready to leave. James watched his father swing astride the horse. "Please be careful, you're riding into a dangerous situation."

His father nodded and spurred his horse into a gallop. John Avery nudged his horse into line behind him.

James stood in the drive, watching them disappear beyond the double row of magnolia trees.

Abigail stood in the hallway, looking out onto the front court. "Shouldn't you send someone for the authorities?"

"Father already has." He looked toward the row of slave cabins. Uprisings were a planter's greatest fear after the threat of a failed crop. He wondered what he should do. Everything seemed quiet. How much did the slaves know? How would they react once they heard of the nearby revolt?

He looked down on the short, stooped figure of Uncle Abrams, feeling his presence long before he spoke. The old man had ambled up to him, not waiting for James to speak first.

"Don't worry, Massa James," he said. "We has good peoples. Dey ain't gonna give yo' no trouble."

With a pensive nod, James replied, "Let's take a walk down there anyway. I don't want any surprises."

The old man nodded his grizzled head, falling into step beside him.

Willow Manor was not a large plantation by some standards, having no more than twenty to thirty slaves at any given time. It did, however, have the reputation of imposing strict disciplinary actions for the most trivial offense.

Andrew couldn't help thinking that the Witherspoons had brought this latest trouble on themselves. They had been warned many times by other planters to stop such harsh treatment of their slaves. He only hoped he and John could get there in time to help prevent what might be a bloody uprising.

He soon lost that hope. Up ahead, fire lit the evening sky.

"Dear God!" Andrew breathed. "They've set the place on fire."

Acrid smoke filled their nostrils when they turned into the lane of Willow Manor. A death-like pall hung over the lane that wound in a crooked path, snaking its way toward the house. It hung in the air ominously, while screams came from the direction of the manor. Andrew pressed his horse harder.

At the upper end of the winding drive, they reined in their horses abruptly. John Avery drew alongside.

Roaring flames engulfed the large house, flicking upwards like grotesque fiery fingers, painting the sky a brilliant orange-red glow. Bodies lay everywhere, brutally hacked, some with gunshot wounds. The house servants, who always felt themselves a rank above the field hands, lay sprawled near the porch and doorway entrances where it was obvious they had attempted to flee. The overseer, Devil Wilcott, lay sprawled in the lane. He had been struck down as he ran. His clothes were ripped from his back, and the length of his body flayed by whips. One person could not have caused so much injury, and Andrew felt sick, visualizing the number of slaves that had no doubt taken part in the frenzied assault. He turned away from the sight.

An agonizing scream filled the air, jerking his attention to the tall French doors standing wide with smoke belching forth. His gaze riveted on Benjamin Witherspoon as he pitched through the doors to the ground, a gash across his chest from the blow of an ax. Nearby lay the bodies of his wife, Alice, and their daughter, Margaret. Both died from stab wounds that bled red into the ground. Andrew dismounted, running to Benjamin's aid. The slave wielding the ax stood over his fallen foe, ready to bring the ax down again to finish the task. Andrew leaped forward, grabbing his arm. They struggled.

From somewhere among the cluster of shrubs a gunshot rang out. The bullet slammed into Andrew, spinning him to the ground. The enraged slave raised the ax over Andrew, whose blood poured from a wound in his stomach.

Among the commotion of the attack, Andrew heard a woman's shrill scream of "Noooo!" and saw Mandy racing to his defense. She struck the ax from the slave's hand, crying out, "No! Dat's Mister Hamilton! He good to his peoples!"

A blast from John Avery's gun interrupted her protest. The bullet slammed the frenzied black man to the ground, sprawling across the blood- stained ax.

Another shot was fired from the stand of shrubs striking Mandy, turning her awkwardly. John Avery aimed below the thin curl of smoke rising from the bushes. He fired. A moan erupted across the way. He ignored it, slipping from his horse and running to Andrew's side.

From where she slumped on her knees, Mandy pulled herself upright, blood seeping across the gray bodice of her dress. She helped John get Andrew to his feet. "Get on back home," she said with an effort.

"Cain't do no good here. It too late."

They helped Andrew into the saddle. He caught Mandy's hand. "Come with us," he said weakly. "You can make your home at Stafford Hall."

Mandy shook her head. "It too late fo' me, Suh."

Andrew felt her hand slipping. "I'm sorry," he murmured.

The woman nodded. "Hurry, Suh. Git on out o' here."

As they rode out, Andrew looked back. Mandy clutched her breast and slipped slowly to the ground. He started to turn back. John Avery reached out, grasping the bridle. "Can't help her now. Best we get on home, Andrew," he advised.

As they trouped up the lane of Stafford Hall, Uncle Abrams came running forward. "Lawd have mercy," he breathed, taking in the situation in a sweeping glance. "Dey done hurt Massa Hamilton."

"Better get Master James," John Avery told the old man quietly. "He's lost a lot of blood."

Uncle Abrams didn't wait for him to finish. He was already loping up the steps, shouting for James.

James came running with Abigail at his side, bounding through the door to Andrew's slumped figure astride the horse. His stride lengthened. He heard him moan as he put his arms about him. "Steady, Father," he said, frightened at the sight of the bloodstained shirt. "We have to get you inside. Uncle Abrams, get Aunt Sallie, and send someone for the doctor." He glanced over his shoulder to his wife, holding back at the top of the steps. "Abigail, waken Mammy Ticey. Hurry!"

He started to lift his father in his arms, but Andrew insisted he could walk. Between John Avery and James, they managed to get him up the front steps and into the house. He was near collapse by the time they got him undressed and in bed.

Mammy Ticey and Aunt Sallie washed and dressed the ragged stomach wound hoping to stop the bleeding until the doctor arrived. Andrew, propped against two white pillows, gasped for breath. James watched him, his heart heavy. His father suddenly looked very frail to him. He felt his lips moving in silent prayer.

Andrew spoke his name, and James went immediately to his side and sat down on the edge of the bed. "I'm here, Father," he said, taking his hand. "Don't talk. Save your strength."

But Andrew ignored his son's request saying with difficulty, "The Witherspoons are both dead. Margaret, too." Andrew drew a ragged breath. "So are most of their house servants, and some of the field slaves. The rest have run away." He closed his eyes. Then opened them, murmuring, "They set the house on fire. Everything's gone. It was a massacre, a horrible scene." He shook his head in agitation.

"Father, don't," James pleaded, accepting a damp cloth from Mammy Ticey and placing it on his father's brow. "You must lay quiet. You've lost a lot of blood."

"James," he whispered, clenching his son's hand firmly. "Send for Jane. I don't think I'm going to make it."

"Yes, you will, " James insisted.

Andrew shook his head. "Please -- must see my little girl --"

"All right, Father. I'll send for her, but you must be quiet. The doctor will be here soon."

Andrew nodded weakly.

James took John Avery aside. "Send someone to Calvert Hall Plantation for Jane."

"I'll send someone right away," the clerk said, hurrying from the room.

Later, when the doctor arrived, Mammy Ticey swept him into the bedroom, barely giving him time to remove his hat. Andrew, though lucid, had grown weaker. By the time the bullet was removed, he had sunk into unconsciousness. Within the hour, he rallied, but soon fell into the fitful sleep of the gravely ill.

With the early morn came the rumble of the carriage bringing Jane home to Stafford Hall and her father's bedside. A rumpled James met her in the drive at the carriage step.

She went into his embrace. "Father?" she inquired quietly.

"He is very ill," he replied.

Jane drew a long breath. As she swept up the steps, she admonished her brother, "You must take care of yourself. I don't want to have to worry about you, as well."

Mammy Ticey waited at the front door. When the pair entered, she gathered Jane into a warm embrace, murmuring, "Prepare yourself, honeychile."

Jane nodded solemnly as she removed her light cloak. Her eyes filled and a tiny stream trickled unchecked down the smoothness of her pale cheek.

Mammy Ticey lifted the corner of her apron wiping it away. "Be brave, honey. Don't go in dere alettin' yor' daddy see tears. Won't be good fo' him. You has got to be brave," she said firmly.

Drawing herself up straight, she nodded. With a thin smile over her shoulder to her brother, she lifted her skirts and mounted the stairs to the bedchambers.

James and Mammy Ticey followed her. Outside the bedroom door, Jane paused. James stepped forward, slipping his arm around her waist. "Do you want me to come with you?"

In answer, she reached for his hand. James opened the door, his eyes meeting Mammy's momentarily, and ushered his sister inside.

Mammy Ticey watched them go, her heart aching for the two she had tended since birth. She knew that sad times were upon them again. Her old head wagged slowly as unabashed tears streamed unchecked down her dark face.

Jane caught a deep breath at the sight of her father lying pale and helpless in the big four poster bed. Her eyes sought James. James and Jane were only barely conscious of the doctor standing across the room.

James touched his father's shoulder. "Father," he said softly. "Jane is here."

Andrew stirred slowly, as though trying to drag himself back from a lethargic state that enveloped him in a grip beyond his control.

Jane took his hand. "Father?" she whispered.

Andrew's eyes opened. Slowly, a smile stretched across his gray features. His eyes rested on his daughter. "Jane," he whispered.

She sank onto the bed, embracing him gently. James heard her weeping softly.

"Now, now, baby. I'm going to be all right," he said with a stab at firmness, that rang false to all of them.

Jane raised up, wiping her eyes stubbornly. "Of course, you are," she returned spritely. She submerged a cloth in water and wiped his forehead soothingly.

Andrew tried to make small talk, asking about her children and Adam.

"They're all fine," she told him. "They send their love." She saw that the conversation was tiring him and she said gently, "You must rest, Father. James and I will stay right here with you."

His eyes closed and he sank into a shallow sleep. The doctor came forward, drawing them outside the room. "Let him rest," he advised. "He needs to conserve his strength."

Jane turned to the comfort of her brother's arms. "Oh, James," she cried, "We're losing him."

"I know," he answered softly.

Hoping for contradiction to their fears, they turned in unison to the doctor. He shook his head. "Your father is in grave condition. The damage was extensive." He hesitated. "You must prepare yourself for the worst."

The confirmation suddenly crumpled Jane onto James' shoulder. He held her as she wept. Tears filled his eyes as he tried to console her.

Collecting themselves, they returned to their father's bedside. The doctor went with them, administering what comfort he could to his patient. Mammy Ticey stood not far away. And though her heart ached for the ill man on the bed, whom she had been with since he was born, it was his children that concerned her most. Resolutely, she stood there, watching them, waiting for the moment when she knew they would need her.

Toward mid-morning, Andrew roused, sought his children's eyes. He raised his hands, clasping one of their's in his own. Each felt the pressure of his hands squeezing theirs, communicating unspoken words. He smiled as only a father can when he looks with love at his children. His eyes closed and Jane, feeling the lifelessness in his hand, looked wildly at James, then collapsed forward onto her father's inert body, weeping uncontrollably.

Mammy Ticey came forward from out of the shadows and pulled Jane into her arms, her eyes holding the misty-eyed blue gaze of her distraught Jimmie-James.

A deathly silence had settled over Stafford Hall since the moment the master had ridden away to try to quell the uprising on a neighboring plantation. It had sunk deeper with the unexpected outcome, as all waited anxiously for word about the man they called master. To every slave on his plantation, Andrew represented a paternal figure who took care of his people with the same dedication that he took care of his family. They looked to him for guidance. He treated them kindly, and only when necessary, dealt out punishment that was neither cruel nor unjust. There was not one slave there who did not mourn his passing. Even Mingo, who was the only slave at Stafford Hall that Andrew ever ordered whipped, was seen weeping softly when word of his death reached the crowd waiting outside.

In the cemetery, at the end of the long cedar-lined drive, they buried Andrew next to his wife EmiLee. The slaves stood in a cluster behind the family and house servants, each of them probably wondering what would become of them now that the benevolent master was gone.

Slowly, not yet comprehending the full impact of their loss, James guided his sister and Abigail past the knot of slaves. He looked at Tilda, their eyes holding in a silent language. A Negro man approached to interrupt the communication. "Is dere anythin' we's can do fo' you, Massa? We is real sorry 'bout yo' daddy."

James was startled at being addressed as "Massa". It left him momentarily speechless. "No, thank you."

And, "I appreciate you asking."

Continuing on their way past the cluster of black mourners, genuine words of sympathy fell on their ears, called out in soft, sad voices. Mammy Ticey and John Avery joined them as they made their way back to the manor.

That night James, unable to sleep watched his sleeping wife with thoughts in his heart and mind he dared not give voice to in regards to their brief and flawed marriage. With a deep, almost weary sigh, he shook his head, aware the fault was not entirely Abigail's. They had married for the wrong reasons. He, by trying to provide Stafford Hall with the proper mistress. And she, he later found out, had quarreled with Carter Stively and sought to make him jealous by announcing her engagement to James. When Carter did not come forward to dissuade her, she resorted to sheer spitefulness. James did not doubt that Abigail often regretted her hasty actions. He, on the other hand, should never have married Abigail feeling as he did about Tilda. A touch of irony gritted in his soul, for James could not help but think that they deserved each other and this shallow, unfulfilled union they had created with misguided intentions. Another sigh dragged up from the lower regions of his belly. He got up and dressed.

Slipping out of the room and down the stairs, his footsteps carried him, unbidden, to Beulah's cabin. He did not hesitate, nor turn back as he had done when his mother died. He needed Tilda. He wanted to hear her voice; to feel her close to him and let his mind and heart run free. He needed the contact that soothed the dull ache within him whenever he was away from her. His knuckles rapped only once, quietly, heard only by the one inside for which it was intended.

Tilda opened the door, holding a lantern with the flickering wick turned low. She saw his anguished look. Neither spoke. Softly, she closed the door and stepped outside. Her hand sought his. He welcomed the gentle touch and the strength of her will as she led him away from the cabin.

She held the lantern before her, leading him into the darkness to the privacy of their secret place. The two shadows moved along the familiar path beneath the light of the autumn moon. And in the solitude of their secret place, Tilda comforted him in the only way she knew how.

11

*What do you suppose will satisfy the soul,
except to walk free and own no superior?*
Walt Whitman

*J*ane returned to Calvert Hall Plantation a week after Andrew's death. James grew increasingly restless with the passage of the days and the vexing thoughts that weighed on his mind. Alone in the study with Abigail, he tried to discuss the problem with her.

"I'm only saying," he repeated patiently, "that there has to be another way."

"The whole idea is ridiculous, James," she snapped. "We need the slaves."

He shook his head. "We need workers -- not slaves," he returned.

Abigail became agitated. "And where," she inquired surlily, "do you propose to get these workers?"

James did not answer, but a minute shrug lifted his shoulders.

His wife frowned. "The whole idea of giving our slaves their freedom is preposterous. What would the other planters think?"

James' head came up sharply. "That is not the issue, Abigail," he said caustically. "I don't care what they

143

think. I am only concerned with what is right for me and our plantation. And holding another man in bondage is not my idea of right. It's degrading."

"It is the way of the South," Abigail argued. "Who are you to try to change the way things are?"

"Someone has to make the first move."

Abigail's exasperation reached its pinnacle. "Really, James! Will you next expect me to work in the fields like a common nigger?"

"I wasn't suggesting that you do," he answered quietly. Then unable to resist needling her, he continued, "However, I don't think either of us should be above doing what we ask of others."

Abigail's mouth dropped open. "Oh!" she uttered with a roll of her eyes, and rushed out of the room, her full skirts flouncing, emulating her turbulent senses.

Silently, James watched her go, a small, appeased smile playing over his mouth.

Late that afternoon, James climbed the stairs to the sewing room where Tilda worked on a gown for Abigail. He looked into the room, saw only Tilda and Annie, the young slave who helped her.

The little girl looked shyly up, her dark face wreathed in a smile. "Afta'noon, Massa," she drawled.

"Good afternoon, Annie," James greeted. "What are you working on today?"

"I's helpin' Miss Tilda make a gown fo' Missus," she told him, proudly indicating the tiny stitches she'd made in the hem.

"That's fine work. Tilda is a good teacher."

"Oh, yas, Suh," Annie agreed.

"Since you've done so well, you may stop for today."

The girl looked up in surprise.

"I saw Gabe outside playing in a pile of leaves," James said. "Run along and join him."

Annie's grin grew wide. "Thank yo', Massa." She fled out the door.

Silence filled the room. James eased down on the corner of a table, as Tilda sat with needle suspended watching him curiously.

"Did yo' wants me fo' somethin', Massa James?" Tilda asked, slipping into dialect in the event anyone should overhear.

James nodded, his gaze lingering on her pensively.

"Yo' likes Missus' dress?" she asked nonchalantly, aware that James wanted to speak of matters having nothing to do with a new frock.

"It's very nice," he replied in an offhand manner. Leaning forward, he spoke in a low voice, "The cave. Can you come now?"

She nodded.

James rose, "Your needle work has always been of the highest quality, Tilda. My mother was quick to notice your talent." With an acute nod, he strode out of the room with a false air of indifference.

In the hallway, he paused. Abigail had locked herself in their bedroom since their conversation earlier that morning. James had made no attempt to placate her. He was well aware that Abigail and he would never agree on the subject of slavery. Though his eyes lingered on the closed door momentarily, he turned abruptly and went down the stairs.

Old Uncle Abrams met him heading toward the stable. "Need a horse, Massa James? Or a carriage?"

"A horse," James replied.

The old man scurried ahead into the barn to saddle the black stallion that young Massa James preferred. He led it out and waited for James to mount.

James swung astride. "Thank you, Uncle Abrams."

The old man nodded, dragging the battered hat off his head, and rubbing it between gnarled hands as he was wont to do when he wanted to speak but couldn't find the right words. He stood silently, worrying the hat between his knuckles, watching as James rode off. Something was festering in the boy's brain like a boil, and was close to popping.

Even though he took the long way around, as he always did, James still arrived before Tilda. He tethered the horse and slipped behind the wall of honeysuckle, now dried and ragged, lying across the opening like a well-worn lace curtain that had grown yellowish-brown with age. He sank into a corner, leaning his head back against the stone wall. Confused thoughts ran through his mind, and he wished he could find the solution to the one that plagued him the most. He waited in the semidarkness, listening for Tilda's footsteps.

Soon he heard the light footfalls that announced her approach. He stood as the brown curtain parted. Tilda stepped inside. James held out his arms and she went to him. Taking comfort from her presence, he held her tightly, without speaking.

She looked up into his face, her eyes questioning.

James' hand slid down her arm to clasp her hand as he drew her down to the earthen floor. He sat on the ground, still holding her hand. Tilda knelt before him.

"What is it, James?" she asked, her brow drawn together. She covered his hand that had such an intense grip on hers. "What is bothering you?"

He shook his head in agitation. "Ever since my father died," he said, speaking in disjointed fragments, "and I became heir, I . . . I am tormented . . . "

"Tormented about what?"

"Everything," he burst out.

"You mean slavery," she said quietly.

He nodded quickly. "For God's sake, Tilda, think of the work I've done -- we've done -- against slavery. How can I continue this way? It goes against everything I feel, what I believe. How can I own slaves feeling as I do? I resent the way you are forced to live. The way *we* are forced to live."

Tilda tried to think of something to say that would soothe his anguish and comfort him. Before she could fashion the words, James continued.

"I tried to talk to Abigail this morning," he said.

"What," Tilda asked softly, "does she say about it?"

James shrugged. "She is angry. She doesn't want things to change."

Tilda made no attempt to comment. James grasped her shoulders, uttering fervently, "Things have to change.

They can't go on this way."

He raised one hand to caress her dark hair, and his tone became softer. "Do you know how it makes me feel, Tilda, when Uncle Abrams looks up at me and calls me Massa? It makes me feel like a hypocrite. We have worked side by side in the antislavery movement, and I am not -- and do not -- feel myself superior to him." He waved his hand in agitation again. "I've trusted him with my life for God's sake!"

"I'm sure he doesn't feel that you are condescending to him. Uncle Abrams loves you," Tilda assured him.

"All the more reason I should do what I feel is right -- and what he deserves," James said acutely.

"But how can you change things?" she asked, perplexed. It all seemed insurmountable to her.

He glanced down at Tilda, his eyes holding hers. "I can't right all the wrongs of my ancestors that have gone on for generations. I only know that I cannot allow this to continue while I am in charge."

Silently, she leaned back on her heels, waiting for him to explain, sensing he had already made a decision. All he needed now was to bring it out into the open, to examine it in a broader light. However, Tilda had no inkling of the magnitude of his decision.

She was shocked at his firm announcement. "I'm going to free all of my slaves."

Tilda's head jerked up. "What?"

"I'm going to free all of my slaves," he repeated.

"All of them?"

He snapped his head decisively. "Every man, woman and child."

"But James, how will you manage the plantation?"

"Sharecropping," he answered simply. "I know of no other way."

"I knew you had made a decision," she stammered, "but this . . . this . . . "

"It's a good idea, Tilda," he assured her.

Despite his confidence, she felt edgy. "If . . . if Abigail disagrees," she began slowly, "how can you do it?"

"I am the owner of Stafford Hall," James said firmly. "Decisions are ultimately mine to make when it concerns the plantation. Abigail must reconcile herself to that fact."

Tilda sat down on the dirt floor beside him. She looked down at her hands in her lap. Her hair fell in a soft cloud, concealing her features.

James tilted her face up. "What is it, Tilda?" he asked, sensing her apprehension. "I do this for you as much as myself. Do you remember," he asked softly, "when you were a little girl and I promised that you would one day be free?"

Tilda nodded, but there was no light in her eyes to show her joy.

"I must do this, Tilda," James said firmly, "not just for old Aunt Sallie and Uncle Abrams and all the others. It's not even for myself." He paused, bending down to her in his earnestness. "It's mostly for you. To fulfill a promise I made you many years ago."

Tilda's mouth trembled, and she looked ready to cry.

"What is it?" James asked. "I thought you would be happy."

"I don't want to be free from you," she answered softly. "You are all I have James. If I am free, I will no longer belong to you."

"That's true," James agreed. "You will not belong to anyone. You will be your own person, to come and go as you please."

The frown did not go away.

"I will offer everyone jobs at a fair wage. They may stay and share in the harvest of the crops or they may go. It will be their choice as it will be yours, Tilda."

"Do you mean I can stay here and work for you and Miss Abigail? It will be just like it is now?"

"You will continue to make your beautiful gowns, just as you always have, only this way, you will be paid a wage. No one can make demands on you. They will ask you to work for them, and you may hire others to work for you."

Her brow was creased as she pondered his words.

"Trust me, Tilda," he said, "this will be best for you."

She wasn't too sure.

Later in the week, in the soft glow of the lamplight, James sat up late into the night signing the freedom papers which John Avery had drawn up at his directions. He had just signed the last one when a light knock sounded at the door.

"You in dere, Jimmie-James?" Mammy Ticey called out.

"Yes, Mammy. Come in," James answered.

She opened the door, and poked her head inside. "You all right?"

He nodded, beckoning for her to enter. "It's late. You should be in bed."

"I never goes to bed 'til you is settled down," she replied matter-of-factly.

James smiled. "Well, I'm glad you stopped in. There's something I want to give you."

Mammy Ticey came toward him, her broad brow puzzled. "What you got, honeychile?" she asked curiously.

James rifled through the papers on his desk until he found the one with her name. He picked it up and handed it across the desk to her.

"What dis?" she asked.

"Your freedom papers," he replied quietly.

Her black eyes met his and she dropped the paper back to the desk as though it was hot. "Don't need 'em," she said evenly.

"Mammy, this means you are free. You can . . . "

"I knows what dey is, chile," she interrupted, "but I don't needs no freedom papers. Always done what I wanted anyways," she stated firmly.

James came around the desk to stand before the old woman. "Mammy," he said softly, "you have always been like family. Jane and I would have been lost without you when Mother died, and even more recently when

Father died. You were always there for us. Loved us in spite of our faults. Please," he said, "let me do this for you."

"Why Jimmie-James?" she asked. "Why you is doin' this?"

"Tomorrow I'm going to give all the slaves their freedom. The papers are signed. " He indicated the stack of documents on the desk. "I wanted to give you yours personally. You have always known how I felt about slavery. I have to find a new way to manage the plantation. For those who want to stay, I will offer sharecropping."

Mammy Ticey cried openly. Big tears rolled down her broad face. "I is so proud o' you, Jimmie-James."

"Father should have done it years ago."

Mammy shook her head. "He always wanted to, honeychile. He jus' didn't know how."

"I'm not sure I do either," James admitted.

"Yo'll be jus' fine," she said, lifing her apron to wipe at the corners of her eyes.

James leaned over to retrieve the papers and handed them to her again.

"Tol' ya once, honeychile, I don't need 'em. Don't need no papers to tell me where I's goin' and what I's doin'," she said firmly. "I's staying right here s'long as you needs me."

"No one will ever take your place, Mammy Ticey." He hugged her, feeling the trail of tears on her face wet his cheek. "I'm going to put your papers in the safe, just in case something happens to me, and you need them. Don't forget where they are."

"Won't need 'em," she said stubbornly. "Ain't goin' nowheres. I's stayin' right here 'til I dies."

James smiled. Old Mammy Ticey reached up to touch his cheek with a gentle hand before shaking her finger at him. "It's late, honeychile. Yo' better be gettin' to bed." She turned and waddled across the room.

"Good night, Mammy," he said, watching her.

"Good night, Jimmie-James," floated to him over broad shoulders that shook with the emotion that echoed in her voice.

He summoned the slaves to the front yard early the next morning. They looked up at the wide porch where John Avery sat at a desk hauled out of his office.

James stood in the background. His eyes roved over the group of dark faces, old Aunt Sallie, Uncle Abrams, Ivy, Mingo, Beulah, the field hands and their families. He searched the crowd, but did not see Tilda. He wondered where she could be. Surely she would not miss such an event. The slaves had a mixture of expressions covering their faces. He knew they wondered why he had called them all together. Most were aware of his feelings about slavery, and he knew that since his father's death there had been rumors of the potential sale of the plantation. They looked up with a trace of fear of what was to come, what their future might hold. There were too many Orem Lemlys and Devil Wilcotts out there for them to feel safe.

James sensed their anxieties and stepped forward to calm them. He spoke quietly, succinctly, so that the person in the very back row could not misunderstand anything he said. He decided to keep it short with little explanation. "Most of you know how I feel about slavery. As heir to Stafford Hall, I have made the decision to give all of you your freedom."

A rumble of surprise ran through the group. James heard "hallelujahs" uttered softly. He continued, "I have had Mr. Avery draw up your freedom papers. As of last night, they have all been signed."

Another excited murmur rumbled over the crowd, amid the initial burst of joyous cries and tears of jubilation. James held up his hand. "I know this news is exciting for you, and I promise you a celebration feast, but first, listen to me. I need your help in running the plantation. John Avery will call out each of your names. When you come up to get your freedom papers, you have a choice. You may either stay or you may leave. No one will stop you. If you choose to stay, you will do so as sharecroppers. I will pay you a fair wage and a percentage of the crops." He paused, waiting for his words to register and to see how many might want to stay on as hired hands. His eyes roved over the crowd, calculating.

"After Mr. Avery has called out all your names, there will be a celebration in the quarters area," he added before going back inside the house.

He watched from the front hall window as the slaves came up to receive their papers. Those who desired to stay lingered while John wrote their names in his account books. James smiled as he observed that most of them were staying on. When old Aunt Sallie accepted her papers, he saw her lips move, murmuring unmistakably, "Lawd be praised! I is free!"

Later, the celebration began in earnest as they slaughtered hogs and placed them on a spit over a glowing fire. The women sang and shouted as they prepared food for the feast. Elsewhere the ex-slaves danced to the sounds of banjos and drums. James looked out an upstairs window onto the festivities below. He saw a woman dancing with a glass of water on her head. Others chanted, encouraging her to dance faster. Several grabbed up containers and joined in. James smiled, knowing he had done the right thing. However, Abigail had locked herself in a room down the hall from their bedroom, having declared he was insane. He dismissed her from his mind refusing to allow her to spoil what he had accomplished.

He did not see Tilda at the gathering. He had held her papers aside, wanting to give them to her himself. He sensed she was troubled and knew he would find her at the hidden cave. Going to the safe, he removed her papers, rolled them into a scroll and tucked them inside his vest. He caught up his cloak, flicking it over his shoulders as he went down the stairs and outside. The noise of the celebration rang out, filling the night. James looked for Uncle Abrams, then remembered that the old man did not have to be at his beck and call. It was just one of many changes to which they must adjust. He smiled and went to saddle his own horse.

James didn't ride out the lane to go the long way around to the cave. He took the shortcut, riding up the perimeter of the field closest to his destination. Striding confidently toward the dried curtain, he pushed it aside, paused in the entryway as his eyes met Tilda's.

"Everything go all right?" she asked quietly.

He nodded, seating himself next to her. "You weren't there."

She made no answer.

"Why weren't you there, Tilda?" he asked.

Still, she made no reply. She held a thin twig that she moved absently in the dirt, making patterns of no consequence.

James watched her scrawling motions, then leaned over, covering her hand with his. "Why weren't you there, Tilda?" he repeated.

"I don't want things to change," she said in a low voice, her dark eyes lingering on his face.

"You don't have to be afraid, Tilda," he said gently. "This is a good change. It is what I have wanted for you since the day I found you."

"But, if I am free," her lips trembled as she fought back tears, "I will have lost you."

"Lost me?" James was puzzled.

Tilda shook her head vigorously. "Being a slave is the only possible way I can truly belong to you," she admitted. "It is all I have. If I am free, then you are also free of me."

She started to cry, and James drew her into his arms.

"Hush, Tilda," he whispered. He cradled her for a moment, then tilted her head up to him. "Listen to me, Tilda," he said earnestly. "Nothing is going to change between you and me. It doesn't matter if you are free or not. I'll still love you, will always love you. And this is going to be so much better for you. Won't you trust me when I tell you that?" He reached inside his vest for the rolled up papers. He handed it to her, but she turned away.

"Take them," he urged.

153

"Don't need them. I'm staying right here." Her words were defiant.

James smiled. "Good. Because that's what I want you to do."

A smile picked at the corners of her mouth. "I belong here. It's where my heart is."

James kissed her. "Do you know you are the second person who's refused their papers? I had to put Mammy Ticey's in the safe for her."

A smile crossed Tilda's face, and James entreated, "So for me, so I won't have to worry, would you take the papers anyway? Just in case something happens to me."

She accepted them, pressing the document to her breast.

That evening, after the long day of celebrations, old Aunt Sallie sat down in her old wooden rocking chair beside the dying embers of a low fire and quietly passed into eternity. They found her the next morning clutching, in both hands, her freedom papers. Just as she had determined to do -- Aunt Sallie met the Lord a free woman.

12

More skillful in self-knowledge, evermore pure,
as tempted more; more able to endure,
as more exposed to suffering and distress.
                                        Wordsworth

A festive atmosphere surrounded Stafford Hall as
they prepared a party celebrating the end of 1860 and the
arrival of the new one.

Since their release from bondage Beulah, Mammy
Ticey, and Tilda worked in the house assisted by others.
While it was Beulah who supervised the servants and saw
that all the tasks were performed, it was Mammy who
took charge from the sidelines, planning and giving
orders. They tolerated her gruffness, smiled and did as
she asked, watching her bustle importantly from room to
room, and in and out of the winter kitchen on the lower
level of the great house. Even though she was aged,
everyone realized that her long years with the Hamilton
family made her invaluable to the smooth operation of the
plantation.

Though Abigail was angry having to pay wages to
former slaves, she was quite happy to leave the duties
of managing the house and kitchen to others. She detested
having to make so many decisions. It left little time for

party planning. The staff knew that Abigail often complained to James about them and their work. She claimed that her personal maid, Delilah, became insolent and lazy since freed. The way Abigail nagged and ordered her about, it was a wonder the poor woman didn't up and leave.

On the afternoon of the party Delilah came into the kitchen quarters in search of Tilda. She found her standing at a long table helping her mother lay out hot pastries to cool.

"Yo' better come, Tilda," Delilah said. "Miss Abigail fit to be tied 'bout her gown."

"What's wrong with it?" Tilda asked wearily. "We did the last fitting yesterday."

"She say don't fit her right in the bosom."

Tilda rolled her eyes, heaving an exasperated sigh. "I'll be there in a minute."

"Don't fit," Mammy snipped, "cause she tries to show too much o' what she's got."

As Tilda climbed the stairs to Abigail's bedroom, she could hear her mistress' high-pitched voice floating down the hall.

"I ought to fire Tilda! She simply hasn't made this gown right!"

"Tilda is the best seamstress to be found, and you know it," James said bluntly.

His wife sniffed. "Of course, you'd take her side. You don't even care how I'll look at the party."

"I'm sure you'll look just fine," James said tiresomely.

Abigail sniffed again, turning her back on him. Tilda knocked, and Abigail jerked the door open. "It's about time you got here. I simply can't wear this dress. You've made a mess of the whole thing."

James nodded politely at Tilda as he left the room. He knew Tilda would eventually soothe his wife's feelings, and that she would endure Abigail's sharp tongue of criticism because she was adamant about staying on at Stafford Hall. He could hear Tilda's soft voice, convincing his wife that she would adjust the dress so that it fit her perfectly. With a rueful shake of his head, he turned slowly and went down the hall.

As snow flurries caught the wind, the guests began arriving. Inside the great house glowing fires flickered in the fireplaces beckoning the new arrivals to the warm hearths. Tables were laden with food and drink. Crystal glasses winked in the soft glow of decorative candles. Gas-lit chandeliers cast dancing shadows over a room filled with chatter and holiday greetings. Waiting to take heavy winter wraps, Mammy Ticey stood behind James and Abigail as they greeted their guests at the wide front door. Beulah and Tilda moved silently around the room serving refreshments and filling empty glasses.

The talk ranged from prices of tobacco and other crops to politics and the differences growing more acute between the North and South. A small knot of planters spoke defiantly about the prospects of a war. Noting the small group of animated speakers which included James, Carter Stively stopped dancing with Abigail to join the conversation.

"We could whip those Yankees in a week," Virg Price said fiercely.

"Right," chimed in another. "We'll send those damn Yankees back where they came from."

"Personally," Carter said haughtily, "I don't care what they do. I have no intention of running off to battle over a bunch of nigras." He yawned delicately to emphasize his boredom of the matter.

"There is more to be considered here than slavery," James said quietly. "The South's honor is at stake."

"Does that mean you would fight for the Southern Cause?" Virg probed. "You own no slaves." Virgil Price held no compunctions about being forthright.

"Why would you expect otherwise?" James returned.

"Well," the man said with a shrug, "it's pretty common knowledge how you feel about slavery." He eyed James critically. "There's not a planter here who has not been touched by your rash act. Whether you realize it or not, it has affected us all -- in an adverse way, I might add."

James studied the man. "You are all entitled to your opinions, and you have the option to do as you please with your own property. I have that same right. If my choice has affected you negatively, I'm sorry, but I do not," he said firmly, "apologize for freeing my slaves."

"Are you saying you would go to war defending the South?"

"I am a southern gentleman. It is my duty to defend my homeland." His glance swept the group. "There is a cause that goes deeper than slavery and it must be defended."

"Southern gentleman or not," snapped Carter, "I have no intention of risking life and limb for any cause. Besides, I have enough money to buy my way out of anything -- and that includes being an officer for the Confederacy."

"You, sir, don't deserve to be called a southerner," Virg Price stated.

Carter Stively shrugged, smoothing his dark brown hair. "Say what you like." He waved a hand denouncing them all. "Play your game of toy soldiers. I will be no part of it." He turned his attention to Abigail at his side. She was visibly huffed at being ignored. "Miss Abigail, shall we dance? These gentlemen sound like children squabbling over marbles."

She smiled, linking her arm through his, as they moved toward the dance floor.

James watched them solemnly.

From the sidelines of the room, Tilda's eyes followed him, her heart aching, cognizant of James' growing discomfort at his wife's blatant show of interest in Carter Stively.

James sensed Tilda at his elbow, and turned. She had a tray of sweetmeats that, wordlessly, she offered up to him. He shook his head in refusal, murmuring a polite, "No, thank you."

Despite the crowded room, his eyes held hers for an infinitismal second. Tilda turned quickly and moved away.

Simon, Stafford's fiddler, played tirelessly as the dancers moved about the great room. He swayed, bending and twisting to the music filling the room. He played as a hired musician, rather than as a slave, and the music came from his soul. His bow danced over the fiddle strings as lively as the dancers flitting around the room. Simon smiled, his teeth gleaming bright against the darkness of his skin.

Toward evening's end, James went in search of Abigail so they could offer their guests a toast to a prosperous, successful new year. Not seeing her in the vast room of the great hall, he slipped out. He had immediately dismissed the thought of her being upstairs in the bedchambers, for she could not have ascended the stairs without everyone being aware of it. Had she claimed one of her frequent headaches that excused her from her duties as hostess? He shook his head, dismissing that thought as well. She enjoyed parties too much -- and Carter Stively's company -- to make claims of debilitating headaches.

James heard voices coming from the library and strode down the hall to peer in. Virg Price waved his arms about, giving an animated account of what he would do when he encountered "those damn yanks." His neighbors, used to his declarations, waited for an opening to change the subject. James wagged his head complaisantly, pulled the door to and continued on his search.

The front parlor at the far end of the hall was cloaked in semidarkness. As he started past the door James heard a low murmur of laughter. A lamp burned low on a mahogany table beneath one of the room's long windows. It cast flickering shadows on the rippled panes of glass. It also threw into silhouette two figures. Abigail and Carter Stively.

Carter leaned over Abigail, his hand cupping an exposed breast that gleamed snowy white in the half-light. His mouth stifled the low laughter bubbling from her parted lips.

James turned away. Affronted and angry, he strode back to the great hall. He saw Tilda across the room balancing a tray of sweetmeats.

She turned, her eyes meeting his steel-like gaze. The tray wobbled. What had caused those deep blue eyes to turn so glacial? Like ponds frozen over with ice. Tilda watched as he crossed the room, and tried valiantly to converse with a guest. She saw Abigail and Carter emerge from the front parlor to the hall. Abigail laughed and her hands fiddled with the tousled curls at the nape of her neck. Carter Stively's hand slid from her waist to his side, but not before Tilda saw the small, intimate gesture. She suddenly knew what caused the coldness in James' eyes. She turned away as James pretended to suddenly see his wife across the crowded room.

"Come, Abigail," she heard him say as he moved in her direction, "a new year is upon us. We must drink a toast to our guests."

Tilda felt a mixture of emotions roll in a confusing wave over her. She had no right to feel indignant over Abigail's infidelity when James had committed the same disloyalty. She felt a sickness well up from the pit of her stomach.

It seemed the evening dragged on forever. Tilda was thankful when it ended. Beulah had long since retired to their cabin, but Tilda had insisted on staying behind to help clean up. Mammy Ticey had gone to bed as well. When finally everything had been put away, and the last lamp was snuffed, Tilda flung a woolen cape over her shoulders and left the house.

On the terrace, she paused to look up at a sickle-boat moon high in the heavens. A light snow lay like a pristine coverlet over the lawn. In the pale moonlight the trees shimmered, adorned in their silvery, frozen ornaments. An occasional snowflake fell, and she felt its vagrant touch on her cheek like the whisper of an angel's breath.

Raising her face up toward the filtering snowflakes, Tilda saw a shadow leaning against the balustrade of the far chimney cluster. It was silhouetted against the deep red brick by the meager beam of the quarter moon.

Recognizing James in the gloaming's dappled, ethereal grayness, Tilda's heart fluttered as it always did when she saw him unexpectedly. She wondered at his isolated refuge that mingled with gray evening shadows to shroud his fixed demeanor. Her heart twisted at the sight of him standing there, alone, in the cold. She turned and slipped quietly back into the house.

Moving through the house with whisper soft movements, Tilda climbed the stairs to the chimney clusters at the top of the house. The door creaked softly as she opened it. James turned at the unexpected sound. Somberness cloaked his features as conspicuously as the cape cloaked his body. His eyes met hers across the short expanse, and held her so tautly, her muscles felt strained. Silhouetted in the doorway, Tilda stood motionless, daring not to approach him. While effectively concealed by his long cloak, she sensed the unrest churning in his body. It seemed an eternity that she stood there.

Finally, without a word, James held his hand out to her. Closing the gap between them, Tilda welcomed his arms drawing her close to him. He held her without speaking, but she could feel his heart beating rapidly within his chest.

She knew what tormented him, what had driven him to the solitude of the chimney clusters, but still she asked, "What is it, James?"

And he felt that she knew, for he replied, "What right have I to feel so angry -- even betrayed? I am no more righteous than she."

"You are the master," she answered simply.

A fleeting smile crossed his lips, and shaking his head, James told her quietly, "That is not a justification, Tilda. And it does not give me the right to condemn Abigail for the very sin that I have committed." He shook his head fiercely. "I have no right to feel so damn indignant."

"But you are the master," she repeated. "It is the way of all masters, and she is the mistress." Her statement implied that a plantation's mistress must be content with her lot and suffer in silence as well as in deed.

James shook his head again. "No, Tilda. Being the mistress of a plantation does not make one above certain behavior. That is just not how things are. And being the master does not make it all right, either," he said adamantly. Looking down at her in the half-light, he said wearily, "Besides, I have told you before, Tilda, I am not your master. If we lived in another time perhaps we would not have this dilemma."

They grew silent.

Tilda sighed. "You hurt because of me," she said.

"No, Tilda. The blame is mine and only mine."

Tilda wondered. The fact that she had no rights as a former slave and now servant made no difference. Her relationship with James had never been one of master and slave. She had always had a choice and now, regardless of what he said, she must share the blame for his pain.

"Did you know about Abigail and Carter?" he asked her quietly.

Having heard the rumors that passed from one servant to another from inside the great house to the quarters beyond, she hesitated before answering. Stories had been rampant from the beginning of his marriage. But until tonight, she had never known for sure whether the truth had been embroidered upon by angry servants and vicious tongues anxious to retaliate against a mistress for whom they had no liking, or if there really was truth to the whispers. But she had no heart to tell James any of this. Instead, she said, "Not until tonight."

James released her and with his back to the balustrade, he stared out into the night.

She watched him solemnly. "I'm sorry, James."

"I never suspected," he murmured.

Tilda's heart trembled. Despite what James said, she still felt he was her superior, yet she knew that she could have turned away from him at any time. He was not like many other planters she had heard about. The fact that she had never wanted to resist him weighed on her heart like a stone. James' suffering was her suffering. She shivered.

James pulled her woolen cloak more tightly around her. "Come, we must go in. The die is cast. There is no changing anything."

Silently, he led her to the door. His anger had subsided. Of a necessity, he had come to terms with it. Besides, it was not an anger that focused entirely on Abigail. It was for his own indiscretions as well. He could blame no one but himself for straying from the marriage bed. Yet even with that admission, he knew that Tilda was firmly instilled in his life. Probably just as Carter was in Abigail's, he thought wryly. Simply having the knowledge was not going to bring about any great changes in their lives. He was cognizant of that irony with a certainty that brewed in the innermost corners of his soul. How could he apologize for Tilda? She was more entangled in his life, in his very soul, than anyone -- even Abigail. Especially Abigail, James thought with a wry, solemn shake of his head. Pensively, James followed Tilda down the stairs. From behind her, she heard his heavy sigh.

13

The line of my horizon's growing thin.
                                    T. Roethke

Spring seemed to be in a hurry in the year of 1861, and while it was only early April, winter's wrath had grown mild, allowing the sun to sift through blue-white clouds and a breeze to whisper among the still leafless trees. The winter kitchen inside the great house had been closed down and the summer kitchen in the outside dependency was once again being made ready.

Beulah and Ivy swept and scoured away the grime and dust that gathers from disuse, and brushed away the cobwebs of a family of spiders that had taken up winter refuge. The large fireplace had been scrubbed clean and already a brisk fire was glowing, roasting chickens grown plump in their fattening cages. The smell of ginger and molasses filled the air, emanating from the large mixing bowl and golden brown cookies baking on the hearth.

Ivy had a small son fathered by Mingo. Even though Mingo had chosen to leave Stafford Hall Plantation when James freed his slaves, Ivy had decided to stay on as hired help, serving in her old capacity in the laundry, as well as assisting Beulah in household chores. Today, as they busied themselves in the cleaning of the summer kitchen, Ivy looked up from where she was scrubbing potatoes.

"I's got to go nuss Tommie. It his feedin' time," she told Beulah. "Gwanna to be back shortly."

Nodding, Beulah waved her away, bending back to the task at hand. She stood at a long marble table making pie crust with a heavy rolling pin. She hummed as she worked. Nobody made a pie crust flakier than Beulah and when Master Andrew and Missus EmiLee were alive, they always insisted Beulah take charge of the pie baking. Beulah smiled to herself. Life had been good at Stafford Hall. She caught a wiff of the ginger cookies and bent to lift them from the grate, setting them aside to cool. While her pies might be the envy of any cook, Beulah's ginger cookies were her pride. They were every child's favorite and Master Andrew had allowed her to sell them and keep the profits, a practice Master James continued. She had always made extra money at holiday seasons.

Her bandanna-wrapped head moved complacently up and down. Yes, life had been good ever since young Master James had rescued them from the auction block and the very real threat of being separated. Beulah's heart gave a little flutter. Much as she liked Master James and truly appreciated everything he had done for Tilda, his relationship with her daughter scared her. Tilda was the most precious thing in the world to her, and she feared for her welfare. Beulah shook her head. The child seemed to be ruled by the blood of her white father. But she knew that there was no place for Tilda at Stafford Hall, except as a servant. How well Beulah knew that. Her own dreams had ended in disaster. The difference was, she had never expected more, but Tilda, looking white, lived in a world of her own making. Should anything happen to the young master, Beulah knew Miss Abigail would waste no time in firing Tilda, driving her out into a world where she had no place, a world that would be cruel and uncaring. Beulah shivered, and a deep sigh drew her shoulders up as the worrisome thought plagued her.

Interrupting those anxious thoughts, a cat came

streaking through the partially open door. Behind it, a dog hell-bent in pursuit crashed inside, knocking over everything in its path. They streaked past Beulah before she could get the broom to chase them out, toppling a can of lard and spilling its contents into the hearth. Some ran in a greasy blob across the floor. All of it quickly caught fire, sending flames up the wall to the rafters. The dried herbs hanging overhead added fuel to the hungry flames. Racing from one side of the room to another with lightning speed, the cat finally escaped outside just ahead of the frenzied, yelping dog. But not before it had knocked over every small stand in the kitchen and toppled a long table, used for cooling pastries, across the doorway.

Beulah grabbed the broom to beat at the flames. The hot grease ran in a path toward the door and the fire eagerly followed it, creating a wall of flames between Beulah and the door. Panic-stricken, she turned toward the window, but as she did so the hem of her skirt swept across the flames licking their way across the floor. The room filled with smoke and Beulah coughed, frantically trying to beat the flames from her dress.

Ivy, strolling nonchalantly back toward the kitchen quarters, saw the smoke curling out of the windows and door. She screamed, running to the well to fill a bucket.

Uncle Abrams heard the scream and joined in, hollering, "Fire! Fire! Good Lawd! Help! Help!"

Tilda came out from the back of the house with Mammy Ticey. She ran toward Ivy standing with an empty bucket in the kitchen yard.

"Where is Mama?" she yelled.

"She in dere!" Her dark eyes wide in terror, Ivy pointed a shaking finger.

"Mama! Mama!" Tilda shrieked, running up to the doorway.

"Stay back, Tilda!" Beulah screamed. Then a more agonized cry reached them. "Oh, Lawd! My clothes is burnin'!"

Tilda heard her mother scream again as she tried to

enter the doorway. She choked and gasped as the smoke pushed her back. Several men rushed to throw buckets of water onto the building. She ran to the window and started to climb through even though the framing was hot to her touch.

"Mama!" she called, trying to peer through the thick smoke. In the haze she saw her mother pitch to the floor. Tilda screamed, "Mama!"

She felt strong hands pulling at her, plucking her from the windowsill. She twisted, fighting against them. "Let me go! Mama is in there!"

"Stop it, Tilda!" James demanded, shaking her. "I'll go in after her! Stay back out of the way," he yelled, turning to the smoke-filled door.

"The door is blocked!" Tilda said frantically.

He turned back to the window, ignoring the blistering wood as he swung his leg over the sill.

Everyone stared as he disappeared into the murky interior. James fell to his knees, and crawled toward Beulah's prostrate figure. The bottom part of her dress had burned. All over the bodice and sleeves were large, blackened gaps where she had managed to smother the flames. He heard her moan as he lifted her in his arms and carried her to the window. His lungs were on fire and he choked from the acrid smoke. Stinging tears filled his eyes. James handed Beulah over the sill to waiting hands.

Overhead, a charred beam broke loose from the ceiling and pitched in a flaming arc to the floor, striking James as it fell. He clutched at the window sill, cringing in pain. Those standing outside saw the beam crashing downward in a fiery descent. Screams of fear erupted amid the chaos of getting Beulah safely away from the burning building. Quickly, many hands pulled James through the window.

He leaned heavily against Uncle Abrams. The old man peered up at Master James. "Caught yo' on de leg?" he asked.

"My ankle. Help me over to that bench." The odor of his singed hair filled his nostrils. Pain seared his burned hands. It was all of no consequence as he watched the scene before him.

They laid Beulah on the ground. Tilda fell to the ground beside her.

Beulah's parched and swollen lips moved. "Tilda --" she whispered, her eyes clinging to her daughter.

Tilda bent to her. "Don't talk, Mama," she begged, trying to stifle her sobbing. "We'll get you to the cabin, and I'll put some of Aunt Sallie's salve on you. That will help until the doctor gets here."

Feebly, Beulah shook her head. "Ain't gonna do no good, chile."

"Mama -- "

"Tilda, baby, I is dyin' -- "

"No, Mama." Tilda shook her head vigorously.

"Ssh, ssh, baby," Beulah soothed. "It all right, honey. I is ready, but you -- you has got to be careful."

"Mama, please," Tilda pleaded. "Don't --" She rubbed her eyes. The tears would not stop.

A low moan escaped Beulah as she lifted her hand to stroke Tilda's hair. "I is sorry for everything, Tilda. Yor daddy loved you. He would have seen to yor care if'n he hadn't died. I is jus' so sorry you has had to live like this -- " She drew a deep, ragged breath.

"No, Mama," Tilda sobbed, "I have been just fine. Please don't think that I have ever regretted you being my mama."

"I knows that, baby," Beulah whispered weakly. Her hand fell from her daughter's soft hair. Her last words were lost in a gasp for breath.

Tilda stiffened, shuddering. "Mama!" she cried, but knew her call was not heard. Tilda fell forward, gathering Beulah's body in her arms. "Mamaaaa!" The agonized word hung in the air, sending a rippling chill over those that stood there in tearful helplessness.

James left the bench, as two women lifted Tilda from her mother's body. Sobbing, she crumpled against him. He held her quietly, his own eyes filled.

Abigail stood at the head of the walk. She looked on the scene passively, displaying no emotion. Then abruptly, she turned and walked back up the path to the front of the house. James shifted his gaze to Mammy Ticey.

"You is hurt, Jimmie-James," the woman said, seeing his blistered hands. "An' likely yo' ankle be busted."

"I'm all right, Mammy. Will you take care of Tilda?"

Mammy Ticey nodded, reaching to draw Tilda into her embrace. "Come, chile," she murmured. "Come with Mammy."

They buried Beulah next to old Aunt Sallie in a corner of the cemetery reserved for slaves and indentured servants.

James had the cloying feeling it was just the portentous beginning of a way of life that was rapidly slipping through the fickle fingers of fate.

And as though some prescience had been whispered to him by an elusive voice, two days later, with irreconcilable differences at the forefront of the politics between the North and South, the country was cast into a state of war.

The entire countryside buzzed with word of it and a flurry of activity was underway to make ready. Men gathered in droves to volunteer their services to drive the Yankees back to where they came from. James, with a sprained ankle, reluctantly had to sit back and wait. He sent word that as soon as he was able, he would join the Confederacy in their stand against the Union forces.

14

The ever-whirling wheel
Of Change; the which all mortal things
doth sway.

Spenser

*T*ilda paused as she swept the brick walk in front of
the house, squinting against the bright sunlight as the
visitor approached. The white horse pranced slowly up
the lane, trotting with measured step. Tilda was sure the
rider was someone important because even at this distance
it was difficult to ignore the distinguished countenance.
From beneath his hat, Tilda could see a thick wave of gray
hair. The gray uniform fit him neatly and he sat erect in
the saddle. She had no idea who he was, but as he passed
by her, he nodded his head and raised his hand to his hat.

Tilda nodded, murmuring softly, "Morning, Sir."

Though he smiled kindly, she thought a look
of concern marked the deeply etched line in his
forehead, and clouded the brightness of the intelligent
brown eyes.

She watched as he rode up to the porch and
swung from the horse. He handed the reins to Uncle
Abrams. "Take care of Traveler, Uncle, we have many
miles yet to go."

Uncle Abrams gave a sharp inclination of his head, saying, "Oh, ah will, Suh. Ah takes good care of all de hosses heah."

The man rested his hand on Uncle Abrams' shoulder. "I'm sure you do."

He turned, climbed the steps and rapped sharply on the door.

Later that afternoon, James met Tilda at the cave. He appeared solemn and she suspected it had to do with the uniformed stranger on horseback.

He put his arms about her, his lips brushing across her temple lightly as though he was preoccupied. Without preamble, he drew her down onto the dirt floor with him.

"You know I had a visitor today?" he began.

Tilda nodded.

"He is Robert E. Lee, commander of the Army of Virginia. He is a great man," he said emphatically, feeling it important to impress that fact on her. "Nearly twenty years ago, during the war between the United States and Mexico, he distinguished himself in skill and undaunted courage. He is considered by many to be the greatest military genius of our time."

"What did he want?" she asked quietly, knowing that the high praise James heaped on the stranger on horseback was for a reason.

"He is fortifying the southern coast against invasion by northern forces." James leaned down to her. "You know that I have to go, don't you?"

She looked down at her hands, not answering.

James lifted her face up to him with a curved finger. "Tilda, I must go," he said earnestly.

"But I thought the South was fighting to keep slavery," she protested.

"There are many more issues at stake now. The very existence of the South is hanging in the balance. General Lee feels as I do about slavery, but he says he is loyal to the South and must do what duty demands. He has asked me to lead a company. He is gathering forces to make a stand in Manassas."

"This war scares me, " Tilda said.

"I know," he replied. "It should scare anyone with any sense."

"Mr. Lee looked sad."

James nodded. "I think he knows that the South can have no victory."

Tilda looked up. "What do you mean?"

"The North has an overwhelming advantage over us," James said. "Not just in money and industrial equipment, but they have nearly four times the number of men than we do. It is a reality that they are finally facing." He sighed. "But, it's too late. War is declared. All we can do now is hope for the best while keeping our honor."

"But if you feel you cannot win, why do you go?" Tilda asked softly. "Why fight to preserve a system you do not believe in?"

"I'm not fighting to preserve this system of slavery that Lee and I both abhor, but to preserve my country. I owe my loyalty to Virginia and the South."

Tilda shook her head. She didn't understand any of it. Her fingers played with the cameo that lay beneath the fabric of her dress. She frowned, angry with this war that she knew would inevitably take James away from her. She wished things could stay the same -- that life was like it used to be -- even slavery was better than this lonely existence that made her feel she was teetering on the edge of doom with no way of stopping her imminent fall.

James covered the hand that worried the cameo with his own and she looked up at him. "I will come back to you, Tilda," he promised.

She smiled up at him, but couldn't stop the heavy feeling that stifled her, encasing her heart in a suffocating way, and sent frightening tremors throughout her system.

"If you go away -- how --" her words were halting, "how will you run the plantation?"

"John Avery will help Abigail. He knows as much about farming and the operation of the plantation as I do," James said. "I know I can trust him to do what is best, and I'm counting on you and Mammy Ticey, too."

Tilda remained silent. James bent down to her lowered face. "You will help me in this, won't you, Tilda?"

Her eyes met his. "Of course, James," she answered. "You shouldn't even have to ask."

"Of course, I shouldn't," he agreed. "You have always been there for me."

She draped her arms about his neck. "You know I would do anything for you, James."

James gathered her close to him.

The outside world was shut out from the soft murmurings of love unfolding in the small enclosure curtained by a thickly woven vine of flowing green and white.

James and John Avery went over the books in the library of Stafford Hall. They discussed the business of running the plantation while James was away.

"Not to worry, James," the clerk told him. "I shall do everything in my power to keep your property solvent, but I fear it may be very hard, indeed."

James nodded. "I am afraid the South is going to undergo an enormous change. But," he drew a long breath, "we'll do what we have to do."

With significant solemnity, they bent over the ledgers and turned their conversation to the operation of the plantation.

Mammy Ticey had been avoiding James. And he knew why. But he had no intention of allowing her to slip into the background and not say goodbye. Two days before he must leave, James entered the library, saw her dusting inside, and with resolute hand quietly closed the door before she could escape.

"Mammy! I've been looking for you," he announced jovially.

The old woman skirted round the desk, making her way to the door. "Cain't talk now, Jimmie-James," she said brusquely, "I's got work to do."

"Now, Mammy," he said softly, blocking her exit,

"we have to talk."

"Later," she mumbled.

James shook his head. "No. Now."

The old mammy looked at him silently, as though considering making a bolt for the door.

"Now, Mammy," James conjoled, "you don't want me to go off without even a goodbye, do you?"

Mammy shook her turbaned head. "Don't like goodbyes," she mumbled. "Dey is too final." She leveled a scowling look on him. "'Sides, I don't see why you has to go off noway. You could get yo'self killed."

James nodded. "True," he answered quietly, "but you wouldn't want me not to do my duty, would you, Mammy Ticey? That would bring dishonor onto the family and you."

She peered up at him, knowing he baited her, but still she felt herself swaying to give in. As long as she drew breath, she wouldn't want none of them white folks talkin' 'bout her Jimmie-James behind his back. Her scowl grew more pronounced. "Well," she drawled, "I guess if you has to go, you has to."

James laughed shortly, giving the old woman a bear hug. "Mammy, you are a gem."

"Yeah," she grumbled in a pseudo-harsh voice, "you just make sure you don't get yorself kilt, and get on back home. We cain't run dis plantation alone forever, you know."

James tried unsuccessfully to hide a smile. "I'll make them bring this war to an end as fast as possible. I'll be back home before you know it."

"See to it that you does," she snapped, brushing past him, and flinging open the door. Just beyond the threshold, she turned back. "And don't," she said firmly, "say goodbye to me, 'cause I ain't sayin' it back!" With a rustle of her full skirts, she flounced down the hall.

That evening when the house was silent, James tapped at Abigail's bedroom door. He stepped inside as she bade him to enter and stood leaning against the door. Abigail sat at a small mirrored vanity, brushing her long blond hair.

Her eyes flowed over his reflection in the mirror. She asked abruptly, "Have you spoken to John Avery?"

James nodded. "He is willing to assist in any capacity." He paused. "Will you be all right?" he asked hesitantly.

"And what would you do about it if I said 'no'," she returned haughtily.

"Abigail, please, don't make this more difficult than it already is."

"You don't have to go, James," she snapped. "This asinine show of honor and duty to the South is getting a little nauseating. You could come up with any number of excuses. Carter simply told them flatly, 'no'."

"I am not Carter," James said firmly, "and duty and honor mean something to me, whether you understand that or not."

"Humph!" Abigail sniffed. "That is all a lot of poppycock!" She had risen from the vanity bench and now she whirled on him. "You don't even believe in slavery, for God's sake! So why on earth are you running off to join the South in fighting for it?"

A weary sigh raised James' shoulders, and he shook his head in consternation. "There is more at stake for the South than just slavery -- "

"Name one damn thing, James," she interrupted scathingly, "something besides your precious honor."

James studied her. "I don't think it is something you will ever understand, Abigail," he said quietly, then turned abruptly and walked out of the room, closing the door behind him. Inside the room, he heard an object smash against the door, flung there by Abigail's angry hand.

The next afternoon on his way to the cave to meet Tilda, James saw Uncle Abrams ambling toward the stables. He held up his hand to detain him.

"I am leaving tomorrow," James said, approaching the old black man whose status as a slave was a mere shadow of the friend and confidant that he had become over the years.

"Yas, Suh, ah knows," he mumbled, not looking

up.

The old man held the worn hat between his fists. James watched him pensively for a moment. "Take care of yourself Uncle Abrams," he said.

"Yas, Suh. Ah will."

"We accomplished a lot of things together that I could never have done alone," James said, referring to their work on the Underground Railroad.

The old man nodded. "Ain't no mo' need fo' dat," he stated solemnly. "Gonna be some powerful big changes round heah, ain't dey, Massa James?"

"Yes, I think there is."

"Yo' started 'em, Massa James, the war's gonna finish 'em," he drawled.

"It's been long overdue," James said.

"Reckon it has," Uncle Abrams replied.

James held out his hand. Uncle Abrams looked up at him, before placing his gnarled, work-worn hand into his. James could not miss seeing the tears that filled Uncle Abrams' eyes and trickled down his cheeks.

"You be careful, boy," the old man muttered.

James nodded. "You take good care of yourself, Uncle Abrams."

The man nodded, pulled back his hand and clamped the old worn hat back onto his grizzled head. He turned away abruptly.

With a heaviness in his heart, James stood for just a second watching the old man's shoulders shake. With a sharp, pivotal step, he turned and continued on his way.

When James pushed back the curtain of honeysuckle at the cave, he saw Tilda sitting on the earthen floor in a crestfallen slouch. She immediately got to her feet and ran to him. He caught her in his arms and she buried her face against his shoulder. He could feel her trembling, could hear her stifled breath that masked the suppressed tears. He held her close.

"Come," he said. "Sit down here where we can talk." He pulled her down beside him. "Please, Tilda," he entreated, "don't look so grieved. Hopefully, this war won't touch you here at Stafford Hall. You will be safe."

"I don't worry about myself," she said.

Seeing the fear reflected in her eyes, he said, "You must not worry about me, either."

"How can I help it, James? You are," she held her hands out, palms up to express the magnitude of her words, which ended on a breathless note, "everything to me. All of my world is you."

James drew her into his embrace. "The country is in a mess, Tilda," he whispered softly, "and I fear it is going to get much worse than we ever imagined. Much worse."

She wanted to beg him not to go, but she knew it would be futile. James was going away to fight in a war that he did not believe they could win, and there was nothing she could do about it. She must remain behind trying to understand the politics of an outside world that few seem to know anything about. She must simply exist until he returned to her. Her fingers clutched at his shirt as her heart knocked within her breast. She saw their way of life slipping through her fingers like the sand that sifted slowly through the hourglass in the library.

James' fingers plucked at the buttons on her dress. "Let's don't talk of war anymore. I want to make love to you, Tilda. I want to take all these special moments with me. I want them to dwell in my heart and sustain me. I want them to carry me through the war, and to bring me back home to you." His eyes roved over her face. "No matter what, Tilda, will you be here when I return?"

Her arms held his head down to her lips as she murmured her devotion. The bodice of her dress slipped from her smooth, ivory shoulders as James eased her to the ground. The gold filigree of the cameo, lying in the small hollow of her throat, caught a small beam of light filtering through the honeysuckle curtain. James bent his head to the twin peaks and kissed their satin smoothness. His lips traveled to the small valley between her breasts, then he lifted the cameo between his fingers. He pressed his lips to the floral engraved back of the gold encasement, and whispered, "I'll love you always." Then slowly, he laid the cameo, warm from his touch, in the valley between the uptilted peaks.

His eyes sought hers and the heart-rending tenderness of his gaze wrapped around her, drawing her body in an involuntary movement up to his. James moved to meet the undulating thrust. His lips nibbled at her earlobe, and seared a path down her neck and shoulders. Her heart pounded, stuttering like the flutter of a bird's wings. The full leafed trees gathered the sighs that came from the carved out rock and tossed them into the air where they mingled with the wind.

Early the next morning, James stood on the porch ready to leave. Uncle Abrams waited at the foot with a horse prepared for the journey. The former slaves gathered in a line at the side of the house. James threw a hand up in farewell as he went down the steps and swung into the saddle. His eyes swept the area, searching for Tilda and one last glimpse of her. She was nowhere in sight. Mammy Ticey came out the door, weeping openly into her apron. She lifted one trembling hand to him. James nodded. Abigail stood at the window, peering through the parted lace curtains. He touched his hat but she stared coldly, giving no flicker of acknowledgment. The curtain fell back into place, and he knew she had stepped aside. He bit back a frown, turning his attention to John Avery, who stood with Uncle Abrams.

James' glance flowed from one to the other. "Thank you for all that you are doing for me," he said solemnly. "Going away is easier knowing you are here."

"Be careful, Massa James," Uncle Abrams murmured.

"I will."

James extended his hand to John Avery. "My thanks to you, as well."

John Avery nodded. "God speed, James."

He could say no more. He swung into the saddle, nudged the horse and started down the drive. Just once he glanced back to wave -- and to see if he could see Tilda.

She was nowhere within sight of his eager glance.

In the woods flanking the long, curving drive of Stafford Hall, Tilda ran breathlessly, hoping to reach the end of the drive before James. She had to see him once more, had to hold him. Tears blinded her eyesight as she crashed through the underbrush. She could not bear to stand idly beside the other servants as he rode off to war. Running as she was, and taking this short-cut, she could reach the end before he did, if he didn't set the horse to a gallop.

Tree limbs lashed out at her, but she paid them no mind as she raced in and out among the branches and tall growth. Her breath came in gasping little noises. Her heart pounded in her ears and, fearfully, she fancied it was the thunder of the horse's hooves racing beyond the drive, carrying James away from her. She ran faster. It seemed an eternity before she plunged through the woods at the end of the lane. She saw the road toward the house. It was empty. Wildly, her eyes raked the lane snaking ahead of her and saw James rounding a bend that would take him to the main road. Soon he would be out of sight.

Her heart rose to her throat even as her barefeet moved over the dusty road. His name bubbled past her lips in a frantic and agonizing cry. James turned in the saddle, saw her running. He turned the horse back. Her breath coming in spasmodic little gasps, Tilda stopped, watching the horse race at a full gallop back up the road toward her.

James brought the horse to a halt and slid from the saddle. "Tilda," he breathed, reaching out to her. "What are you doing? Where have you been?"

She fell into his arms, sobbing, her body trembling. "Please, James, just hold me once more."

James held her tightly, his lips caressing her temple. "I looked for you," he murmured. "I did not see you."

"I couldn't go. I couldn't stand there and watch you ride off without . . . " She looked up at him, a sob catching in her throat. "I . . . I couldn't let you go without . . . I just started running through the woods, trying to catch you at the end of the drive, away from them, away from everyone. I was so afraid I would miss you. And I had to tell you . . ." She paused to catch her breath.

"Tell me what?" he asked gently.

"That I love you. Wherever you go, James," she whispered, "you take my love with you."

"I know, Tilda," he answered softly. " I love you, too." He gathered her tightly in his arms, holding her as if they could meld into one. Some moments later, he held her back from him. "You must go back now," he whispered.

She nodded.

He said nothing as he swung back into the saddle, but bent down to her as she raised one small hand up to him. He caught it in his own, pressing it to his lips. Then he released her, turned the horse's head toward the end of the lane and moved slowly away.

At the bend in the road, James turned and looked back. He saw Tilda sitting in the middle of the dusty road with tears streaming silently down her beautiful face, and her arms locked around her body as she rocked to and fro trying to quell her grief.

That last sight of Tilda froze in his heart and haunted his memory through the many months to follow.

15

Between the idea and the reality
Between the motion and the act
Falls the shadow.
                              T. S. Eliot

*A*bigail did not share with anyone the contents of the first letter received from James after he left to join Lee's army. Tilda, Mammy Ticey, and the others could only assume that he was well, for no one dared ask the formidable Miss Abigail about the letter. It was not long after that first letter arrived that two more were delivered to Stafford Hall. One for Abigail and the other addressed to John Avery. It was from Mr. Avery's letter that they learned James had engaged in a bloody, hard-fought battle on the outskirts of Manassas along a small stream called Bull Run. The battle, fought under the guidance and strategy of Robert E. Lee, had resulted in a Confederate victory, and successfully ended the North's proposed plan to march on Richmond. While James had lost several of his men which greatly grieved him, he wrote that he was, otherwise, well.

Tilda sighed with relief as John read the contents of the letter to them. Hearing a sniffle, she glanced over at Mammy Ticey, who wiped at her eyes with the corner of her apron. She couldn't resist reaching out to comfort the old woman. Probably no one understood better than Tilda just how much the old mammy loved James.

When Uncle Abrams left the house, he looked up at the sky and murmured jubilantly, "Praise 'de Lord, Massa James is all right!"

That evening Tilda was surprised to see John Avery appearing at her cabin door.

"I have a message from James," he said quietly.

"Come in," Tilda said calmly, though her heart was knocking about inside her chest.

She closed the door quickly, indicating for John Avery to have a seat on the single wooden chair in the room. She stood near the end of the bed, watching him, waiting.

Though clearly ill-at-ease, he withdrew an envelope from his vest pocket. John Avery's name was written on it in James' bold script. "He sent it to me," John said, "to make sure you received it." He withdrew the single page that had been folded and sealed with a drop of wax. Forgetting in his self-consciousness that she could not read, he handed the letter to her.

Waving it back, she murmured, "Please. Read it," and sank onto the bed, leaning forward in her eagerness to hear James' words.

"My Dear Tilda,
I know that John will see that you receive this, and so it is that I have addressed it to him.
We engaged in a long and horrendous battle near Manassas, but it ended in a victory for us. I fear this war is going to drag on much longer than either the North or South realizes. Many lives will be lost. But we must not think of that. We must pray for an end to this madness, and we must think of tomorrow. Do not despair, Tilda. Remember 'always.'"

Tilda sat enraptured, absorbing every word, clinging to them as though she could hear James' voice. Silently, she stared into space, in her own private reverie, and Avery glanced back down to the paper he held. The words meant something intangible and precious to Tilda. He sensed in the significance of that single word that there lay a message that wrapped around the gentleness of her heart, simultaneously bringing her comfort and hope.

Softly, John continued to read the last few lines:

"Give Mammy Ticey a hug for me and let her know that I am all right. Stay well, Tilda. Please, do not worry about me. I shall be home as soon as possible."

Forever and Always,
James

Silence filled the cabin. The wick flickered in the lantern as John Avery looked over his small, round spectacles, studying Tilda. He handed the letter to her, speaking quietly with measured words. "It was important for James to get this note to you. I'm sure he knew Abigail well enough to know that she would never share her news with those of us she considers beneath her."

Tilda glanced up, her sparkling eyes holding his dove-gray surveillance, even as her fingers closed around the paper that carried James' thoughts to her. The paper, crinkling beneath her clutching fingertips, invaded the silence. Her eyes continued to hold his.

"What I mean, Tilda," he said, rising, "is don't feel embarrassed that I must read James' words to you -- that I know how he feels." He moved his feet with the uneasy shuffle of a man unused to a woman's company, a man who spent his hours alone with his account books. He ran his fingers through thinning gray hair. "I've known for many years -- since you were a little girl -- how James feels about you." He paused. "What I'm trying to say is, that I'm your friend."

Tilda rose. "I know that, Mr. Avery. And I thank you for that friendship. It is very kind of you to bring me James' letter."

She clutched it to her bosom.

He turned to go, pausing at the door. "Should you like to send him a note, I'd be happy to pen it for you," he offered softly.

Tilda smiled, shaking her head. "Thank you, Mr. Avery, but there's no need for that."

The man looked surprised.

"I saw him before he left," she told him. "He knows I cannot read or write. To have you write down my words would seem to make them less mine."

"No less than me reading his to you," he replied gently.

But still she shook her head. "No. James will not expect a letter from me. He knows that wherever he goes, I am with him. I live in his heart, as he lives in mine."

John Avery's graying head nodded slowly up and down. A feeling of melancholia flowed over him. A dark sadness for something that was not, but should be. Yet, at the same time, he felt overwhelmed with a definitive sense of futility. He reached for the door handle. "Good night, Miss Tilda," he said, according her the same courtesy he would have shown Abigail. He slipped out the door and into the evening dusk.

At President Lincoln's direction, blockades were set up at many southern ports, which brought an immediate halt to the shipments of goods from the South. Effectively, commerce and the daily life in the confederate states were literally being choked by the war.

By the year's end, Abigail was fed up with trying to manage a plantation that had become stagnant with no outlet for selling their crops. Sharecroppers, who had been former slaves, were leaving every day, which frustrated and angered her even more because she could not force them to return. Even when they were able to get the crops harvested, they were unable to get them to a viable market. Visible signs of the war were beginning to show across the South.

In the spring of 1862 when James had been gone for a year, Tilda came from the sewing room where she had just finished pressing a gown for Abigail. In the hallway outside Abigail's room, she knocked at the door.

"Who is it?" The voice sounded irritated, but that was nothing new to any of the servants' ears. Abigail was nearly always surly with them.

"It's Tilda, Miss Abigail. I've brought your new gown."

"Come in," her mistress called out.

Tilda pushed open the door and entered. She was surprised to see Abigail packing a traveling case. Her mouth gaped but she quickly collected herself.

"Don't look so shocked," Abigail said without pause, as she continued to fold items into the case. "You might as well know now."

Tilda looked blank. "Know what?" she asked.

"I'm leaving," Abigail replied, turning to lift a gown that had been thrown over a chair back. "I've had enough of this plantation and godforsaken war. I'm leaving with Carter."

Tilda's mouth formed a round circle at that admission. "But Mr. Hamilton will be coming home soon -- "

"Mr. Hamilton," Abigail interrupted, "will not be coming home for a long time. " She threw up her hands. "Who knows how long this damn war will last. It is showing no sign of ending. Besides, I'm sure he will be relieved to find that I have gone."

"Miss Abigail," Tilda began, "I'm sure that's not true."

"Oh, spare me the homilies, Tilda. You, of all people, must know who James hopes to find when he returns."

A light flush washed over Tilda's face.

"He always wanted you, anyway," Abigail flung at her.

Tilda's eyes grew wide, and speech escaped her.

Shaking her head, Abigail said wearily, "Oh, don't think I didn't know it."

Standing numbly, Tilda saw no point in trying to deny a truth that nestled in her own heart, but was something she had not considered being obvious to her mistress.

Abigail leaned across and snatched the freshly pressed gown from her hands. "Don't bother to make excuses," she told her in indifferent tones. "It makes no difference regardless. You're welcome to him. After this damn war is over, I don't suppose it is going to matter anyway." With a loud bang, as though to emphasize her words, she slammed the lid down on the traveling case.

She rose slightly, staring into space across the room, announcing in serious tones, as though she held some foreknowledge, "Everything is going to change." Tilda's bewildered gaze followed her and she heard her sigh. "Nothing will ever be the same again," she said softly. "Nothing." There was a wistful note in her mistress' voice.

"Where will you go?" Tilda asked hesitantly. "It will be dangerous. I have heard there are renegades roaming about, and deserters -- "

"Nonsense," Abigail said sharply. "I shall be perfectly fine. I am meeting Carter. In fact, he is waiting for me now." She reached for a small hat that matched the dark green traveling suit she wore and bent to the small vanity mirror to put it on. It had a small black feather that curled around the emerald green velvet crown, and a black, wispy veil that feathered across Abigail's forehead, reaching below her eyes. As she straightened, she said, "Carter said we might go to Paris. Do you know anything about Paris, Tilda?"

Tilda shook her head.

"No, of course not, " Abigail responded with her characteristic touch of hauteur. "How could you?" She smiled as though seeing images that Carter had painted in her mind with his eager, descriptive words. "It is a city that never sleeps," she whispered estatically. "They dance on the tables there, did you know that?" she asked of the startled Tilda, but did not wait for an answer. "It is full of music, and laughter, and fun." She snatched up a hatbox, saying, "And I, for one, cannnot wait to get there!" She sailed out of the room, leaving a perplexed Tilda to stare after her.

No one knew what to say or do, and consequently stood silently with varied degrees of expressions as their mistress' trunks were loaded. They watched with those same mute expressions when she placed her hand in Carter Stively's so that he might help her into his carriage. And they continued to stare in wide-eyed amazement, their heads turning in unison as the driver flicked a whip to the horses. Abigail and Carter rode away, rumbling down the drive without so much as a backward glance.

Abigail laughed gleefully. "I can't believe we finally did it!" She flung herself into Carter's arms. "I am so thankful to be free." She looked up at him. "Where are we going?"

"I have a friend who can get us safe passage to Maryland. From there we will set sail for New York, and from there to the beautiful and fabulous Paris."

"How did you manage that with all the ports blocked?" she asked.

"My dear," Carter said with his exaggerated air of importance, "I have told you before, there is not a single thing that money cannot buy."

Abigail snuggled next to him, pleased with their good fortune. "What did you do about your plantation?"

"I turned it over to my brother, Martin." He winked down at her. "For a price, of course." He nudged a small case at his feet. "The world is at our feet, so to speak," he said jovially, and laughter filled the small coach.

"Everyone was shocked that I was leaving," Abigail confided in him, "though I can't imagine why they should be." She tossed her shoulders. "It was quite laughable to see their faces." She smiled, settling back into the leather seat. "I don't care if I never see another plantation as long as I live," she said vehemently. "I'm afraid James is going to find his in shambles when he gets back -- that is, if he gets back."

Carter nodded. "I am sick of this stinking war, too. Chaos everywhere you turn. No way to get products to the North, the slaves in an uproar and running away every day."

"I know," she agreed. "The cotton has gone

unattended, tobacco is rotting in the fields -- frankly, I'm tired of it all."

"This wretched war has stifled our lives, destroying the aristocracy as we know it." Carter said. "I'll be glad to put it behind us."

The carriage rolled along beside a dense forest. Just as Abigail and Carter fell silent, feeling they had made the most fortuitous decision of their lives, they heard approaching horses. A shot rang out. It slammed into the upper part of the carriage. Abigail's scream rent the air.

From the coach window, they saw three riders in tattered, gray uniforms.

Abigail clutched at Carter. "Yankees?" she breathed.

"Confederate deserters," he muttered.

They fired again and the driver groaned, slumping audibly to the floorboard. Almost immediately, the carriage came to an abrupt halt.

Carter leaned toward the side window, demanding, "What is the meaning of this?"

A brawny hand yanked open the door, reached inside and grabbed Carter by the front of his jacket. The scruffy, bearded man's glance fell on Abigail. "Well, well, fellas. Lookee what we got here."

The beefy hand dragged Carter to the ground and reached back for Abigail. She shrank back into the corner of the coach. "Come on, girlie, get out here," the bearded man growled. "Let's have a look at ya'."

He made a caressing movement across her bodice and she slapped his hand away. "Take your filthy hands off me," she demanded, drawing herself up into her usual stance of hauteur.

With a quick flick of his wrist, the man slid his hand under her dress to grasp her ankle. "Don't get so bossy, gal," he snarled. "You and me are gonna get to know each other real well." He jerked her foot, bringing her roughly off of the seat and onto the floor. Her hat fell askew over perfectly coiffed curls. With a leering grin, the man ran his hands under her full skirts to her waist, which he grasped with ham-like fists of iron, and lifted her out of the carriage, as though she were a ragdoll.

Skirts billowing, he swung her around for his companions to see their prize.

The other two men cheered as he stood her on the ground, taking his time to allow his hands to slide down her thighs. A deep red spread over Abigail's pale, frightened face. She cowarded beside Carter in absolute terror.

Carter was cognizant that this was the most crucial moment of his life, and he did what he always did. He fell back on trying to buy what he wanted, and this time it was the most important thing in the world -- his life, and that of Abigail's.

"Look, if it's money you want, we can help you," he ventured.

"You got money?" one of the men on horseback asked.

Carter nodded vigorously. "Yes. Lots of it. Let us be on our way, and I'll give it all to you."

The three scruffy deserters, who looked as if they had not bathed in months, looked at each other. One of them on the horse, said, "Let's see how much you got."

Carter turned back to the carriage and withdrew the case from the floorboards beneath the seat. He turned slowly back, praying silently that the small fortune he held in his hands would be enough to satisfy the three men. With a shaking hand that he found hard to control, he opened the case and turned it for the men to see.

The two men on horseback dismounted and came forward. Three pairs of glazed eyes stared at the case that held more money and sparkling jewels than they had ever seen. Their eyes met once again, for they were unable to disguise their delight, their mouths stretching into gleeful grins. One of them hooted joyfully.

Carter breathed a sigh of relief as he gave a slight nod to Abigail. The bearded man leaned toward him, snatching the case from Carter's hands. Folding it closed, he tucked it under his arm, and strode over to his two companions. They conversed briefly, then turned back.

Carter met his cold glare stoically. "Now, may we be on our way?"

"Sure," the bearded man agreed. "You can go." He pulled a revolver and fired, shooting Carter in the chest. "Straight to hell!" A loud guffaw resounded round the small area, reverberating mockingly off of the treetops. Carter pitched to the ground, a startled and horrified look on his face.

Abigail screamed his name and fell to his prostrate form. One glance told her the horrifying truth. Carter was dead. Her cries of anguish were interrupted by the trio, who had closed in on her. One of them yanked her up from Carter's body. Another licked his tongue over thick lips, and his eyes struck a renewed terror of a different kind into Abigail's heart.

"Been a long time," he drawled, "since I had a lady."

"Hell!" snapped his friend, "you ain't never had a lady!"

All three burst into raucous laughter.

Suddenly they grew still, and three pairs of eyes were on Abigail. The look renewed her initial terror. She turned and tried to run. In seconds, they were on her, flinging her to the ground and tearing at her clothes.

She pleaded with them to shoot her, and they did -- when they were through with her. The single shot that ended her misery, resounded through the forest and up and down the roadway.

Because of its close proximity to Richmond, Fredericksburg, and other strategic points, Stafford Hall had been chosen by the Federal States to confiscate and use as a Union headquarters. And so it was, at that moment, that a regiment of Union forces was traveling toward the plantation. The gunshot brought them into the wooded area to investigate. They rode up to the scene of the triple murders en masse. The three Confederate deserters were spotted immediately and shot without preamble.

Surveying the grisly scene from astride his horse, the regiment commander shook his head in dismay. From the confines of the small group of black soldiers, riding in their own company behind the Union troops, a tall man came forward.

He approached the regiment commander. "Colonel Bradley, Sir, I am certain that I recognize this woman." He indicated Abigail's body that lay sprawled where the deserters had left her, her clothing awry, and a gaping, bloody hole in her chest. "She's a friend of James Hamilton of Stafford Hall. He's the man responsible for getting me to the North. If it hadn't been for him, I'm sure the slave trader would have killed me." He paused. "I'd like to take his friend back for a decent burial," he said quietly.

Colonel Bradley threw a glance up and down the length of Jubal Stafford. He was a good soldier. The men respected him. He kept his men in line, and had proved himself more than courageous in the last skirmish they fought. The colonel had heard his story of being rescued by James Hamilton and his helpers. Sergeant Stafford deserved the chance to repay a debt, and so, as commanding officer gave a nod of agreement. As a gentleman, and for his own peace of mind, he felt it was the least he could do for a man whose property he was about to seize.

"Set a detail to bury the others," he ordered. "Put the lady in one of the wagons. We'll go ahead. You can catch up with us."

"Thank you, Sir," Jubal said, turning to direct some of his men to start digging the graves.

Sometime later, the detail rode away from the death scene that they encountered too often in a war of mixed causes. Behind them, lying in the grass on the roadside, was the small green hat with the black feather curling round its crown. It was a forlorn sight, a mute testimony of the horrendous events that had just taken place. A sad little breeze whispered across the ground. It seemed to sigh woefully. Its mournful breath ruffled the feather with a seemingly half-hearted gesture, and then the little breeze went on its way.

At mid-afternoon, Tilda, Mammy Ticey, John Avery, and Uncle Abrams were startled to see the long procession of horses and wagons winding up the drive toward the manor house of Stafford Hall. They were the only ones left at the plantation now, and with Abigail gone, they turned to John Avery.

With a slight nod, he took one step forward to the top step, and waited as the military forces drew abreast.

The officer in front, drawing adjacent, addressed him. "I am Colonel Bradley of the Union Army. We have been sent here to secure the area. We will be making our headquarters here at Stafford Hall. I am asking you all to cooperate. As long as none of you interferes with our operation, you may go about your daily business as usual. However, no one is to leave the property without permission. Any of you living in the house, we ask that you make your living arrangements elsewhere. We will be requiring the entire premises for our officers. Do I make myself clear?"

John Avery nodded, turning to the trio standing behind him. "We have no choice but to do as he says," he said quietly. His gentle gray eyes swept over them one by one. "I know this is difficult for all of us, but we must cooperate."

Tilda and Uncle Abrams nodded in agreement, but Mammy Ticey had a frown on her broad face, and he heard her grumble as he turned back to the union officer. "We understand."

The officer turned in the saddle, and called over his shoulder, "Sergeant Stafford!"

A man broke ranks and rode forward. The quartet on the porch was startled to see that he was black.

"Jubal?" Tilda uttered in astonishment.

Jubal looked up at her, and tipped his hat. "Yes, ma'am."

He cast a glance up at his commanding officer, and received a minute nod. "I'm afraid," he continued quietly, "that we have bad news." He turned his look onto John Avery. "I think we have found a friend of Mr. James Hamilton's. She has been murdered. I thought it the least we could do to bring her here, so that you could notify her family and give her a decent burial." He indicated that

John should accompany him to one of the wagons.

Standing at the back of the wagon, John Avery waited as Jubal leaned into the interior and threw back the wool army blanket.

John's eyes grew wide. "Dear God," he breathed. "That is not a friend. She is James Hamilton's wife." He gulped to still his swirling stomach. "What in God's name happened?"

"Confederate deserters apparently stopped them on the road. They robbed and murdered her companion. She appears to have been assaulted. We heard the shot and went to investigate. We . . . we found her and her companion." He flung the blanket back over Abigail's ashen face. "I'm sorry. About everything," he murmured, indicating this new turn of events that they must deal with concerning the Yankees' imminent encampment. "I will try to help you as much as I can, but I don't have much authority."

"I understand," John Avery told him. "We owe you a debt of gratitude for bringing Mrs. Hamilton home."

"You owe me nothing. I am the one who owed a debt," Jubal replied solemnly. "Tell Miss Tilda and the others not to worry. Colonel Bradley is a fair man."

With a slight nod, John Avery strode back to the small group waiting on the porch. His grave features and clouded eyes told them what they all had feared.

Abigail was buried in the small cemetery on the hill overlooking the Potomac. There were only four people attending. Ironically, they were the very ones whom she had been the least kind to during her time as mistress of Stafford Hall. They were respectful, probably because of the way each felt about James. The solemn ceremony was brief. Unlike any previous funeral on the plantation, there was not a tear shed.

16

*U*nder Colonel Bradley's command, the Union troops moved onto Stafford Hall Plantation. They began by taking shelter in the empty slave quarters, and when those were filled, a tent city sprang up over the once neatly maintained lawns. The officers took over the big house. Mammy Ticey moved into Beulah's cabin with Tilda. She was exceedingly vocal about, "dem Yankees, takin' over James' house," and she went about scowling and muttering everytime one of them came into view. Uncle Abrams managed to hold onto his living quarters over the stables. John Avery's small rooms above the offices were left to his disposal, but the office rooms were invaded upon, causing him to scurry about collecting his prized accounting books, which he carried to his upstairs rooms.

Horses were tethered everywhere and supply wagons rumbled over the dirt roads daily. The blue-clad soldiers seemed to be everywhere one turned, and the once serene plantation became noisy and disquietening.

When Tilda realized that the northern troops would set up an encampment on Stafford Hall grounds, her hand closed with uneasiness over the cameo beneath the bodice of her dress. It was all she had of James, and she

194

would not allow the dreaded Yankees to take it from her. Immediately, she took action to ensure its safekeeping. She recalled a loose brick in the mortar of the hearth in Beulah's cabin. She would hide it there. No one but herself would know of its hiding place.

The day after the Yankees began their encroachment, Tilda made her way to the kitchen dependency that still bore the scars of the fire. There had been no time to make repairs, and with the start of the war, no one available to do it. Her heart dipped painfully when she entered the partially burned room. Tears welled in her eyes. With a resolute hand, she swiped at them, determined not to think about her mother and how much she missed her.

In the cupboard, among various kitchen tools, bowls and containers, she found a small metal box. She pulled it out, brushing the dirt and grime from its lid. It was perfect, just large enough to put the necklace in. She hurried back up the path.

In the cabin, she knelt on her knees, her fingers wiggling at the loosened brick. Finally, she worked it free and lifted it out. She used a stick to scrape the soft dirt aside, making the hole deep enough to hide the box. On the floor beside her lay the metal box in which she had put a small piece of velvet to cushion the necklace. It was open in readiness to accept its keepsake. Also on the floor lay the three letters she had received from James. She'd tied them together with a bit of narrow lace left over from one of her sewing jobs. Tilda picked them up, pulling at the bit of lace that bound them. Slowly, one by one, she looked at them, touching the words written by James, as though absorbing with her fingertips that which she could not read. With infinite care, she refolded each letter, returned it to its envelope and retied the scrap of lace around them. With a reverent touch, she placed them in the hole of the hearth.

Then with quiet determination, she unclasped the gold chain of the necklace. Cradling the cameo in her palms, she remembered her promise to James that she would always wear it. Her heart trembled and she sighed a deep, distressful breath at having to break her promise.

It could not be helped. She would leave it there until this dreadful war was over and James returned. She simply did not trust these Yankees that James was fighting. How could she trust them? Unbidden, Jubal came to her mind. He was now also a Yankee. But she dismissed him with the thought that he was different, since he had once been a slave like herself. He had made a new life for himself in the North.

The fact remained, to her way of thinking, that she must protect James' gift from those very people that he was fighting. And these were not men like Jubal. She would rather put James' token of love in the earth and cover it with a brick then to have some Yankee take it and give it to someone else. She could not bear the thought of anyone else wearing James' gift.

Her fingertip traced the curly-cues on the back and she imagined she could feel James' breath on her skin and the warmth of his lips where they had been pressed to the back of the cameo, before he had placed it in the valley between her breasts, whispering, "I'll love you always." Tilda sensed she could feel that warmth now, and involuntarily she held the cameo pressed next to her skin. She closed her eyes and from beneath the black fan of lashes, glistening tears slipped out and ran in an irridescent trickle down her pale cheek.

Slowly, she bent to her task and placed the cameo on its bed of velvet. She clipped the lid on, sealing it tightly, and placed the box in the hole on top of the letters. Another sigh dragged from her as she lifted the brick and tamped it back into place. She sat there motionless staring at the secret of the hearth.

The door opened and Mammy Ticey came in. She hesitated before closing the door behind her. The irridescent trail of tears on Tilda's cheek did not go unnoticed by Mammy Ticey. "You all right, honeychile?" she asked gently.

"I'm okay, Mammy Ticey," Tilda answered, getting to her feet.

"You look so sad."

Tilda shrugged.

"It's dis terrible war," Mammy lamented. "It draggin' on fo' such a long time." She leveled a steady gaze at the girl. "Guess you misses James," she ventured.

Tilda met her look, but didn't answer.

"You doesn't have to be afraid to talk to me, chile," she said softly. "I has known fo' a long time how Jimmie-James feels 'bout you. Fact is," she said abruptly, "I think I knew it fo' he did." She had crossed the floor to where Tilda stood in front of the fireplace. "I think it started the first day he brought you home." Her words were almost a whisper, as her dark eyes surveyed the girl. She put out her arms and drew Tilda into them. "Don't be afraid to cry, chile. Sometimes it eases de pain."

Tilda succumbed to the warmth and kindness. Words tumbled from her mouth, guided there by her heart. Tears spilled down her cheeks. "I know it's not right for me to love James, but I can't help it. I think I loved him from that first day. It just seemed to keep growing and I didn't seem able to stop it. It was -- just there."

Mammy Ticey shook her head in understanding. "It's okay, baby. Cain't nobody no mo' tell you who you can loves an' who you cain't. If you loves my Jimmie-James -- then you jus' does. Ain't gonna change nothin' noways. You cain't help what you feels in yo' heart, and he cain't help what he feels in his." She paused in thought. "Sides, I reckon Jimmie-James needs to know you is here thinkin' 'bout him, prayin' he be safe, and lovin' him. So you jus' go right on, chile, and keep that love in yo' heart fo' him. Reckon you both needs each other."

They were silent for a moment, then Tilda kissed Mammy's cheek, and whispered, "Thank you, Mammy."

The old woman set her aside brusquely. "Come on, chile, 'nuff o' this talk. We has got to fix supper," adding with a flash of anger, "if dem Yankees has left anything!"

Several days later, coming up the path from the quarters, Tilda shook her head at all the visages of war that scarred the beauty of the grounds. She saw Jubal in the distance and waved in acknowledgment of his nod.

He strode toward her.

"Morning, Miss Tilda. You all right?"

"Good morning, Jubal," she replied. "Yes, I am as well as can be expected."

"I hope we are not making things too difficult for you," he waved his hand around. "So many people and tents, and all the noise and confusion."

"They are killing off so much of the livestock every day," Tilda lamented. "Very soon it will all be gone."

Jubal nodded sadly. "That is what war is, Miss Tilda. We must feed the men who fight."

"But they're Yankees!" Tilda spoke the word distastefully.

Again Jubal nodded.

"How can you help them?" she asked, her brow furrowed in puzzlement.

"They fight to save our people," the man replied quietly.

"But they are fighting James and his people," Tilda uttered. "James is the one who helped you."

Jubal's head moved up and down in a slow, sad movement. "I know. And I will be forever in his debt -- and yours. But, Miss Tilda, the South must change. And I must do what I can to help bring about that change."

Tilda shook her head. How could it be that the very person James helped to get to freedom, must now fight against him. The frown deepened.

"It's war, Miss Tilda," Jubal reminded, as though reading her mind. "And it's ugly and not always fair," he added.

In the face of her downcast silence, Jubal spoke again. "I will always be grateful for Mr. Hamilton's actions. That is why my name is now Jubal Staffford."

Tilda looked up. "From Stafford Hall?"

He nodded.

"Why?" This was even more bewildering.

"I got my salvation here. The start of a new life. So you see, Miss Tilda, James did not act in vain. He was helping in a movement that was necessary. Every little step brings us closer to freeing all men."

"But war?" Tilda whispered.

Jubal frowned, his dark-eyed gaze cast upon the ground. "It's sad, but it seems the only way men know to settle their differences."

A great sigh escaped Tilda. Thoughtfully, she watched Jubal stride away.

17

Like as the waves make towards the pebbled shore,
So do our minutes hasten to their end.
                                        Shakespeare

*T*he war dragged on, and it seemed like the Yankees would never leave. All the chickens, cattle, and hogs had been slaughtered. Everything had been killed to feed the troops. The root cellar had been depleted long ago. The plantation lay in total devastation. The fields lay barren, rutted from wagon wheels and trampled with the footsteps of horses and men. The outbuildings had become eyesores. Tilda found it difficult to remember a time when there had been no war, when all of their lives had been different, and when the grounds of Stafford Hall had been green and beautiful. The only thing that stayed alive in her heart was James and her love for him.

One morning, she awoke to the sound of wagons gathering and orders being shouted in tones that carried across the plantation. She had grown accustomed to the noise and chaos of the Union troops, but something told her this was different. She dressed quickly and ran outside.

The Yankees were leaving!

Tilda saw John Avery standing at the foot of the porch talking to Colonel Bradley. The wagons had been loaded and were drawn into a line ready to move out. She saw Jubal break away from his men and ride over to her. He slid from his horse, took her by the elbow, and drew her away from the crowd.

"I wanted to say goodbye, Miss Tilda," he began.

"That is kind of you, Jubal."

"I know these many months have been difficult for you, but hopefully this war will soon be over." He paused. "I hope Mr. Hamilton returns safely."

"Thank you, Jubal. I wish you a safe journey, as well."

"I've left you something at the mill. I am sorry I couldn't do more."

"What?"

"You will soon see, but please, don't go there until we are well on our way. If the colonel finds out, he will probably have me shot." Before she could ask further questions, he swung back up into the saddle. He touched his fingertips to his cap, "Please let Mr. Hamilton know that I tried to help you, even though I know I can never repay what he has done for me."

Tilda watched him ride away. When he rejoined his company, she began to thread her way among the wagons and milling troops, to the front of the house and John Avery.

By the time she reached the porch, the colonel had ridden away. She watched as the soldiers on horseback fell into line behind him and the wagons took their place behind the troops.

It seemed to take forever for the long procession, snaking its way down the lane, to finally wind out of their sight. Tilda looked at John Avery, and a smile wreathed her face. It disappeared quickly when she saw his grave look.

She hurried to where he stood. "What is wrong, Mr. Avery? Aren't you glad the Yankees are gone?"

"With them goes the food," he replied quietly.

Tilda frowned, looking back at the empty road.

Later, old Uncle Abrams came running up to the

house. "Yo' all has gotta come see what's at de mill!"

Tilda remembered what Jubal had told her. "Jubal said he left us something," she said, "but I forgot to look. What is it, Uncle Abrams?"

But the old man shook his head beneath the battered, ancient hat, refusing to tell them, insisting they come with him.

At the mill, they clustered at the doorway. Uncle Abrams stood aside, grinning from ear to ear, watching them as they peered inside.

First, he heard Mammy Ticey say, "Well 'pon my soul!"

John Avery uttered, "I'll be damned!"

"Jubal hid them away for us!" Tilda said. "He asked me not to come down here until they were well away. He risked being shot to help us. He is a good man."

Uncle Abrams joined them as they stood admiring a fat hog, and four chickens cooped up inside the mill.

John Avery and Uncle Abrams set about preparing the meat. There was no telling how long this food would have to last. As soon as the Yankees were off Stafford Hall soil, Mammy Ticey and Tilda planted a small garden with leftover seed that Mammy had managed to hide. It was late in the season, but they had to try.

An early frost came, and with it destroyed their hopes of more provisions from the garden. As the days and months dragged on, life became even more difficult. Their food supply grew more scarce each day. There was no meat except for fish or an occasional rabbit. Even the wildlife seemed to have been chased away by the war.

Winter was setting in, and they were all aware that the days ahead were going to be hard. The Yankees had used the meager furniture in the cabins for firewood. Despite the fact that Beulah's cabin had remained intact, they all decided they should take up residence in the big house. It had suffered the least amount of damage, and even though it was in dire need of repairs, it still provided them the best shelter. John Avery moved his things into the study. Mammy Ticey and Tilda shared a room at the back of the house, down the hall from one occupied by

Uncle Abrams.

As the months wore on, there were more and more visual signs of the war that plagued the nation. It was a blight that was evident all across the South. Slowly, slipping into view from the horizon, the spring of 1865 dawned across the battle-scarred land and a war-weary people.

Tilda had been sick with a fever and congestion off and on for much of the winter. She was just recovering from the most recent bout, but insisted upon getting up and moving about a bit.

"You has had 'namonia," Mammy Ticey scolded. "You should stay in bed."

But Tilda refused, insisting she felt well enough to sit on the riverbank and try to catch enough fish for their dinner.

John Avery offered, but Tilda stubbornly refused. He and Uncle Abrams were already doing more than their share.

Late in the afternoon, she returned from the river carrying a string of fish she'd caught from the wharf at the end of the rolling road. Tilda walked slowly, feeling fatigued. As she started around the house to the back entrance, a noise in the drive, which had been silent for many months now, caught her attention. She looked down the brown ribbon road, still hard-packed from the winter's icy temperatures. Her heart skipped a beat. She almost dropped the fish. A horse and rider came into view, heading straight toward the house.

Tilda hurried inside, calling to Mammy Ticey, John Avery, and Uncle Abrams.

"Quickly! Take cover! A rider is coming up the drive. It could be a Yankee or a deserter."

John Avery reached for the rifle he always kept nearby.

Adrenaline pumped through Tilda's veins, giving her renewed strength. She grabbed up a rifle from the corner behind the door and ran to the front entryway. Instead of taking cover as she had directed, the others followed her. Tilda shoved the tip of the rifle barrel through a broken window glass, aiming it toward the rider.

She watched as the exhausted horse plodded slowly toward the house. The rider rode slumped in the saddle. She strained to see if he carried a gun, refusing to allow herself to feel any concern for his weariness. Suddenly, the rifle she held clattered against the window opening and her hands began to tremble. She stared at the rider.

"James!" she murmured. "It's James!"

She dropped the rifle on the floor and ran to the door, flinging it open.

Behind her, she heard Mammy Ticey mutter, "Lawd be praised!"

Tilda ran headlong down the steps, calling his name over and over. Tears of joy streamed down her face.

A smile spread over the rider's gray features when he caught sight of Tilda's thin figure running toward him.

She reached him just as he collapsed and slid from the horse, whispering her name. John, Uncle Abrams and Mammy Ticey had followed her outside. John hurried down the steps. Uncle Abrams, moving at a much slower gait, followed. Together, they helped her get him into the house.

James lay on the small bed in the study that John had been using. Tilda sat on the bedside, holding his hand and stroking his cheek. Mammy hovered nearby, constantly changing the cool, wet cloths she lay on his brow. John and Uncle Abrams had helped remove James' clothing and Mammy had washed and dressed his wounds. Tilda had to grit her teeth to keep from sobbing when she saw the ragged tears in his side.

James was extremely ill and they all knew it. Tears rolled down Mammy Ticey's broad face as she tended the man she loved like her own child.

Seeing her tears, James spoke in a raspy voice, "Don't cry, Mammy. I'm going to be all right."

"Don't talk, Jimmie-James," she said, using his old pet name. "Jus' rest, chile."

James eyes roved the room restlessly. "Where is Abigail?" he asked.

A look passed among them, but no one answered.

"Tell me," James insisted.

Tilda bent to him, smoothing his hair back from his forehead. "She ran away with Carter Stively," she said quietly.

"I'm not surprised," James admitted. "She should never have married me. It was him she really cared for." After a pause, he asked, "Where did they go?"

There was a strained silence before Tilda answered. "They didn't get very far. Deserters were in the area, and they were robbing and murdering people all around. They stopped Carter and Abigail on the road. Carter was robbed, and then murdered. They -- " she hesitated, seeing no reason to burden James with the horrible details of his wife's death. "They also killed Abigail."

James closed his eyes, and she saw his mouth set in a firm, grim line of acceptance. She watched him closely, and seeing no movement, shook him gently. "James -- " she began, frightened.

He opened his eyes, covering her hand that lingered on his chest. "I'm all right, Tilda," he murmured, taking a deep breath. "The war is nearly over. General Lee has retreated from Richmond. He is on his way to Appomattox to surrender."

No one said anything, yet all drew a sigh of relief. They were weary of the death and destruction that the South had suffered over the last few years. It didn't matter that they were not victorious. They were just glad it had finally come to an end.

Uncle Abrams fought the tears that would not stop welling in his black eyes. Once he ventured close to the bed, asking, "Is dey anythin' I's can do fo' you, Massa James?"

James reached out to touch the old man's arm. He made no attempt to correct the "Massa James," for he understood that as far as Uncle Abrams was concerned, it meant more than the words connoted. They had been friends for too long for it to mean anything else. James also knew that Uncle Abrams would have given his life for him had their participation in the Underground

Railroad been discovered, and it became necessary. Gently, he said, "No, thank you, Uncle Abrams. I'm going to be all right. I just need to rest." He looked the old man over solemnly. "And so do you," he said gently. "Go on. Sit down. I'll call you if I need anything."

"Good," the old man bobbed his head. "Yo' do dat, Massa James. Ol' Uncle Abrams be right heah." And he took a position near the bed in the event James should call out to him.

James looked up at his old nurse. "Mammy," he asked, "are my old diaries still around, or were they destroyed?" His eyes swept the threadbare furnishings.

"I saved 'em fo' you, Jimmie-James," Mammy Ticey assured him. "I put dem where no sorry Yankee could ever find 'em." She bustled out of the room to get them.

"The Yankees set up headquarters here," John Avery told him, as if he felt he had to explain the condition of the house. "They killed all the livestock we had on the place to feed the troops. Anything left, they took with them. A lot of the furniture was broken up and used for firewood, as well as most of the planks off the barns. Most of the outbuildings have fallen into disrepair from lack of attention. The house survived simply because they used it as their headquarters. We should be thankful they didn't burn it down before they left, which is what I've heard they did at many other plantations," he finished solemnly.

Mammy Ticey returned with the volumes of diaries, which James had begun as a small boy. Weakly, he searched for the most recent volume.

"Must you do that now, James?" Tilda asked. "You need to rest."

He shook his head. "Need to bring them up-to-date." He tried to make her smile, making an attempt at humor, "Someone may need them when they try to reconstruct the history that we have all just lived through."

John fetched him a pen and ink, and James began to write while they went about their work, leaving Tilda to watch over him.

Tilda's heart ached when she looked at him. His

color was death-like, and he was dangerously weak. Mammy Ticey brought him a bit of broth from the stew she had prepared with the chicken John had miraculously found somewhere. He did not eat much of it.

Her eyes searched Mammy's fearfully. The stark look in those old dark eyes made Tilda's heart quiver. She looked back down at James. There was so much she wanted to say, and she sensed there was little time. Something was driving her from deep within, to say it one more time. To say the words just once more, when he could hear them. She didn't care that Mammy, Uncle Abrams and John Avery looked on. They all loved him, too, and she knew they would understand.

He had stopped writing, and she leaned down to him, kissing his temple. "I love you, James," she whispered.

James gathered her to his chest, unmindful of the book lying between them. "I love you, too, Tilda. It was that thought that kept me going. I had to get back home to you." He paused, gasping for breath. The diary fell to the bed.

"Don't," she whispered. "Don't talk. Save your strength."

But there was a burning desire in James that would not be still. "This was all wrong, Tilda," he whispered.

"What, James? What was wrong?"

"Us. We belonged together. I should have found a way for us." He paused, drawing a shallow, rasping breath. "I want you to know that I will come back to you. Wherever you are, I will find you. We will be together. Always." His voice drifted off, and his eyes closed.

Mammy Ticey looked at Tilda. "The fever talkin', chile," she told her.

But Tilda wondered.

James stirred again. This time he reached up and pulled Tilda down to him, holding her with a renewed strength. She could barely feel his lips moving against her temple. "I love you, Tilda," he whispered with an ardor that flamed in his soul, "and I will come back to you." His lips brushed her forehead, and his arms fell away from her.

Tilda jerked her head up. "James!" she whispered. "James!" She saw the deep blue eyes staring, and knew he could no longer see her. "No! No! Jaaaames!" she cried. She collapsed to the floor.

They buried James Hamilton on the hill next to his mother and father, with the four remaining people of Stafford Hall attending, Mammy Ticey, John Avery, Uncle Abrams, and Tilda. Once again, the treetops sighed woefully, echoing the sobbing that floated upward from the four below.

In the days ahead, Tilda felt hopelessly lost. One evening John Avery came to her in the parlor. He carried James' diary. She looked up from where she was sitting beside Mammy.

John shuffled his feet. "I thought you might like to know what James wrote in his journal," he said quietly.

John sat down across from them. "He writes first about the war and the impact it has had on the South. He speaks of a South that is changing, and will never be the same again." He paused. "It's the last thing he wrote that I thought you would like to hear." Softly, in a subdued voice, he began to read the last entry James had penned.

> *"I am very ill. Tilda, Mammy Ticey, Uncle Abrams, and John Avery are here with me. No one is saying it, but they, too, know in their hearts that I am dying. I am sad to see them so worried. Dear Mammy. She has been as much a mother to me as my own. Uncle Abrams was my friend and partner. John Avery, loyal employee (but I never thought of him as that), has been my friend and confidant, someone I knew I could trust. And Tilda. My beautiful, darling Tilda. I was so wrong to allow her to stay on here, but I could not bear to let her go. It was selfish of me. I hope she will forgive me. But of course, she will. I know in my heart*

*that she loves me. It is that which has
sustained me and given me strength to return
to her. How sad that it is too late. I should
have found a way to marry my dear Tilda,
and be with her forever, for I know that if
ever two souls belong together, it is Tilda's
and mine. It can't end this way. I won't let
it! I must promise her. I will come back to
you, Tilda. Wherever you are, I will find
you, and we will be together always."*

The diary ended with the last word barely written as
though it had been done with great effort. When John
finished speaking, Tilda was weeping softly.

"I just wanted you to know how he truly felt," John
said, as though apologizing for making her cry.

"He truly loved you, Tilda," Mammy Ticey said,
reaching out to draw Tilda to her bosom. "Even when
you was a little chile." She shook her head sadly. "He
jus' didn't know how to change the way things was in his
world."

"I know," Tilda said, wiping at her eyes. "I don't
blame James. It was the way of the South. There was no
way for us," she finished sadly.

Two weeks later, Tilda fell ill again with a recurring
bout of pneumonia from which she did not recover. Her
death left the others grief-stricken once again, and brought
to an end an era at Stafford Hall Plantation and all that had
gone before.

With tears in his eyes, John Avery told Mammy
Ticey, "I think she lost the will to live when James died."

"When Jimmie-James died he took her heart and
soul," Mammy agreed.

Uncle Abrams wept silently to himself.

They decided it was the right thing to do to bury
Tilda next to James, rather than in the section once
reserved for the slaves. After all, they said, who was left
to stop them.

The three mourners walked out of the cemetery,

weighed down with this most recent loss, and wondering what lay ahead for them. It was evident to each that the future of Stafford Hall teetered on the edge of abandonment. There was no one left to bring it back to its former glory. And even if there were, could it rise again from the crumble that was the south? A south that lay in tatters, devastated by a lost cause that had taken its toll, not just in lives, but also, in a way of life.

The sun had been hiding behind gray clouds for days, adding immeasurably to the sullen pallor that lay over the plantation. A heavy mist hung in the air, echoing the tears on their faces and the crying in their hearts. A great sigh dragged up from deep within John Avery's soul, as he paused to shut the iron gates of the cemetery. The metallic clink resounded with such a note of gloomy finality that Mammy Ticey covered her face in her grief and wept inconsolably. Old Uncle Abrams turned a tear-stained face to John Avery, but John had no words of consolation for them. He felt the same sense of bereavement that they did, and unabashed tears ran unchecked down his face. Silently, he fell into step beside them.

EPILOGUE

*A*ustin James Hamilton sat doggedly through the hours, watching various emotions run rampant over the journalist's face. He'd watched strickened, as tears spilled from beneath the black feathery crescent of her eyelashes and ran in a desolate rivulet down her fair cheeks. He saw her flinch as though in pain, and later, saw a sense of peace and happiness rest on her features. There was a riot of different emotions registering, as he sat beside her, unconscious of the passing hours, mesmerized into a state of vigilant observation.

For one brief second, her eyelids fluttered open, and dark brown eyes stared out at him with -- what? What was it he had seen so fleetingly? Recognition? They closed again before he could decide.

Austin watched her as she tossed feverishly in a curious, fitful unconsciousness. Again, the feeling that he had looked into those eyes before swept over him. He scoffed at the thought. Perhaps he had a touch of the fever, as well.

He had poured over old papers and the diaries of James Robert Hamilton until he felt he knew him well. Too well. Sometimes it was as if he knew what the next passage was going to be. Had he absorbed James' feelings through all those diaries? At times, it seemed as though he had taken on his personality. Did osmosis work so thoroughly? How else to explain this cloying emotion that engulfed him? He felt that he knew this beautiful girl, stranger though she was, lying on his couch in a restless sleep. Was it from another time? Another place? The admission of such thoughts surprised him. He drew a deep sigh, thoroughly confused. Especially after his unsettling experience yesterday.

On a leisurely stroll over the plantation, he found his feet carrying him across the field, beyond the old slave quarters, through a field of wildflowers, to where he paused at the edge of the woods beside a huge jutting rock. Without hesitation, his hand reached out to the thick wall of honeysuckle that was just beginning to bloom. He jerked the heavy woven curtain back, hoping to find nothing more than a benign rock wall. His mind reeled, as his wild-eyed gaze fell on the carved out, cave-like room. He knew, without a doubt, that he had found the "secret place," a reference in James' diaries that had lingered in his thoughts. How had he known? His logical mind did not want to accept what his heart suggested.

Suddenly, his legs felt weak. He went inside and plopped down onto the dirt floor. His gaze swept the area, squinting in the dusk. What was he expecting? To see Tilda sitting among the shadows? Austin sat there for a very long time, trying to come to terms with his discovery. Was he so plagued by James' diaries that he had somehow tuned into an inexplicable aura that surrounded the plantation?

The last passage in the diary, James vowing to come back to Tilda, haunted him even more than the discovery of the "secret place". *I will come back to you, Tilda. Wherever you are, I will find you.* The words rang in his ears, and he fancied they echoed round the stone walls, reverberating in their intensity. Somehow he felt they were more than the hastily scrawled words a dying man wrote in a journal. They held the ardor of a promise.

And what about that first week, after he had begun to read James' diaries. He had become so consumed by the bittersweet love James had shared with Tilda, daughter of a slave and white planter, that he had gone to the cemetery to find her grave. Of course, he had looked in the slave section first, but there was no marker, and finally, he ventured into the main part in search of James' resting place. It was there that he found Tilda. As he looked down on her grave, he felt a sharp pain hurl through his heart. He reached out, touching the stone with a gentle caress, his index finger moving to trace the letters of her name. A strange flutter began in his chest -- as if his heart was crying.

Austin found it all quite unsettling.

And now, here was this woman journalist, with haunting, dark eyes smiling up at him as though she knew him. He saw her stir again, and bent toward her.

He leaned over her as her eyes slowly drifted open. Her lips moved. He bent closer.

"James, you have come back to me," she murmured, and the joyful light in her eyes seemed blinding to Austin.

He stared at her.

She smiled and he was startled when, in her bemused state, she reached up and put her arms around his neck, drawing him down to her.

Tugged by the magnetism of the moment, he hovered over her parted, inviting lips, then slowly bent to meet them.

Suddenly she stiffened, her arms falling to the bed. Austin drew back from her.

"I . . . I," she stammered, throwing a puzzled glance around the room. "What has happened?" She pulled herself up in the bed. "Are . . . are you Mr. Hamilton?"

"Yes."

"I . . . I have had a dream, I . . . I think." She put her hands to her face. Her cloud of chestnut hair fell around her.

"You were struck by a tree limb when you got out of

your car," Austin said. "You don't seem to have been injured, except for the bump on your head. Do you know what your name is?"

"Yes. It's Laura Townsley," she answered, but some inward voice was whispering: *Tilda. My name is Tilda.* She shook her head trying to dispel the echoing whispers.

"What? What is it?" Austin asked, seeing the curious look on her face.

"The dream I had was so strange. It was so real -- more like a memory," she murmured. "It was like a lifetime flashed before my eyes."

"Dreams are like that sometimes," he said with a nonchalance he did not feel.

She shook her head. "No. It wasn't like that. It was like a lifetime that I remember in detail. I was here. On this plantation. I was a slave. My mother was black and my father was white. My name was Tilda." The words tumbled out of her mouth, as though she couldn't say them quickly enough, like she had to get them out into the open to examine them. She lifted her head to Austin Hamilton who stared at her.

"What?" she whispered. Then, "I suppose I sound crazy to you, right?"

Ignoring her question, he asked warily, "How do you know about a slave named Tilda? Did you find that in your research?"

"I haven't done any research yet. I was to do that when I arrived."

He was silent a moment, studying her, then said, "You mentioned James."

"James?" she whispered, and the name sounded so familiar to her lips, familiar and sweet. She raised her hand, brushing her fingertips across her mouth, as though she could feel the name printed indelibly. And at the same time, she wanted to weep. She couldn't explain the melancholia that swept over her, nor the simultaneous sense of hope that leaped to her heart. Austin Hamilton's voice drew her eyes to his dark, suspicious visage.

"Yes," he said, shaking his head. "You called me

James when you awoke."

"I did?" she mused softly.

"Yes. You did." His brow knitted. Questions lingered in his eyes. She sensed he was also confused. "Why did you call me James?" he persisted.

She shrugged.

"You said, 'James, you have come back to me.'" Austin waited for her answer. He watched as her shoulders lifted beneath a deep sigh.

Her eyes met his. She felt drawn to this man that she sensed in some inexplicable way, was not a stranger to her. Instinctively, she knew she could share her thoughts with him. Softly, she said, "Tilda loved James Hamilton and he loved her."

"So I've read in his journals," he said.

"When I awoke," she said slowly, "I thought you were he."

"And now?" he asked quietly.

She shrugged.

"This is all very strange," he muttered.

She nodded in agreement, knowing that, once put into words, what she was about to say would be startling to them both. She began apprehensively. "I'm very sure about one thing."

"What?" His voice was almost a whisper.

"That I was Tilda," she blurted.

"What do you mean?" he demanded, forcing volume to his voice. "How?"

She shrugged. "I don't know how. But I know what I saw was real. I know what I felt was from some secret corner of my heart -- and my soul."

"But it's not possible," he breathed, losing the volocity of his vocal chords again.

"How do you know that?" she asked quickly.

Austin didn't answer, for he was confronting an inner struggle with his own volitive emotions. At the moment of her revelation, at her strong conviction that she was Tilda, the urge to take her into his arms was so strong that he had to force his arms to remain at his sides. The desire to feel her body against his, to hold her in his arms was overwhelming. He could sense the pressure of his lips against hers, almost as though he knew how they would feel and that he had done so before. The impulse to hold her was so powerful, he stepped back, his breath catching over the rapidity of his heartbeat. He wanted to reach out to her, to soothe her anxieties. He felt a strange need to tell her he had returned and that this time they would be together -- always. If he did not know better, he could almost believe, as well, that she was Tilda come back to James -- himself. Austin immediately chided himself for considering such foolishness. He glanced down as she spoke.

"If you have read his diaries then you must know James gave Tilda a cameo."

He did know that, and he became even more confused. How did *she* know it? His eyes were questioning.

"Tilda hid the necklace from the Yankees." Her gaze met his. "I know where it is," she said softly.

Her assured manner told him she spoke the truth, but it was the feeling in his soul that made him believe her. But still, he asked, "Where?"

"Come," she offered him her hand. "I'll show you."

Austin stood, clasped her hand and assisted her to her feet.

Laura's feet trod the same path from the house to the slave quarters, just as she had done so recently, as Tilda, in that strange state from which she had just wakened. When she pulled her hand out of his, Austin wanted to snatch it back again. He did not like losing the contact that made him sense a realness about this whole incredible phenomenon.

Laura stopped in front of one of the slave cabins. "This was Beulah's cabin," she said quietly, in response to his questioning eyes. "She was my mother."

Austin nodded, remembering the many references to Tilda's mother in James' diary. Without comment, he reached around Laura to release the rusted latch of the door. He pushed it with his palm and it swung back with a squeak.

Laura stepped gingerly over the threshold, feeling like she was still walking in the curious phantasmagoria which held her in its possessive grip for so many hours. She put out her hand to touch Austin, needing the contact, and most of all, needing to know he was there. Without a word, he clasped her hand in his.

Austin's gaze swung round the dusky interior and came to rest on Laura. "Where?" he asked softly.

Laura pointed to the hearth.

He saw her draw a deep breath, then pull him eagerly toward the fireplace. "There is a loose brick here," she pointed again, falling to her knees. Her fingers wrapped around the proposed brick, and in her eagerness she broke a tapered, manicured fingernail. But she ignored it and pulled frantically at the brick, trying to tear it loose from its mooring. It wouldn't move. She stared at Austin, her heart beating so vigorously that it was painful. Tears sprang to her eyes in frustration. This *was* the brick! She was positive of it.

Austin ran his hand over the brick and she held her breath as his fingers worked at the dirt and grime of more than a century. When the handmade brick shifted, she saw it and leaned forward to help him pull at it. Finally, the brick became loose enough to lift out. Austin drew back.

Laura's hand shook as she lifted the dusty red brick and set it aside. As she raised it, she could see the rusted metal box lying beneath it. Tears streamed down her face, as she looked up at Austin. His own features were frozen in awe. Laura reached for the box, drawing it out and into the light.

Breathlessly, she whispered, "I knew it was there! I *knew* it!"

"This is absolutely amazing," he said, with a perplexed shake of his head.

She pulled at the lid, but it was stuck tight. Austin took it from her and pried it loose with a penknife. Wedging the knife beneath the lip, Austin pushed, and the lid flipped off and landed across the room. Its shiny interior gleamed like a beacon in the half-light, but neither paid any attention to it. Their eyes were riveted to the cameo necklace lying in the box on a scrap of faded velvet. Austin lifted it out. Suspended from its chain, the gold filigree mounting caught the light. Laura reached out to it, a rapt expression on her face. Her eyes met his.

"Come here," he said, leaning toward her. He undid the clasp and held it out to her. She bent down and Austin reclasped the necklace around her throat. "There," he said softly. "It is back where it belongs."

Tears filled Laura's eyes as she met his gaze. And suddenly she was in his arms.

Looking up; she whispered, "You believe me now, don't you?"

"There was never any question," he replied softly. "I think, deep in my soul, I knew there was a reason why I was drawn back here. I seemed to have an affinity for the plantation from the moment I set foot on it. Perhaps this explains the overwhelming sense of longing -- of expectancy -- that I felt when I arrived. It was like -- " he paused. "Like I was waiting for something." He brushed a light kiss across her temple. "I admit I was scared to admit it -- it seems so preposterous -- but I saw the truth in your eyes. Some part of me seemed to recognize you the moment I saw you."

They were silent, absorbing all that their discoveries meant.

"This is scary, but wonderful, too," Laura ventured.

"I don't know how, and I don't want to question it. I am merely thankful," Austin said gently. "Tilda and James -- we have another chance. He had to want it desperately to make such a thing happen."

"We -- they both did."

After a moment, she whispered, "I -- Tilda," she corrected herself, "also hid the letters James sent her. They were tied with a bit of lace she had left over from a gown she made." She returned to the hearth, put her hand into the hole dug so long ago. But too many years had passed. The letters had long since disentegrated from the years of moisture and tiny insects that fed on them. All that was left was a fragment of lace, which she held up into the light. She looked up sadly at Austin.

"It doesn't matter," he said softly, drawing her to her feet. "Our hearts are telling us all we need to know."

He led her to the door, stopping at the threshold. "I found the secret place yesterday," he said quietly.

"Our carved-out rock," she said with delight.

He nodded. "Let's go back together," he suggested.

A smile flickered over her face. "Together," she repeated.

They stepped out of Beulah's cabin into the growing dusk of evening. He caught up her hand in his as they started up the path.

Weeds, growing in wild abandon, encroached onto the handmade bricks, laid so many years ago by slave hands. They stepped from the path into a clearing. Beneath the wide-spreading branches of a tree, where James had once danced with Tilda, she smiled up at him in the half-light. He drew her close to him and gazed down into the dark depths of her eyes. "What they had -- what we have," he whispered, "is for always."

She smiled. Their hearts resounded like a symphony echoing the word -- always.

She leaned into his embrace. His tall figure bent forward over her upturned face. They stood, dark images poised in silhouette, against the background of the plantation. The whispering winds of yesterday swirled round them, and evening shadows played sensuously over the two still figures.

Yesterday and today melded into one. Beneath the dipping branches of the wide-spreading tree, James bent over Tilda's slight figure, his black woolen cloak swinging from his shoulders and her full-skirted fashion of a century past flowing round her ankles and slender bare feet. The twilight held them momentarily suspended in time -- two dark shadows silhouetted against the darkening sky.

Drugs and dealers infest a small Georgia town, determined to destroy three generations of a family—except they underestimated a battle-scarred old man.

The Third Season

With determination, the old man slowly forced a path deeper into the swamp. In the distance, wild dogs gathered for a killing hunt. He knew dangerous men were trailing him, and he left clear signs for them to follow. It was all part of his feeble plan. Elmer Goodhand shifted the bags of angry rattlers, hoping he could save the life of the five-year-old granddaughter he raised from a baby. If he were lucky, he might even save himself.

This is the story of one man's devotion for a child and her worship of the one who is her world. Hauntingly and brilliantly, it portrays in a unique tenderness, the best of us and the worst of us.

You may purchase copies of *The Third Season* at a 20% discount, postage paid. Complete the coupon below and mail to the publisher.

===

Name_____(3-5)

Address_____

City_____State_____ZIP_____

I am enclosing ($17.56) per copy $_____
GA residents add 6% sales tax ($1.05) $_____
Total amount enclosed $_____
Valid in U.S. only. All orders subject to availability

Use your ___Visa ___MasterCard #_____

Exp.date_____Signature_____

GoldenIsle Publishers, Inc.
2395 Hawkinsville Hwy
Eastman, GA 31023

The Texas brushland wilderness springs to life under the pen of Don Johnson, a cattleman who owned and operated a ranch in la brasada *bordering the Rio Grande.*

Brasada

In the latter days of the Civil War, a lifeline of the South was made up of wagon trains loaded with cotton bound for the neutral ports of Mexico to avoid the Union blockade. This cotton, traded for gold or hard foreign currency, fueled the hungry looms of Europe, kept the Confederacy solvent, and enriched the merchants of Matamoros, known as the "Baghdad on the Gulf". Mexican outlaws attack and decimate a train, leaving three enlisted men to protect and hide the gold. They take refuge in *la brasada,* a crescent of brushland wilderness where Lance Morgan is determined to build an empire of land and cattle, fighting off thieves, killers and crooked officials. He meets his match in the vivacious Colleen who is a product of the harsh environment.

You may purchase copies of *Brasada* at a 20% discount, postage paid. Complete the coupon below and mail to the publisher.

==

Name_____(3-5)

Address_____

City_____State_____ZIP_____

I am enclosing ($17.56) per copy $_____
GA residents add 6% sales tax ($1.05) $_____
Total amount enclosed $_____
Valid in U.S. only. All orders subject to availability

Use your ___Visa___MasterCard#_____

Exp. Date_____Signature_____

GoldenIsle Publishers, Inc.
2395 Hawkinsville Hwy
Eastman, GA 31023

A note to our readers

Thank you for spending time with us. We hope your visit has been an enjoyable one.

The staff of GoldenIsle Publishers, Inc. is committed to bringing you some of the best in contemporary, adventure, and historical romance stories by writers who know their craft and instill deep feelings in the characters that bring life to a book.

If you have enjoyed sharing the adventure with the people who moved throughout this novel, write and let us know. Your comments will be forwarded to the authors who constantly strive to entertain their readers with carefully researched and intricately plotted stories.

GoldenIsle Publishers, Inc.
2395 Hawkinsville Hwy
Eastman, GA 31023